DON'T MAKE A SOUND

BOOKS BY H.K. CHRISTIE

One In Five

On The Rise

Go With Grace

Flawless

H.K. CHRISTIE

DON'T MAKE A SOUND

bookouture

Published by Bookouture in 2024

An imprint of Storyfire Ltd.
Carmelite House
50 Victoria Embankment
London EC4Y 0DZ

www.bookouture.com

ISBN: 978-1-83525-624-4
eBook ISBN: 978-1-83525-623-7

For Dusty

PROLOGUE

CLAIRE

When our eyes locked, I knew my life and everything I had ever known would be over, unless I acted immediately. I lunged toward the countertop and grabbed the largest knife from the block. Filled with resolve, I charged at the threat but within moments I was caught in a struggle. I should've known they wouldn't go down without a fight. The blade sliced my finger, and I was forced to relent, losing both the fight and the weapon. The desperation and determination in my attacker's eyes sent a shiver down my spine. But it wasn't until I saw the glint of the blade, the one I'd just been holding, now aimed at me that I realized how quickly it would all be over.

Instinctively, I shielded my face with my bloody hands, a futile effort to prevent the inevitable. The knife pierced my forearm, a searing hot pain that jolted through my body like electricity. I raised my arms in defense, trying to regain control but then came another strike, and then another, each one battering down my attempt to survive. The attacker was relentless and didn't stop until I lay still on the floor, a crumpled heap of heartbreak and disbelief.

I couldn't move, and I couldn't see through the haze of pain and shock, but I could feel the hot, sticky liquid—my own blood —dripping from my forehead and snaking down my neck. In those moments, I could've asked why: Why me? Why now?

I could've begged, promised anything to make it stop. But deep down, I knew it would all be for nothing. And maybe I deserved it.

I could have pleaded for mercy. And maybe I would have if I had even the slightest will to live anymore. But I wasn't sure I wanted to live. Not when I knew what was coming next.

As I lay on my once-loved kitchen floor, the cold seeped into my body and my mind focused not on the horror and regret, but on the past.

The best of times. The day my baby girl was born. The light of my life. My son. A mini version of his father. My wedding day. The joy I had felt as he lifted my veil and slid the ring on my finger. The faces of all the teens I had taught about Shakespeare and essay structure.

The images were quickly replaced with the worst of times.

In these final moments, as the life drained from my body, I pondered on the what-ifs. What if I had paid closer attention? What if I hadn't been so selfish? Would I have then made different choices?

But now, as my breathing began to slow, the weight of my past life pressing down on me, I realized all the could-have-beens were merely fantasies, as fleeting and intangible as the life slipping away from me.

I was so cold and tired, so very tired.

Maybe I would just rest here for a moment in the darkness, praying for heaven but fearing there would be no place for me.

ONE

VAL

The living room door opened and two women, dressed head-to-toe in red and purple, burst in. My mother sat in her favorite chair, a sparkle in her eyes that I hadn't seen since her stroke. It wasn't the first time Julie and Diane had visited, but it was the first time they wore their Red Hat Ladies regalia. Mom, finally resembling a bit of her former self, seemed uplifted.

The Red Hat Ladies, a women's organization my mother was an active member of, had been a godsend, bringing casseroles, cakes, fruit, and even a mouthwatering lasagna. Thanks to them, I had hardly needed to cook over the past few weeks and wouldn't for a while still. The majority of the food lived in the freezer, as I didn't have much of an appetite these days. As an FBI special agent, my job had revolved around dealing with serial killers, but it was my recent capture by the Bear that had been unquestionably one of the toughest times in my life.

Mom's health was improving, but she still faced significant challenges in her daily life. She couldn't walk or bathe unassisted. But being able to use the toilet independently seemed to restore some of the dignity she felt she had lost. It pained me to see my mom, once a symbol of strength, in such a fragile state. Thankfully, her lifelong commitment to the community in Red Rose County meant we weren't alone. The outpouring of support when she had suffered a stroke had been overwhelming, and her regular visitors kept her going.

Julie and Diane enveloped Mom in long, heartfelt hugs as she sat in her recliner. "Maybe that's what I'm missing—some red and purple," Mom remarked with the faintest smile.

Julie, her green eyes sparkling, responded playfully, "No fear, let's get you set up. You can wear my hat." She took off her red sequined baseball-style cap and gently placed it on Mom's head. The three women, all in their seventies, chuckled like schoolgirls. As I looked on, a part of me envied my mother, despite her current health status.

"Can I get anybody tea or coffee?" I offered.

Diane, giving me a knowing look, replied, "Sure, but let me help you," and followed me into the kitchen. As one of Mom's best friends and frequent visitors, she was familiar with every corner of it.

"How are you holding up, honey?" she asked as soon as we were alone.

"I'm doing okay. She's getting better," I said, trying to sound convincing.

Diane looked me in the eye, her gaze piercing yet empathetic. "I've been in your position, Val. Taking care of your parents when they're not themselves is one of the hardest things you may ever do. I was my mom and dad's caretaker at the end. By the time they passed, I thought there would be nothing left of me. You're doing something noble."

"I don't know if it's noble, but I'm glad I'm able to do it," I said, my voice a mix of exhaustion and resolve.

"You know we can stay with your mom anytime, don't you? You could maybe go out and have a drink, have a night off?"

Lately, my life had revolved entirely around taking care of

Mom. I hadn't left the house, except to take Mom to her doctors and physical therapy appointments. "I don't even know what I would do with myself."

"You and Brady could grab a bite to eat. He's such a nice young man. And pretty cute too," Diane said, smiling mischievously.

She wasn't wrong but I hadn't really seen that much of Brady, except when he had been kind enough to stop by and check on Mom and me. Which he had several times. "Maybe I will."

Changing the subject, Diane walked over to the pantry. "About that tea, let's see..." She pulled out packets of chamomile and switched on the kettle. I leaned against the counter, my thoughts heavy. "How do you get through it?" I asked.

She set down the packets and looked at me, her expression sincere. "You just do. When someone offers you help, you take it. Elizabeth is one of us, and so are you. Anytime you need a break, even if you don't think you need one, we're here for anything and everything you or your mom needs."

Mom was lucky to have such a strong, supportive group of friends, and I supposed I was too.

"Have you heard from Harrison? Is he enjoying his trip?" Diane asked, as she prepared the tea.

"Yes, he's having a blast," I said. "He's been in Europe for just over a month now and he's already been to London, Budapest, the Czech Republic, Spain, and Paris. I wish Mom and I could go and visit him." Before Mom's stroke I had put forward the idea of meeting up with Harrison during his trip. Harrison had liked the idea, but there was no way it would happen now, given Mom's condition. The next time I would see him would be when he was back from his European adventure and getting ready for the next chapter of his life at MIT. Hopefully, I would find someone to stay with Mom so I wouldn't miss such an important milestone in his life.

With the tea prepared and set on a tray, I followed Diane back into the living room. She set it down on the coffee table and took a seat on the sofa next to Julie. Like two peas in a pod, Julie and Diane had both aged well and easily passed for being in their sixties with their denim and rhinestones. Like my mom, they had kept in shape—mentally and physically. Watching the trio, I was jealous of their close friendship that was more akin to sisterhood. I didn't have girlfriends like that and suddenly wished I did.

"Elizabeth, I was just talking to Val. I think it would be good for her to get out of the house for a bit. What do you think?"

Mom nodded.

Diane continued, "I told her to call up Brady and ask him out to dinner."

There was a slight curl in Mom's lips; she liked the idea. She said, "Now there's an idea. And I've got Julie and Diane to keep me company."

"Sure, maybe I'll give him a call this week." It would be nice to get out of the house.

Mom said, "He told me he was stopping by tomorrow. Maybe just ask him then. You two were such good friends in school. And you were great when you worked on Scarlett's case together. Quite the team," Mom added, her tone hinting at something more.

The insinuation wasn't lost on me, but for now, my focus remained on her recovery and keeping us both safe.

TWO

VAL

Standing on the front porch, I squinted as the sunlight nearly blinded me. Shielding my eyes with my hand, I glanced around the quiet street. None of the neighbors were out yet; there was nobody working in the yard or going for their morning stroll. More importantly, there were no signs of the Bear. It had been several weeks since I'd received a note from him—at least, I suspected it was him, despite not being able to prove or disprove it. But something inside me knew he wouldn't let me go so easily. If he was done with me, I didn't think he would have sent me that message. I couldn't let my guard down, especially with Mom in her condition. Satisfied the coast was clear, I bent down and picked up the morning paper. Before I'd come to stay with my mother, I hadn't picked up a physical newspaper in years.

Going back inside, I shut the door behind me and joined my mother at the kitchen table. She was already sipping her coffee, eagerly awaiting the newspaper. I took the front section, and she took the second—the financial news. It had become our morning routine to each read a section, then switch and discuss it over our first cup of coffee of the day. Sometimes we were joined by Julie, Diane, another one of Mom's friends, or the neighbor from the house to the left.

Suddenly, Mom gasped and placed her hand against her chest. "Oh dear."

"What is it?" I asked, unnerved.

"Did Brady tell you about this?" she asked, her voice tinged with shock.

"Tell me about what?"

She set the paper down and pointed at an article. "Claire Nelson was murdered in her own home."

I had no idea who Claire Nelson was, but it was obvious she was someone my mother knew. "And who is she?"

"She is a teacher at the high school in Hectorville. She's married to Jordan, who owns the local hardware store. How awful," Mom lamented.

"That's terrible. When did she die?"

"Just yesterday."

"Do they have any suspects?"

"I don't know. Brady really didn't tell you about this?" Mom looked surprised.

"No. Does it say how she died?" Brady had mentioned a suspicious death a few weeks ago, which turned out to be a suicide, but he hadn't said anything about Claire Nelson when I spoke with him the night before.

"Says here she was stabbed to death in her kitchen," Mom replied, her voice somber.

An awful way to die. "Did you know her well?"

"Well, yes, of course. I know most of the teachers in the towns within our county. She was a delightful woman, two children too. Gosh, how tragic. Who would do such a thing? I can't imagine she had any enemies."

The most dangerous person to a woman was typically her spouse. "Did she have a good marriage?"

Mom glared at me. "I don't know. I'm not running the investigation. But I do know Jordan, and he's just not the type. They always seemed happy, and I've never heard any rumors of affairs or any reason for him to want to get rid of her. But I guess you never really do know anyone, do you?"

A knock on the door signaled the arrival of more of Mom's friends. I opened the door, and sure enough, there stood Julie and Diane.

"Good morning," they greeted in unison.

"Good morning."

The women stepped into the kitchen, helped themselves to coffee, and joined us at the kitchen table. Julie sat next to my mom, and Diane sat next to me. "We just saw the news about Claire Nelson. Isn't that terrible?" Julie said.

"It is. I was just discussing it with Val. She thinks Jordan might have had something to do with it. Can you believe that?"

"I was merely asking if there were any suspects. Statistically, the most dangerous person in a woman's life is her husband. But I don't know the facts of the case," I clarified.

"Well, I know Jordan Nelson. That's who we get all of our tools from, and he's always willing to help us fix up the house if something goes wrong. He's just not the type to murder his wife. He adored Claire," Diane interjected.

In my mind, that didn't rule him out. Of course, I didn't know any of the case details and hadn't seen photos of the crime scene. That wasn't my job anymore; I had left that kind of work behind when I retired from the FBI.

"Maybe you should offer to help out with the case, Val," Diane suggested.

"Oh, I don't think I could right now." Mom was my focus. And it wasn't like the Red Hat Ladies were in charge of assigning homicide investigations in Red Rose County, despite the fact that my mother had been sheriff before she retired. I hadn't even met the new sheriff yet, although I had heard good things. He had requested my help on Scarlett's case last month, but nobody was asking for my help now, and I wasn't about to offer. I had enough on my plate.

"Well, have you had dinner with Brady yet?" Julie asked, changing the subject.

"Since yesterday? No. But he said he would stop by today." Staring down, I found myself wondering if Brady's visit was why I had subconsciously chosen to wear a pair of nice jeans and a button-down shirt, as opposed to my typical attire of FBI sweatpants I had acquired during my time at the Academy.

"Well, you definitely should. Get out of here. Maybe throw some lip gloss on ya," Julie said with a smile.

"I haven't even asked him yet." If it wasn't obvious these ladies were Team Brady before, it was loud and clear now.

Diane said, "When he gets here, you can ask him. We'll stay here with your mom. Go hang out with Brady. I don't know, maybe help solve a murder. That's what you like to do anyway, isn't it? You've already solved one since you've been home."

"Yeah, you don't want to lose your winning streak now," Julie added, encouragingly.

"If the sheriff is hesitant, I could put in a good word," Mom offered, supporting the idea. "He's a good guy. A little green, but smart."

I stared at my mother in disbelief. I had retired from the FBI to take care of her since her stroke. Not to mention I was still talking to a therapist once a week to deal with the trauma of being imprisoned by the Bear. Why on earth would I want to rush back to work?

Although Mom was regaining her strength and didn't need me as much as she had in the first week, she still needed me around. Following my captivity, and with Harrison growing up, I had to admit I didn't mind having Mom around too. There was a certain comfort in being back in Red Rose County, with its gorgeous forests and lakes, a paradise.

"I don't think that's necessary, Mom. If they want my help,

they can ask. And if they do, I'll see what I can do," I said cautiously.

Mom tipped her head at me and said, "You can take time away from caring for me. I've got Julie and Diane, and I'm getting around a little more on my own. Sure, I would love to be out of this chair, but all in good time. Really, I'm pretty well taken care of. I can heat up meals, make coffee, and use the bathroom. I just need these legs to work again, and I'll be good as new."

I didn't want my mom rushing her recovery, but she insisted on doing everything she possibly could on her own. It was just in her nature to be independent, and I had to let her be. She was remarkable.

There was another knock on the door. "I'll get it," I said, as the ladies giggled among themselves. Definitely at my expense.

I hurried to the front door and looked through the peephole. Sure enough, it was Brady. "Good morning," I greeted him as I opened the door.

"Hey, Val, how's it going?"

"I'm doing just fine. Fair warning, Mom's in there with Julie and Diane, and well, they're darn near back to their normal selves," I said playfully.

He cocked his head. "Should I be worried?"

"Well, they're saying that the two of us should go out to dinner, and my mom wants to put in a word to the sheriff so I can start working cases."

Brady stifled a chuckle. "She must be feeling better."

"I think so." I led him into the kitchen where Mom and her friends eyed Brady with interest.

"Morning, Brady," they greeted warmly. He was clearly a favorite among my mother and her friends.

"Hi. Elizabeth, how are you feeling?" he asked Mom.

"You know, Brady, I'm doing pretty good. I was just telling

Val, once I can get out of this chair, I'll be good as new," she replied with determination.

"Already?" he asked, surprised.

"Yep, I'm getting around just fine, thanks to you and your friends, who moved me down to the first floor and built a ramp outside," she said with a hint of gratitude.

"That's good to hear."

"We just read in the paper about Claire Nelson. What can you tell us about her death?" Julie asked, her brown eyes wide.

Brady swallowed, visibly uncomfortable. "It's an active investigation," he replied.

"Come on, Brady. Tell us something. You must know what's going on. You don't suspect Jordan, do you?" Mom pressed.

"Nobody's been ruled out yet," Brady admitted.

Mom continued. "The paper said Claire was stabbed in her home."

He sighed, as if resigned. "Multiple times. It was brutal."

"Did you go to the scene?" I asked, curiosity piqued.

He shook his head. "No, but I saw photos. The sheriff's department has it as a high priority, but they're not getting very far. The team's in the process of verifying Jordan Nelson's alibi."

My mind raced ahead. If the husband has an alibi, who else would have wanted to hurt Claire? This could be an interesting case.

"Maybe you and Val could go out to lunch and talk about it, or breakfast. Look at that, it's still breakfast time. What do you say?" Mom was relentless.

Brady's jaw dropped ever so slightly; probably reminiscing about our high school years when Mom would boss him around then too. I said, "I think they're trying to get rid of me."

"Val, you're so dramatic. We're not trying to get rid of you, but you do need to get out of the house," Mom chided playfully. "And I'm sure the sheriff's department could make use of Val's insight, even if just to consult on the case. You could use the help, right, Brady?" she added.

Brady looked like a deer in headlights. My mom and her friends were a force to be reckoned with. "If you want to go to the diner, I have time for breakfast," he offered.

I was about to agree, when I remembered something. "Oh, shoot, I can't. Mom has physical therapy."

"We can take her," Julie said immediately.

"Do you know how to drive a van?" I asked, somewhat concerned she wouldn't be able to drive the van we'd acquired to accommodate Mom's wheelchair.

"Of course. What do I look like, a spring chicken?" Diane retorted.

"Mom, if I'm quick, I can be back to take you to physical therapy," I insisted.

"Nonsense, you know they can take me," Mom said, dismissing my concern.

"I used to take my mother. I am more than capable of helping out. You two go. Have fun, talk about the case, and we'll see you later." Diane's voice grew higher with each suggestion.

"Okay, okay, we'll go," I conceded, feeling slightly over-whelmed.

They were all smiles, waving goodbye to Brady, and wiggling their eyebrows at me the moment he wasn't looking. Mom was *definitely* feeling better.

THREE

VAL

Despite my hesitation, it was nice to get out of the house, though I couldn't help but worry about Mom. Maybe I didn't need to be so concerned. She had proven time and again that she could take care of herself, even in her current state. Not completely, of course, but probably better than most. I sat across from Brady in a booth at the downtown diner, which was like stepping back in time, to the fifties, with its vinyl booths and checkered floor. The smell of grease mixed with berry pie filled the air.

"I'm sorry again that you got roped into this," I said.

"Stop apologizing, Val. It's nice to see you out. We haven't had much time to talk since Scarlett's case closed."

Was that true? He'd come by the house several times over the last few weeks, but I guess we hadn't had a proper conversation or even talked about work. "True, it's nice to be out and about, and those hash browns smell incredible," I said, although I feared my pants were getting a little tighter than I liked without my normal workout routine. My exercise was limited to pushing Mom around the neighborhood to get her and me some much-needed fresh air.

"They are," he agreed.

"Well, then, I'll have two eggs and hash browns," I decided.

"And I know it's only ten o'clock in the morning, but their pie is amazing. The apple walnut is the best."

"Let's call it brunch," I said with a smile.

"So, how are you really doing?"

Tired. Mentally and physically. It had been nearly two months since the Bear, a serial killer I'd been hunting, had captured me, but the nightmares were persistent and cutting into desperately needed quality sleep. "I'm all right. Mom is doing a lot better, and I'm starting to see that. Maybe I do need to get out of the house and not fuss over her. She's made incredible progress since the stroke." I was giving Brady the sugar-coated version of my life. I couldn't tell him the truth, and I didn't know why. Something was stopping me from being completely honest with him.

"She does seem to be in good spirits."

"She is. How about you. How are you?"

"How much have you read about the Nelson case?"

Not as much as I'd like. Not that I enjoyed gruesome murders but being able to discuss an investigation made me feel like my old self. Being home with no job and taking care of my mom, I feared I would forget who I was. Thankfully, Brady was reminding me.

"Not a lot. Are you bringing it up because you want to share details?"

That boyish grin appeared. "I am. How could I pass on getting input from the great Val Costa?"

"I don't know how great I am, but sure, I'll let you know what I think."

Before we could get into the groove, a server arrived. She was older, with a fifties-style updo and horn-rimmed glasses, fitting right in with the style of the diner. She looked vaguely familiar.

"Deputy Tanner, good to see you. And you too, Val," she greeted us warmly.

I hesitated, wondering how she knew my name. Did she remember me? She leaned over with a coy smiled and said, "Of course everyone here knows who you are. You're the only new face in here, although I feel like I used to see you in here perhaps thirty years ago with the same gentleman." I realized then that she had worked here when I was a teenager. She was considerably older now, but her style hadn't changed.

"Yes, Brady and I went to high school together and we're good friends."

"Well, welcome back! What can I get for you?"

After we'd ordered our breakfast and a double dose of caffeine, she said she'd be back in a jiffy.

"So, let's hear it," I urged Brady.

Brady cleared his throat. "I was just brought onto the team, so I've only just reviewed the file. It was bad. I'm sure in the FBI you saw all kinds of gruesome, demented things, but we're not used to that here in Red Rose County."

This sounded unusual. "How so? Just lay it on me, give me the details."

"Claire Nelson, she's a high school English teacher, married to Jordan Nelson, who owns the hardware store in Hectorville. They both attend the local Lutheran church, and their two kids grew up in town, both are away at college. The husband comes home after closing up the store for the day and finds her body. There was blood everywhere. She had been stabbed multiple times."

"Has the sheriff's department come up with any theories?" You had to get up close and personal to stab someone.

"Not yet. They're still processing the scene, trying to see if there's any evidence to point to who could've done this."

"Did you know her?"

"Not well. I met Claire and her husband a few times at some of the community fundraisers."

"Any known enemies? I'm guessing since it was yesterday, there's no forensics back yet? Fingerprints? DNA?"

Brady shook his head. "Not yet. No murder weapon either, but they think it's a chef's knife that might be missing from the block of knives."

"Defensive wounds?" I tried to picture the scene.

"ME's not done with her assessment."

Interesting. An argument between husband and wife; he snaps and grabs the closest thing he can use as a weapon. "Sounds like it could be a crime of opportunity. Anything else missing?"

"Her car, her house keys, and her wallet."

A robbery. That didn't fit with the husband. A random crime? "Does anybody believe it's anything other than a home invasion, a robbery gone really, really wrong?"

"That's the working theory. That's why they're processing the scene, to see if we can get any prints."

"And you have a BOLO on the car?"

"We do. No sightings yet."

Basically, the sheriff's department knew nothing about the crime, which was understandable as it had been less than twenty-four hours.

I stared at the display case full of freshly baked pies and was suddenly really looking forward to that apple walnut. Brady interrupted my thoughts. "So, what do you think?"

"I would need to see the crime scene photos and any reports on similar crimes recently committed in Red Rose County and its surrounding counties. It could have been someone passing through."

"Or persons."

"Exactly."

"What are you thinking? Someone high on drugs?"

"Too soon to tell." I needed a lot more information than Brady was giving me to be able to put together an accurate assessment of the perpetrator.

"Where would you look first?"

"I'd walk the scene, look at photos. Interview the husband and the community. Speak with the family and friends. Look for traffic cam footage... There's a lot of things I would do."

"Would you?" Brady's eyes twinkled. After a sip of coffee he said, "Truth be told, I had an ulterior motive for checking in on your mother this morning."

Sneaky. "Oh?"

"As you can imagine, the sheriff's department is rattled by the brutality of the crime."

Of course it was. We all wanted to believe bad things didn't happen where we lived. But the truth was it could happen anywhere.

"The sheriff would like you to come in for a meeting. See if we can talk you into helping us, officially, with the case. He wants this closed. Fast."

If Mom didn't need me, I wouldn't hesitate. But she did. "I need to take care of my mom."

"Your mom has a strong support system that would be more than happy to keep her company if it meant we might find out who killed Claire."

"I'll have to check with Mom."

"Talk to her," he said, with a smile.

Brady knew my mother almost as well I did; she would want me to work the case. Maybe I could work just a few hours a day so I could still be there for her. "I'll talk to her and let you know."

Brady took another sip of his coffee. "I'm looking forward to working with you again."

Brady Tanner needed to watch himself. I hadn't agreed yet,

but maybe, even after all these years, he knew me better than I thought he did.

FOUR

VAL

The sheriff's office was just as I remembered it, except there was no longer a photo of Maxine, Harrison, and myself on the desk. A bookshelf lined the back wall, adorned with plaques, awards, and photos of the Red Rose County's current sheriff with the governor of California. Behind the desk sat Sheriff Kingston Phillips. I was surprised Mom had failed to mention that a Rosedale High School alumnus had taken her spot. It had been a long time since we'd met, but I couldn't be sure we had ever had a conversation.

"Agent Costa, thank you for agreeing to meet with me about the case," he said, extending his hand.

With a firm handshake, I replied, "Sheriff Phillips. I'm not with the bureau anymore, so Val is fine."

"Thanks, Val, and please, call me Kingston."

Brady sat, and I followed suit. As I had expected, and Brady had too, when I had approached my mother about the idea of helping the sheriff's department find out what had happened to Claire Nelson, she didn't hesitate. She immediately insisted I help because, according to Mom and her friends, Claire Nelson was a wonderful person, and so was her husband. The whole family was held in high regard by the community.

Julie and Diane promised to take turns staying with my mother, which of course she brushed off, saying she didn't need someone to be there all the time. She could get around in her wheelchair, in the kitchen, and to go to the bathroom. Bathing was a challenge, as she needed help getting in and out of the tub, but I explained that I would still help her with that. She relented and agreed.

I would still be there every day, and I would try to work from home as much as possible, bringing case files back with me and working off the laptop computer, just in case Mom needed me. The doctors warned us that although the progress she had made was remarkable, having one stroke meant she was more susceptible to having a second, and really, Mom shouldn't be left alone in the event she suffered another stroke and needed immediate medical attention. But I didn't think Mom minded. She was always more social than Maxine and me, and I think she enjoyed all the company.

My mother had approved the plan, so there I sat, across from the new sheriff. Kingston had replaced the spot where our family photo used to be with his own—a picture-perfect young family. It depicted him with two little fair-haired children and a matching blonde wife. I didn't remember much about Kingston from high school as he was a few years younger. We didn't interact much back then, but I recalled his name and that he had been a star athlete.

"How can I help, Sheriff?" I asked.

"Kingston, please," he corrected gently.

"How can I help, Kingston?"

"Well, as you can imagine, I'm impressed, as is the whole department and our community, with how you worked alongside Brady Tanner on the Scarlett Douglas case," Sheriff Kingston Phillips began. "Exposing an organ-trafficking ring and finding those missing teens was beyond impressive. We will find the budget, and as much as we can utilize your expertise, we'll take it."

Not to be a stickler for logistics, but I had to ask, "Will I be on the payroll? Would I be working in an official capacity?"

"There are a couple of ways to handle it. But my initial thoughts were that we would give you the title of consultant. It's up to you how long you'd like to work with us, but we're hoping at least for the Claire Nelson murder investigation. Hopefully, between the three of us, we won't need your services after this one."

After a bit of back-and-forth on the terms, I accepted and said, "For now, assume it's for the duration of the Claire Nelson case."

"Very well. Brady will work with you in a similar capacity as in the Scarlett Douglas case. We'll get you access, show you around the file room. Sounds like you've already met our ME and some of our lab techs. Brady will introduce you to the crime scene team shortly so you can get acquainted with everyone. I assume the first thing you'll want to do is see the file and know what we've done so far."

"That would be great."

"If you like, Mr. Nelson is in an interview room right now, if you want to talk to him, get his first-hand account of how he found his wife and go from there."

"I'd like that. Who will be taking the lead on the case?"

Kingston smiled, showing off perfect white teeth. "We have a few detectives working the case. But, with your experience, we feel it makes sense for you to take the lead."

That was exactly what I wanted to hear. Mom was right, he was a smart one. "I agree."

"Excellent. As soon as we're done here, I'll send an email to the team, to tell them officially."

The sheriff was in a hurry to close the case. I didn't blame him. If the community began to believe that there was a murderer on the loose, they'd fear they might be next. Not to mention the effect it would have on the tourists who came here to get away from the hustle and bustle of city life and enjoy the scenery of Red Rose County with its dazzling lakes and dozens of hiking trails. "If there's nothing else, I'd first like to talk to Mr. Nelson about his wife's murder."

"One more thing. I'd like regular updates as the case progresses."

"Sounds reasonable. I look forward to working with you."

"And I with you."

Back on the job. "Thank you, Kingston. I won't let you down."

"I don't doubt it. You've got quite the reputation."

The media hadn't stopped reporting that we had solved the Scarlett Douglas case as well as a string of missing persons cases, but they hadn't broadcast the fact that I'd been captured by the very serial killer I had been hunting. Thankfully, because it was a reputation I didn't want, but it seemed it would stick until I caught the Bear. There hadn't been a peep from him, and Kieran reported that it seemed as if the killer had stopped altogether or paused temporarily, but that didn't fit with what we had uncovered about him. If he had stopped, he was likely hunting and hadn't yet caught his prey.

Speaking of which, I was looking forward to meeting Mr. Nelson.

FIVE

VAL

By early afternoon I had a gun on my hip and I was back in my element. From outside the room, I watched through the one-way window and assessed Jordan Nelson's demeanor. His face was beet-red and there were tears in his eyes. His silver hair was in disarray, and he rubbed his beard as he answered the detective's questions. At first glance, he appeared to be in shock at the death of his wife.

At a knock on the door, the detective glanced up at the mirror. He was about fifty and wore a dark suit and had a buzz cut, resembling someone who had served in the military and had decided to keep the hairstyle long past his time served. As he rose from his seat to open the door, I watched Mr. Nelson bury his face in his hands. Was he distraught because his wife had been killed, or was he was afraid he'd be found responsible for her death? The detective stepped out into the hall and shut the door behind him.

Brady said, "Hey, Allan. This is Val Costa. She's a consultant, former FBI, and will be leading the Claire Nelson case. Val, this is Allan, he's one of the detectives working on the case."

We shook hands and I noticed his chiseled chin resembled a heroic comic book character.

"Oh yes, the sheriff told me you'd be coming in. Thank you for helping out with the case. We could definitely use your expertise. Welcome to the team."

"Thank you. How's he doing in there?"

"I haven't worked a lot of homicide cases. I mostly handle robberies, home invasions, grand theft. Before Red Rose County, I worked near the border handling drug crimes, a few homicides, but nothing like this. Between the three of us, I'd say he seems genuinely upset about his wife's death."

"Any criminal history? Alibi? Have you checked financials yet?"

Allan smirked playfully. "You like to dive right in. No, yes, and yes. Nothing unusual in his financials."

Recalling he owned the hardware store, I said, "Did you check his business financials too? Or just his personal accounts?"

"Just personal so far. We have Lucy working on a full inquiry into anything connected to Jordan and his wife."

Lucy, a researcher I had met during the Scarlett Douglas case, was good at what she did, and if I remembered rightly, she had worked in New York before settling in Red Rose County. "Sounds like you could use a break."

"Nah. I'm good. As soon as we got the call, we started working and we haven't stopped since."

Good to know I'd be working with a dedicated team. "Well, then, wish me luck."

"Luck," he said as he opened the door to the interview room for me.

I said, "Thanks," and stepped inside.

Mr. Nelson glanced up and I offered a tight-lipped smile before taking the chair across from him. "Hi, Mr. Nelson. I'm Val Costa. I'm sorry for your loss."

He cocked his head.

"I'm Elizabeth Costa's daughter."

"Oh yes, the FBI agent, right?"

"That's right. I was formerly an FBI agent, but I've moved back home to help take care of my mother. But I'll also be helping the sheriff's department to find out what happened to your wife."

"That's awfully good of you to take care of your mom." He lowered his head and shook it. "Sorry, I'm heartbroken, but my kids... They've lost their mother."

"I'm so sorry. I lost my father when I was young, so I understand. Are your children at home currently?"

"No, they're on their way home from college. Sarah is at UCLA, and Jake at San Francisco State."

"You must be very proud."

He nodded.

"I know you've probably been asked this several times, but I'm just coming into the investigation. Could you please tell me what happened last night?"

His eyes met mine. "I understand. I left the hardware store around eight. I was closing that night. It only takes me about ten minutes to drive home. When I got home, I noticed Claire's car wasn't in the driveway, so I assumed she'd gone out to the store. I walked inside the house and there were no lights on, but that wasn't unusual. It wasn't until I stepped into the kitchen that I saw her."

Mr. Nelson paused, visibly trying to compose himself to continue his story. Based on his speech pattern and movements, I would say that everything he was saying seemed genuine. "Take your time, Mr. Nelson."

He nodded again. "I found her on the floor, and she was gone. I tried to find a pulse, even though she was already so pale and cold to the touch. I knew not to touch anything else, and I called the police right away. I still can't believe this has happened. You will find out who did this to her, right?"

As I stared into his eyes, there was a flicker of something that I couldn't quite place. Everything had seemed straightforward about Mr. Nelson except that look in his eyes.

"I will find out what happened to Claire."

"Thank you. I can't believe this," he cried.

"Can you tell me about your life with Claire? Were there any problems in your marriage?"

He shook his head. "No, we were happy. Married thirty years. Of course we had our ups and downs over the years, but we were in a great place. We had just become empty nesters as our youngest had gone off to college last year. We were starting to think about traveling, what we would do next. She loved her job at the high school, and the students loved her."

His account matched what my mother and her friends had told me about Claire. "Were there any students, other teachers, or neighbors that she might have had a scuffle or disagreement with?"

"Not that I know of, but you might want to talk with the school. She never mentioned any issues, but you never know." He hesitated. "Teenagers can be temperamental."

His remark made me wonder if he suspected a teenager had killed his wife. "Can you think of anybody who may have wanted to hurt your wife, or you?"

He shook his head again but didn't meet my eyes. "No."

I glanced behind at the mirror, to signal Brady and Allan to take note of his behavior.

"Is there anything you can tell me about Claire and her routine that may have been different over the last few weeks? Were there any new habits, new hobbies. Maybe she joined a new gym?"

Jordan shrugged. "I don't think so. I mean, she usually got home from school between 3 and 4:45 p.m. It just depended on if she was going to do grading at home or stay at school for a meeting. I usually came home around eight, and then we'd have a late dinner. We were night owls. For the life of me, I can't think of anyone who could've done this."

There was that flicker again. "Is there anything else you can tell us that might help us figure out what happened to Claire?"

He shrugged again, his gaze falling sadly to the floor. "No, I can't think of anything."

I thanked him for his time, but I knew this wouldn't be the last time I would be speaking to him. There was something there that I couldn't quite put my finger on. If my instincts told me anything, it was that he wasn't telling us everything.

SIX

THE SECRET ADMIRER

"Well, well, well, it must be my lucky day."

She was magnificent, not in a flashy kind of way, but in a manner that captivated me and probably everyone she encountered. Slender, with soft dark hair cascading down to her shoulders, she was remarkable.

The first time we met, I sensed she was special.

And here we were again.

She strutted across the parking lot with Deputy Tanner. Initially, I wondered why she was at the sheriff's station, but then I quickly realized the obvious. Knowing that she was staying in town with her mother, I knew it wouldn't be long before she got involved in another investigation. She was probably itching for a case to work on. She had already proven she couldn't sit still very long when she had taken over the Scarlett Douglas case after being in town only a couple of days.

She had done an excellent job on that one.

A true hero, the unstoppable Valerie Costa.

A stunning specimen.

I must admit, she had occupied my mind more than all the others. She intrigued me. It wasn't like that with the others.

There was something about her that set her apart, drawing me to her. I liked to think that the day we met, it was fate.

Fate had brought me a worthy adversary, or perhaps a partner. I had no doubt that Valerie Costa had taken on the Claire Nelson murder case. Would she solve it? What would she discover? I was looking forward to watching her in her element. Shining like a diamond in the back of a dark cave, illuminating the path for all to follow.

I had her only briefly, but I would have her again. She was smart, but not as smart as me. I couldn't wait for us to be together again, but not yet. Patience was key, for the next time we were together, I wouldn't let her go. I had big plans for Valerie Costa.

SEVEN

VAL

Despite the warm late summer air, I felt the hairs on the back of my neck stand up as I reached for the car door. Glancing around the parking lot at the Red Rose County Sheriff Station, I saw it was relatively full of cars, but it was just Brady and me in the lot. What was it that was making me uncomfortable?

Brady stopped and stared at me. "What is it?"

I hesitated before replying, "Nothing, let's go."

My therapist had warned me about possible paranoia after my encounter with the Bear. Perhaps "being more on edge" was a better description. But I couldn't let those feelings interfere with the Claire Nelson murder investigation.

As the doors of Brady's SUV unlocked with a click, I climbed into the passenger side, trying to shake off how creeped-out I felt.

"All right, partner, let's get going," I said, forcing a smile.

Brady said, "How is Harrison enjoying his trip?"

"He's having the time of his life."

"Is he excited about starting college?"

"Honestly, I don't think he's thinking too much about it right now. I've heard there's been lots of sangria."

Brady hesitated and gave me a look. "Well, if I didn't say it before, I'll say it now: I'm glad you're here. It's nice to have a friend in town."

Shifting in my seat, I said, "You haven't made any new friends in the last three years? That's not like the Brady I remember."

"No, I've met new people. I've joined a hiking club and, don't laugh," he took his eyes off the road to glance at me, "I'm on a bowling team."

Suppressing a laugh, I said, "Just like your dad." We had joked about Brady's father incessantly when we were kids, thinking bowling was the dorkiest of all the sports. Everything from the shoes to the team shirts and the brightly colored balls.

"Yeah. It's more fun than you'd think. But I don't know... I just feel comfortable with you."

We had been really good friends in high school, competitive in all areas. But was it something more now? "Well, since my mom is being looked after, we'll have to try to socialize as opposed to just work on murder investigations."

"Deal. Hopefully, we can solve this one quickly. The sheriff's under a lot of pressure right now."

Of course he was. We had a brutal murder on our hands, the likes of which I couldn't recall in all my years of living in the county. While Scarlett Douglas' death was tragic, it hadn't been particularly violent.

As we drove toward Hectorville, I gazed at the tall pines that lined the road. We were in forest land, and it was gorgeous —a stark contrast to the urban landscapes of Washington, DC, or the FBI's headquarters in Quantico.

I opened the case file and studied the details of the Nelson home. I didn't know the area particularly well since it was two towns over from Rosedale. But all the towns within the county had similarities: they were small, people had large lots and usually enjoyed an outdoor lifestyle of hiking, fishing, and hunting.

Brady made a left onto a gravel road. It was private, and I suspected that the property itself had to be at least five acres. It was back from the road by some 200 yards.

Brady parked the SUV next to a couple of black-and-white cruisers, and I found myself studying the house. It was encased in natural beauty, surrounded by towering trees with a cobblestone path leading to the two-story house. It was a bright, sunny yellow with white trim and a wraparound porch. It was nothing like the crime scene photos.

"Has CSI finished collecting evidence?"

"Not yet," Brady said. "They worked up to a certain point last night. From my understanding, the common areas have been completed, but the bedrooms and the back of the house are still being processed."

Stepping out of the vehicle, I inhaled the fresh scent of pine and cedar. The front door of the house opened, and a man clad in black and white, with "CSI" emblazoned on his front pocket, appeared. Brady approached him.

"Swanson, how's it looking in there?"

"We're just about finished up."

"Good to hear. Have you met Valerie Costa?"

"Not yet. Haven't had the pleasure. Nice to meet you. I am Bernard Swanson, head of the CSI team."

He had a firm handshake. "Good to meet you. Call me Val."

"I'd been told you'd be helping out with the investigation. Ex-FBI, am I right?"

With a warm smile, I said, "And Sheriff Costa's daughter."

"I heard. Word gets around fast here. Welcome to the team, Val."

"Thanks. What can you tell me about the samples you've collected?"

"We can walk through the house together if you prefer," Swanson suggested.

From his satchel, he pulled out booties and gloves, handing them to Brady and myself.

We covered our shoes and hands, the gloves snapping into place.

Swanson said, "After me."

As we stepped over the threshold, I noticed the deadbolt and the lock on the front door were undisturbed. If the assailant had forced entry, it wasn't through the front door. We stepped into a clean hallway, and as we continued, we came to a living room with a giant fireplace. The mantelpiece was adorned with what looked like family photos, and a cozy couch that was large enough to seat an entire family. To the right was a sitting room or a library, with floor-to-ceiling bookshelves.

We continued behind Specialist Swanson until he came to a stop. "This is the kitchen, where we found Claire Nelson."

I eyed the doorframe and looked inside. The kitchen was large, with an island in the center and gray tile on the floor. It had been updated recently, with white cabinets above and below, and stainless-steel appliances. The cabinets and floor were covered with yellow evidence markers, and there was blood splatter on the cabinets and floors, along with a large pool of blood where Claire had taken her last breath. Bloody footprints marked the floor.

The scene in the kitchen had been meticulously marked by the CSI team, with indicators on everything from shoe prints to fingerprints. The amount of blood and the apparent disregard for leaving fingerprints on the refrigerator door handle, the cabinets, and the pantry suggested a frenzied attack and aftermath. "What about inside the refrigerator?" I asked.

"We picked up prints in there too," Swanson replied.

The countertops were clear, except for a pool of blood next

to a roll of paper towels and bloody prints on the drawer directly below.

"What's in the drawer?"

"Kitchen towels," he responded.

A sign that the suspect had bandaged a wound, but there were no remnants of a snack. In several cases I'd investigated, the perpetrator, exhausted from the exertion, had pulled out a container of orange juice or made a sandwich, leaving crumbs or an empty bottle behind. But this kitchen, aside from the blood, was completely tidy. It didn't make sense.

I continued to explore the home, trying to understand how the suspect might have gained entry. The rest of the house appeared relatively undisturbed. I examined each bedroom, two of which clearly belonged to the Nelsons' children, their rooms adorned with posters, still on the walls as if they hadn't been touched since they had left for college.

Turning to Brady, I asked, "When exactly are the Nelson kids due back?"

"I believe in a few hours," he answered.

That meant they hadn't been home yet, as their father had said, and the crime scene remained sealed.

Entering the primary bedroom, it was typical: dressers, wedding photos on the wall, and a king-size bed neatly made. The Nelsons were meticulous housekeepers. In the bathroom, I studied the soaking tub, the sink, and the floors. Nothing seemed to have been disturbed.

"Has everything in the house been photographed?" I asked Swanson.

He nodded. "Oh yeah, floor to ceiling. Photographs of absolutely everything." This wasn't typical; usually, the focus was on the actual scene of the crime, but this time their thoroughness was beneficial since some things still weren't quite adding up.

After checking the upstairs bedrooms, which included what looked like an office or study, I headed back downstairs, moving toward the back door, passing through the laundry room. Waving Swanson over, I asked, "Did you get a picture of this?"

"Yep, interesting, right?"

It was. Near the back door, there appeared to be a set of muddy footprints. "Perhaps this is how they gained entry?"

The dirty prints stopped after a few feet. Did the assailant change into clean shoes? If so, had they brought the shoes with them, which would make it premeditated murder?

Swanson said, "Maybe. No sign of forced entry, but it's the only dirty thing in the whole house, other than the kitchen."

I continued to study the walls, doors, and handles as I made my way back toward the front of the house. That's when I spotted it. The bloody handprint on the doorknob. The perpetrator might have come in from the back, but they had left through the front.

"When will we get the prints back?" I asked.

"Any minute. They're being processed and put through AFIS to see if we get a match."

AFIS, the Automated Fingerprint Identification System, is a database of fingerprint data used by government agencies, including law enforcement, to help identify individuals by their fingerprints. I had a nagging feeling we weren't going to be lucky enough to get a match from the fingerprints. That would be too easy. The suspect clearly hadn't been concerned about leaving them, which made me think they probably weren't in the system. Either that, or the killer had panicked and forgot all about forensics.

With a gloved hand, I opened the door and stepped outside.

Brady asked, "What do you think?"

Based on what I had seen, I began to piece it together. "It's possible Claire Nelson's attacker entered through the back, caught Claire by surprise in the kitchen, pulled the knife from the block and stabbed Claire repeatedly until she was dead, and then looked for something. Maybe they even asked her for it.

They left through the front door with her keys, her wallet, and the car. Did Mr. Nelson say anything else was missing from the house?"

"He said it didn't look like anything was missing," Brady responded.

Something didn't feel right. I walked down the steps and turned to look back at the house. There was no surveillance system in place. "I'm going to check out the back entrance," I announced as I made my way around the house. If a car had pulled up, Mrs. Nelson would've likely heard it. So why had they bothered going through the back door?

EIGHT

VAL

After a thorough inspection of the backyard—with its patio chairs, table, barbecue pit—and the expanse of forest land covered in grasses until the tree line, we returned to the front of the home. Brady leaned on the hood of his SUV, while I stood next to Specialist Swanson.

"What do you think, Val? Is there enough here for a profile?" Brady asked.

"I need some time to think about it and review the case file again, but my first impression is that it's an unusual scene."

"How so?" Brady inquired.

"Well, you saw the place was covered in fingerprints. That alone tells us that it wasn't a sophisticated killer. And the killing likely wasn't planned."

Staring out at the house and surrounding forest, I continued, "In my mind, there are a couple of scenarios. One possibility is that there are two suspects. One drives up, goes to the front door, talks to Mrs. Nelson. While this suspect keeps Mrs. Nelson occupied, the second suspect enters through the back door, not wearing any shoes, slips on shoes once inside, and then surprises Claire in the kitchen and attacks her, stabbing her to death."

"While suspect number one stands outside, waiting? There was only one set of bloody shoe prints inside the home though," Swanson countered.

"Maybe."

"What's your second theory?" Brady prodded.

"The dirty prints at the back door have nothing to do with this. Perhaps Claire had been out there earlier that day. She comes in, maybe she had slippers by the door or outdoor shoes—not uncommon. She slips them on but doesn't get a chance to clean up her own footprints because she hears someone at the front door. She goes to answer it, and it's someone she knows. Maybe they get into an argument in the kitchen. The assailant picks up a knife from the knife block and stabs her."

Swanson chimed in, "Do you think drugs might be involved?"

"It's possible. However, given the remoteness of their home and how far off the road it is, I just don't see this as a random act. You don't just walk down the road, decide to go two hundred yards off the highway, knock on the front door, and start attacking someone, especially when the rest of the home is completely undisturbed. Unless it was a hitchhiker."

Brady said, "We don't get a lot of those these days."

Swanson nodded. "Trucks tend to keep to the main highway and those are the only folks who are likely to take a risk on a stranger."

My thoughts were racing with the possibilities.

"If a hitchhiker is out of the suspect pool, I'd say that based on the remoteness of the location, it's likely the killer was familiar with Claire or the property. She likely let the assailant in the house, or they slipped in through an unlocked door. Mr. Nelson said nothing was missing from the home. If that's true, then it wasn't a robbery. Or maybe it was but they didn't find what they were looking for. If they searched the house for something, they were neat about it. Or they just needed a car and went inside the house to find the keys, encountered Claire, and killed her before fleeing in the stolen vehicle. But how did they get there? There is no public transport for miles. But if it wasn't a robbery, based on the intensity of the kill and lack of another motive aside from killing Claire, the next theory is that it's personal." Pondering that, I knew what our next task would be. "We need to interview everyone who knew Claire. Her children, husband, neighbors, colleagues, and the kids she teaches."

"You think one of the teens she teaches at the high school could have done this?" Brady asked, skeptically.

"It's possible. Jordan Nelson said something odd in his interview this morning. He commented that teenagers were temperamental. Perhaps he was suggesting Claire might have been having problems with one of her students. Perhaps something pushed them over the edge to come here to kill her."

"Are you thinking it *wasn't* a robbery?" Swanson interjected.

"I'm not sure yet. We'll know more once all the evidence has been processed."

It didn't look like a robbery, considering the only thing missing from the house was likely the murder weapon, the missing chef's knife, and Claire's car, keys, and wallet. How had they arrived at the house if they didn't have a car? Could it have been a neighbor?

"Sounds irrational," Swanson commented.

Brady said, "It does, sort of. Maybe one of the teens who had a problem with her also had a drug problem, didn't think everything through, leaving fingerprints everywhere."

"It's possible. They didn't break in, unless the Nelsons typically left their doors unlocked. And we don't think they brought a weapon to the scene. They grabbed the first thing at hand, which suggests an inexperienced killer. My guess is they cut themselves during the attack, hence the makeshift first aid station with the paper towels on the countertop," I concluded.

There was something else about the scene, something more. A sense of desperation, almost. The frenzy didn't start in one room and end in another; it was a singular, concentrated attack.

If Claire had known her attacker, how had they got there? They had to have walked there or had an accomplice. Or a friend had dropped them off, not knowing they would be aiding a killer. Maybe it was a student she'd taken home to tutor? Or someone she was having an affair with? She'd tried to break it off and he'd got upset and killed her, taking her car to flee the scene?

The lack of a weapon or escape vehicle all pointed toward someone close to her. Or someone who was familiar with her schedule. Someone like her husband. Had he killed her himself or had he ordered someone to do it for him?

NINE

VAL

Based on the location of the Nelson residence, the only people who could have realistically got there on foot were neighbors. From what we could tell, the nearest neighbor was about a tenth of a mile from their private drive. Could it have been a neighbor? I didn't know much about Claire Nelson. Only after interviewing her coworkers, children, and her husband again would I get a clear picture of who she really was, what her daily comings and goings were.

"Have you canvassed the neighbors?" I asked.

"Just the ones on either side."

"What are you thinking?" Brady asked.

"I'm thinking whoever killed Claire either walked to the house or was dropped off by an accomplice. If they were able to walk there, they had to live within walking distance. I think we need to canvas the neighbors three to five miles on either side."

Brady gritted his teeth. "That's quite a bit of work."

"Well, then we better get started."

"Yes, ma'am."

We waved to Swanson and headed back into the SUV.

Brady said, "Do you think it could be a neighbor?"

"It could be anybody who knew Claire, even you, Brady," I said with a smirk.

"I have an alibi."

"Is that right?"

"That's right. My butt was in a chair at the sheriff's station doing paperwork at the likely time of death."

"Has the ME confirmed time of death?"

"Right now, it's a pretty big window. Between four and eight in the evening. She told me she'll be able to narrow it down after the autopsy."

"But we also have your fingerprints on file, so you're probably safe."

Brady gave me his famously boyish grin and said, "I wouldn't say I'm safe. I'm a bit of a bad boy these days."

I couldn't help but laugh. Brady had been a lot of things in his youth, but a bad boy wasn't one of them. Sure, we both snuck alcohol and smoked a few cigarettes behind the gym at school, but he was *not* a bad boy. He'd always been one of the good ones, always looking out for the underdog, stood up to bullies—the whole nine yards.

"Can we pull in help from other departments?"

"Probably. I can ask the sheriff."

"Good. It'll cut down on the time it'll take to get through all the neighbors."

"You don't think it's a neighbor?"

I shrugged. "Not unless she had a close relationship with one of them. But questioning them will give us a better idea if she did or not."

"It's a good thing you're in town, Val."

"Beats watching courtroom TV with Mom."

He laughed at that and pulled into the first driveway. As we drove down the private drive, the setup was very similar to the Nelsons' house, nestled among the forest. But this home looked more reminiscent of a giant log cabin.

We pulled up, and before Brady had even turned off the engine, our presence had been noted. The homeowner stood on the porch, and I immediately thought that this was exactly how Claire would've reacted if she'd heard someone drive up to her house. Unless, of course, she had been expecting someone. Brady waved to an older woman with chin-length gray hair and wire-rim glasses, wearing a shapeless floral dress. Recognizing Brady, she waved back.

"Deputy Tanner, what can I help you with? Is this about Claire next door?"

He nodded and introduced me to Doris. She smiled. "Good to meet you. I've heard all about you. Welcome home!"

That was small-town living for you. My guess was that Doris was a long-term resident and knew my mother. "Thank you."

"How's Elizabeth doing?"

"She's getting better every day."

"That's wonderful. You give her my best and let her know we're praying for her."

"I will."

"So, what can I help you with? Did you want to come in? Or we could have a seat on the porch?"

"No, that's okay. We don't expect to take up much of your time. But we did want to ask whether you had noticed anything unusual in the past few days, or if anybody in your household is unaccounted for."

She nodded. "I haven't seen anything unusual. And it's just me and my husband who live here. He's taking a nap right now. Definitely not missing."

"Did you hear anything yesterday late afternoon, early evening?" I asked.

She shook her head. "No, I was as shocked as everybody else when I read the news in the paper this morning. She was such a lovely woman. It's such a shame. Have you met Jordan and the kids? Such a lovely family."

"Did you ever hear the Nelsons arguing?"

She shrugged. "If they fought, I wouldn't have heard it. But no, I mean, I've seen them in town, and we go to the hardware store at least once a month. They're just the nicest people. Such a tragedy. We're going to miss Claire. She would bring us a pie every Christmas. Apple, my favorite."

"Thank you, Doris."

Before we could say our goodbyes, a tall, frail gentleman, maybe eighty years old, with large glasses, emerged. "Deputy Tanner! Oh, you must be Valerie Costa. All grown up."

Slight recognition flashed through my memory. Mr. Brown, the high school auto shop teacher. "Good to see you, Mr. Brown."

"You two were students?" Doris asked us.

We nodded and after a few pleasantries, we said our goodbyes and headed back on the road.

From the look of Mr. and Mrs. Brown, I wouldn't have thought they were capable of the carnage I'd seen in the crime scene photos. Maybe Doris had the strength, but Mr. Brown moved slowly and I doubted he could have overpowered Claire. And they didn't seem to have a single negative thing to say about the Nelsons.

My twenty years in law enforcement told me they had nothing to do with it. After three more grueling hours, we had questioned every neighbor in either direction of the Nelsons.

Not a suspicious one in the bunch. Each neighbor expressed the same positive opinions about the Nelsons: a wonderful family—just the nicest people. Nobody had a bad word to say about Jordan and Claire Nelson.

From the interviews we conducted, we learned that Claire was a caring and devoted teacher, and she cared for her neighbors. Like Mrs. Brown had said, she brought her an apple pie every Christmas. Other neighbors reported she brought them casseroles when their spouse was sick or when they had lost a loved one. Claire didn't seem to have any enemies.

My thoughts kept drifting back to her husband, and more than ever, I was looking forward to having a follow-up conversation with him. After everything I'd seen at the house, I had several questions. And I needed to get to the bottom of that twitchy feeling I had about him. There was something familiar and unsettling about our conversation that I couldn't shake.

TEN

VAL

Reviewing the crime scene photos, I was reminded of the viciousness of the crime. What could have precipitated inside the individual who had killed Claire? Claire had been stabbed in the chest, shoulder, and neck. My guess, just from the photographs, was that it may not have been overkill so much as the person wanted to make sure she was dead. But why? Why did this person want Claire Nelson dead? From the neighbors' accounts, she was a pillar of the community, a warm individual who went out of her way to take care of others. The only person it could have been, therefore, was someone who knew her intimately, someone full of rage, or someone under the influence of drugs. But if it wasn't someone she knew, then who?

After walking the scene and reviewing the crime scene notes and photos, I wondered if the research team had searched for similar crimes in the area. Maybe not within Red Rose County, but the surrounding counties. I got up from my seat and stretched my arms overhead. My makeshift office was a very small conference room, comprising of a round table and two chairs.

We needed a task force room, and a murder board, but I

doubted anyone had started one. Feeling more limber, I headed over to Brady's desk.

"Find something?" he asked.

I shook my head, looking at his desk, which was piled high with documents. I was suddenly grateful for my tiny office because I didn't know how well I would do out in the open, with so many distractions—phones ringing, people talking.

"Is it possible we can set up a conference room, get a murder board going?"

"Oh yeah, of course. Let's go talk to Allan and see how far he's got."

From my understanding, Allan had taken the first shot at the investigation until I was brought in. "Let's go."

Brady stood up and waved Allan over.

"How's it going, Val?" Allan said.

"It's going okay. I wanted to know if you'd started a murder board. Or if we had a conference room we can set up in?"

"Not yet, but I have a room designated. Follow me."

We followed Allan into a conference room, considerably larger than my makeshift office. There was a whiteboard on one wall, a projector on the other, and an oval table with seating for eight. The room was drab, with no artwork, posters, or anything to break up the monotony of the gray walls, but it would do.

"Any new developments?" I asked.

Allan said, "The research team is pulling surveillance footage to confirm Jordan's alibi. The CSI team is working on the forensics, and the autopsy should start tomorrow morning."

"It'll be useful to have a more concrete time of death."

"Let us know what you need."

"How about we have everybody who's working on the case meet here in an hour, if they're still around?"

Brady raised his eyebrows. "It's almost four o'clock, Val."

Allan said, "I can stay."

"Sorry, I'm not used to taking breaks on cases. Allan, if you want to join me, great. Brady, if you can too. And a member of the research team, if possible. How about Lucy?"

Brady said, "I'll check with her."

"Great. I'll grab the file and start marking up the murder board."

Allan looked at me eagerly. "You want some help?"

He must be an adrenaline junkie who loved a tough case, just like me. "Sure."

Brady said, "I'll talk to Lucy and be back to help too."

"The more, the merrier."

An hour later all the information we had so far had been set up visually on the murder board: a timeline, potential suspects, people to be interviewed. There was still a tremendous amount of work to do.

A knock on the door turned our attention. It was Lucy, with those giant glasses and a giant brain to match. She waved sheepishly, and I waved her inside. "Hi, Lucy."

"Hi, Val. Good to see you again."

Lucy had been invaluable in the Scarlett Douglas case. After we'd exchanged pleasantries, I had everybody take a seat as I stood next to the murder board and outlined everything we had found so far and what we needed next. "So, you want a background on Jordan Nelson, the kids, and everybody Claire worked with?" Lucy asked, a hint of hesitation in her voice.

I said, "Is that too much? We can prioritize."

"Yeah, let's prioritize. That way, we can get the most important information first."

"Okay, we'll do backgrounds on the suspects first. Tomorrow, I'll start interviewing Claire's coworkers and students at the high school. We've already met with the neighbors. There are a few I want you to check out. You'll see it on the notes here." I pushed my notebook toward her.

She nodded.

"The autopsy is being done tomorrow. Hopefully, we'll get confirmation of the timeline of her death, as well as anything else of interest that Dr. Edison may find."

Allan tapped his pen on the table. "Does the report say what time the husband called in the murder?"

I realized we hadn't written it on the board. I flipped through the pages of the report until I found the information. My heart skipped a beat.

Looking up at Allan, Brady, and Lucy, I said, "He called it in at 9 p.m. last night."

"Almost an hour after he got home?" Lucy asked, with widened eyes.

When I spoke with Jordan before visiting the scene, he said that when he found his wife, he knew she was dead, and he called the police. But according to his own statement, he left work at eight o'clock and it was only a ten-minute drive home. That meant he would have found Claire at 8:10, but he hadn't called 911 until nine o'clock. Why had he waited almost an entire hour before calling it in? "Okay, new top priority. Confirm from traffic cams what time Jordan left the hardware store and the call logs from when he called 911."

"I'll do what I can to get it done tonight."

Brady shot me a look. Overtime hadn't been approved.

"Tomorrow morning will be fine. I'm about to head home soon, too," I quickly said.

I had promised Mom we'd have dinner together each night. I couldn't blow that promise on the very first day.

"After the autopsy and confirmation of time of death, we need to re-interview Jordan. Where is he staying?" I asked.

Allan said, "Hectorville Hotel. His kids should have arrived by now too."

"Good. Let's get them all in first thing tomorrow morning." After a slight pause, I said, "After we confirm the timeline,

Lucy, if you can find out if there's been any similar home invasions-type of crimes in the surrounding counties, or even in Nevada or Oregon, that would be good."

A random burglary or stranger killing was always a possibility. But if the person knew Claire, we needed to find out the reason they wanted her dead. Understanding why she was killed would lead us straight to our suspect, or suspects.

ELEVEN

VAL

"I love you too, honey. Have fun." I ended the call, and Mom glanced at me across the kitchen table.

"How is Harrison doing? I'm guessing he's having the time of his life?"

"He absolutely is."

And I had to admit, it was invigorating to be running a case again. It was a great distraction from my own worries. Although I still checked the security cameras at least every hour on my cell phone, just like I did when I was home. I knew I was likely being paranoid, but what if I wasn't? "How are you feeling, Mom?"

"You know, I'm a little better every day," she replied with a gentle smile.

Julie, who was busy at the sink washing the breakfast dishes, chimed in, "She did great at physical therapy yesterday."

"That's what Mom was telling me last night."

"Yep, the doctor thinks she'll be walking in no time."

"I don't know about that, Julie," Mom said, a hint of skepticism in her voice.

"Well, I'm so glad you're doing well." Julie paused, drying

her hands on a towel. She looked up, her expression resolute. "And look, we've got everything under control here, Val. You find out who killed our Claire. Work late if you need to. You don't need to worry about anything here," she said, her tone commanding yet reassuring.

Mom eyed me, her gaze filled with gratitude. "It's true. They're doing a great job taking care of me. Julie is going to help me try to... take my own bath today."

Surprised, I said, "I was going to help you with that, Mom."

"I know, and you're such a lovely daughter. Don't tell Maxine, but right now, you're my favorite daughter."

I would absolutely tell my sister when I talked to her. "Are you sure you're ready for that?"

"I'll be right outside the bathroom. If she needs any help, I'll be right there."

As proud as I was of the progress my mom had made, a part of me was cautious. She couldn't be left alone while in the bath. If she had another stroke, she could drown or not get to the hospital in time. "If you're sure, Mom."

"Val, I appreciate everything you have done. It is more than you should've done. Giving up your job at the FBI... You loved that job. I guess I was selfish to let you stay and take care of me, especially now that you're working with Brady at the sheriff's department. I can tell it's been good for you to be working and not stuck in this house with us old ladies. I love seeing you sparkle again, Val."

So much for hiding things from my mother. That was one drawback of having a mother who had spent her life in law enforcement—she knew your tells as well as just about everybody else's. I suppose Harrison felt the same way; he couldn't get anything past us, or if he had, he'd been so good at it that we hadn't figured it out. "Yes, I loved the FBI, but I love you more."

"I love you too, Val."

To avoid tearing up, I said, "And Julie, I really appreciate everything you and Diane have been doing for my mom."

"Elizabeth is family, as are you. We look out for each other here in Red Rose County. We've got your mom; you've got the murder investigation. Claire Nelson was one of ours. You have to find out what happened to her. We can't let her killer run free in our county."

I wanted to broach a sensitive subject, but I was hesitant as I knew they wouldn't hear a bad word about Jordan. But I couldn't understand why he had waited so long before calling the police. He had supposedly arrived home, saw his wife had been brutally murdered, and yet he didn't call 911 straight-away? Why not? I took the plunge. "And you're sure Claire and Jordan didn't have any marital problems?"

"Oh, no," Julie insisted emphatically. "They were like a fairy-tale couple, married for thirty years, still happy and smil-ing. They held hands at the Fourth of July parade. And those kids, such good kids. Have you talked to them yet? They'll tell you the same thing. Great parents, very much part of the community."

Mom added, "Honey, I know you've got to look at the husband, but it wasn't Jordan. He just isn't the type. They were happy, as strange as that sounds. There are some couples that get married, stay married, and stay happy."

Was that directed at me? Or was she just annoyed I was still asking about Jordan? I was aware that some couples stayed married. And I knew Nathan and I weren't one of those couples. I had thought we were. For many years. How could I have predicted that after Harrison was born, my husband who had always been supportive of my career would expect me to quit the FBI to become a full-time mom?

We'd always talked about having a nanny, because we both had careers we loved. But as soon as Harrison arrived, Nathan suddenly thought the idea of a nanny was ridiculous and that it was my responsibility to look after our child. He didn't want our child to be brought up by a stranger. The first time he mentioned the idea, I thought he was joking. Many arguments later, I realized he wasn't. In the end we employed a nanny because I refused to give up my career and Nathan wouldn't even consider giving his up. It was at that point that I realized maybe Nathan wasn't the man I thought he was.

I honestly thought Nathan and I would spend the rest of our lives together—a perfect family living in DC—with me in the FBI and Nathan at the State Department.

Instead, we spent a decade arguing and growing apart. All of our differences rose to the surface and formed a bridge between us. *Surprise*, love isn't enough.

It was a rough ten years, but we chose to focus on watching Harrison grow up. Like the first time he rolled over, crawled, walked, said "Mama" and "Dada." His crooked smile on his first day of kindergarten. The artwork he'd bring home. The soccer games.

We fought hard to keep our marriage going for Harrison's sake, but neither of us were happy. I felt duped, as though my husband had tried to change me and had never really known me at all. It was as if our entire relationship had been a charade. How I had missed all the red flags, I'll never know. I was a profiler. An investigator. I should have known better.

It wasn't until Nathan said he was done with me and our marriage that I truly understood heartbreak. And what it was like to have my family, my hope for a perfect family, and my world shattered. Everything I went through when the Bear kidnapped me didn't even come close to that kind of pain.

In time, the wound began to heal. Nathan and I came to terms with coparenting and were able to build a good relationship for the sake of Harrison. But some wounds, like the "S" carved on my chest, would never fade completely.

Choosing to ignore the jab, I said, "Well, we have a good

team working the case. We'll find out the truth and bring her killer to justice."

Mom placed her hand on top of mine. "I know you will, honey. Now you go. Julie's got your coffee ready to go. Find out who killed Claire."

Mom was definitely feeling better, bossing me around, telling me what to do. It was like I was fifteen again. It was good to see, and she was right. Even after only a day of working a homicide investigation, I felt more like myself again.

Not scared, not looking over my shoulder all the time, fearing the Bear would be waiting for me. Working a new case definitely helped shift my focus. Before, I was consumed with Mom's care; now, I would be consumed with the case, knowing that Mom would be safe with so many friends always dropping in to check on her. I could finally relax a little.

Back in the conference room, or the war room as we liked to call it, Lucy rushed in, her energy infectious.

"Wow, you're here early," I remarked, impressed.

"Yeah, well, you wouldn't want to miss what I found." Her excitement was palpable.

"Oh?"

"Should I wait for everyone else?"

"You can tell me, but that means you'll have to repeat it all to the team. It's up to you."

"Okay, I'll wait. That way we'll have more minds to tell us what could be going on."

I nodded in agreement, understanding the value of a collective brainstorm. "How have you been? I haven't talked to you since... well, since they closed the Scarlett Douglas case. You were such a great help."

"True. It was kind of fun to be working a tough case again. I've got to admit, I kind of miss NYPD and the big city, but I wouldn't trade it now. I love being out here. It's like you're in a different world, but not totally. I still work for the sheriff's department, and since you've been in town, I've worked on two death investigations. So, overall, pretty good."

"Well, I'm going to say this before the team gets here. We should go out, you know, a girls' night out. Does that sound cheesy? Can I say that?"

Lucy chuckled. "I'd really like that. You know, we should invite Sally, I mean, Dr. Edison too. I think she'd be fun."

That was my impression of the medical examiner as well, with her bright red hair and insistence on being referred to by her first name, claiming that "Dr. Edison" made her sound old. "Let's do it. We can go talk to Sally after we finish up here."

"I can't wait! This is going to be fun," Lucy said.

The day I resigned from the FBI, Brady had told me that when something ended, maybe it wasn't an ending but possibly the beginning to something even better.

It felt good to be home and making plans, something I didn't do much of in DC. Not that I didn't have coworkers to socialize with, but it was usually post-hard-day kind of drinks, commiserating with the guys. It'd be nice to have girlfriends, like Mom had. Her fellow Red Hat Ladies were more than friends, they had become her family, who would drop their sparkly red hats on a moment's notice to help her.

Now in my mid-forties, I thought the end of my twenties signaled the end of our girls' nights. When all my friends, and myself, started having kids the happy hours became a thing of the past. But now, Harrison was a grown-up, and I was back in my hometown. And I was really looking forward to getting to know Lucy and Sally better. Perhaps this was exactly where I belonged. My new beginning.

Brady stepped into the war room with Allan and Deputy Baker.

"Good morning."

"Morning," I responded.

Brady gave me a look, but I couldn't quite decipher it. There was something about him that felt different from when we were in high school, like there was still a familiarity, but it was different, like we were discovering each other, getting to know one another like new friends but with a shared past.

And Allan, he seemed cool, confident, and attractive, but married. And Baker, I'd met him before. He had worked with my mom, but I wasn't quite sure why he was here. "Deputy Baker, good to see you," I greeted.

"Hey, Val," he replied.

Before he could explain further, Brady interjected, "We spoke with the sheriff and he said we could have a few more bodies to help interview students, coworkers, anyone associated with the investigation. He says it's a bit tight, but we'll find more if needed."

"Excellent, because there's a lot to do."

Lucy added, "For sure. Wish we had a few more researchers, too."

"We'll all help out," Allan offered, a sign of a real team player.

Everyone was rolling up their sleeves to get the job done. There was very little formality at the sheriff's department, unlike the bureau. Here, nobody wanted to call me by my last name, which was pretty unusual for law enforcement.

"Okay, I think that's everybody for now," Brady said. "Once we start doling out tasks, we'll see who is available if we need more help."

"Perfect." Eyeing Lucy, I said, "Lucy has an update."

"First of all, the financials are back for Jordan's business. Nothing unusual there."

That told us that if Jordan had hired someone to kill Claire, he hadn't used funds from his personal or business accounts to pay for it. Although, it was also possible that the person he hired hadn't been paid yet. "What about life insurance policies?"

Allan said, "The only policy Claire had was through the union."

Roughly equal to one to two times her salary, it wasn't enough of a motive considering that, based on their personal finances, the couple weren't short of money. They had saved and invested wisely. It was a good update, but I doubted that was all Lucy had found. "Lucy, anything else?"

She stood up and said, "Yes." Without another word, she walked over to the whiteboard, grabbed a dry erase marker, and began recording her findings. After a few minutes, she stepped back and said, "I was able to confirm from the traffic cam footage that Jordan left the hardware store at 8:10 p.m., likely arrived home ten minutes later, but didn't call 911 until 9 p.m. Jordan Nelson waited forty minutes after discovering his wife to call 911."

What on earth had he been doing for forty minutes before calling the police? Well, that would be a question to ask Jordan when we interviewed him again.

"The autopsy starts in about an hour. Dr. Edison will confirm the time of death. Jordan might have had time to kill her before calling it in."

Allan cocked his head. "Except we know the killer cut themselves during the attack. When I was interviewing Jordan, I didn't see any cuts on his hands, they were clean."

That was a good point. Perhaps he didn't cut his hand. Maybe he cut himself somewhere else. "Well, either way, we'll get a time of death to make sure that there was no way he could've killed her. Maybe the killer didn't cut their hands. Maybe they accidentally stabbed too hard and got their own leg or their arm or something else."

Allan said, "True."

"Did any of you know the Nelsons personally?" I asked the room, curious about their connections.

"I knew them from community events. I think everyone kind of does."

I glanced over at Deputy Frank Baker. "Did you know them?"

"I knew them."

"Any red flags?"

"No, well..." Frank hesitated. "I think you're wrong on this one. I know we usually have to go after the people closest to them first, but Jordan is the least likely to have killed his wife."

Nods from the gentlemen in the room followed. Lucy didn't nod. Maybe she didn't know the Nelsons well enough. "How about you, Lucy? Did you know them?"

"I've seen them around, but I didn't know them personally," she admitted.

"You get any weird vibes from Jordan or Claire?"

She shook her head. "But that doesn't mean he wasn't weird. I mean, come on, I think we've seen enough headlines to know that people are capable of terrible things with no prior history. Something could've made him snap and kill her for whatever reason."

Lucy's insight resonated with me. She was right. It happened all the time. "All right, let's come up with a game plan and then head over to the autopsy suite."

It was progress. I was glad to have a good team, especially Lucy and Brady. Any homicide investigation could be taxing, and it was important to have a supportive partner. Allan and Frank were capable too, but they were too close to the people in this town. I was from a small town but had been away for a long time, just now returning with a fresh perspective, not completely intertwined with the community yet.

With all the talk about me around town—the sheriff's

daughter, the retired FBI agent who had solved the Scarlett Douglas case—they knew about me, but I didn't know a whole lot about the town, not anymore. And that was about to change.

TWELVE

VAL

Claire Nelson's gray face was eerily flawless. Her killer hadn't touched her face. That could be significant. If it was someone who truly hated her, they likely would have wanted to destroy her, especially her face. It didn't fit with the profile I had been building in my mind.

Taking a closer look at the wounds, now cleaned by Dr. Edison, I could see the full extent of the victim's injuries. The knife wounds were concentrated mostly on her chest and at shoulder level, with only a few at the neck. And there was a nasty slice on one of her fingers. The rest of her body was nearly pristine.

"If you look here," Dr. Edison, the medical examiner pointed out, "this cut to her neck was likely the final, fatal blow, severing her carotid artery, and she bled out."

"What do you make of the fact that the majority of the stab wounds are at chest level?" I asked, trying to work out their significance.

"In my experience, it indicates the killer was of average height, and roughly, and I mean give or take several inches, a similar height to Claire. Claire is five feet, two inches, so the killer probably would not have been more than five feet, eight inches. If they were any taller, the direction of penetration would have been downward, likely onto her head and neck if the aim was to kill her."

That was what I had figured. When I had met Jordan Nelson, he was sitting down, so I couldn't be certain of his height. "Any sign of sexual assault?"

Dr. Edison shook her head. "No. There are no bruises or cuts to indicate that. Based on the condition of the body, I would say the perpetrator's sole intention was to kill her."

It wasn't a lust killer or somebody who wanted to deface her, humiliate her. They simply wanted to kill her. That still didn't exclude her husband. It was common in homicides where the husband killed his wife for the victim to be killed but not sexually assaulted. The lack of emotional factors made me believe the killer had one goal. Perhaps a hired gun? I could see it. Jordan wanted to get rid of his wife, so he convinced a young person, inexperienced in killing, to do the deed. Or it could have been a robbery gone wrong, where the suspect simply killed her to not leave a witness.

Dr. Edison lifted Claire's body, showing us her back—a gruesome, purplish black—and then set her back down gently.

"When I arrived at the scene at ten o'clock, she was in full rigor mortis. Rigor mortis usually sets in between two to six hours after the time of death. Obviously, there are things that can affect that, but that, mixed with livor mortis—which, as you can see, is the pooling of the blood in the part of the body that was laid up against the tile—begins two to four hours after death and fixes around twelve hours. Add in her body temperature calculation, and I can confidently say she died between four and six o'clock on Monday evening."

Turning to Lucy, I said, "Does the traffic cam footage confirm Jordan was inside the hardware store between four and six p.m. on Monday?"

She nodded. "He couldn't have killed Claire."

But he could've had someone else kill her. If the time of death was accurate, anybody available between 4 and 6 p.m. could've killed Claire. That would fit the lifestyle of a teacher or a student.

Was it possible Jordan had persuaded a teenager to commit the crime for him? His comment about teenagers being temperamental echoed in my mind. It wouldn't be the first time an older person had manipulated a vulnerable teen into doing such a thing. Or was one of them having an affair? It wasn't out of the question.

Brady chimed in, "Sounds like it clears Jordan Nelson of the crime."

Our eyes met, and I said, "Not necessarily."

Lucy added, "I'm doubtful too. Just because he didn't strike the blow doesn't mean he didn't have a hand in it."

I nodded at Lucy's insight.

"I'm inclined to keep investigating the husband too," Dr. Edison said, rather unexpectedly. "I always got a weird vibe from him."

"Really?" I asked, more than a little surprised.

She nodded, though hesitantly. "I can't really put my finger on it, so I probably shouldn't have said anything. I take it back."

One's own intuition was real. "Don't forget it, Sally. What kind of feeling did you get?"

Sally removed her latex gloves. "I can't really explain it. There were times I felt he was staring at me for too long. It made me uncomfortable. I don't know how else to describe it."

I had felt the same unease around Jordan Nelson, a twitch that I couldn't quite decipher. There was something not right about him, and I was determined to uncover what that was, along with the truth behind who killed Claire Nelson.

With our protective gear in the trash, Brady said, "Back to the war room?"

"In a minute. I'll catch up with you."

He hesitated before saying, "Okay," and heading down the hall.

Alone with Sally and Lucy, I said, "So, Lucy and I were talking..." A few minutes later we had solid plans for a girls' night out on the town. We'd have a glass of wine, dinner, and most likely a discussion about the investigation. And I couldn't wait.

THIRTEEN

VAL

Sarah Nelson bore a striking resemblance to her mother with her high cheekbones and long, flowing blonde hair. She was the eldest and most distraught of the Nelson children.

"I'm so sorry for your loss, Sarah. I know this must be an incredibly difficult time."

She sniffled, her voice trembling. "Yes, I can't believe it. It's like a nightmare. I just wish I'd wake up."

Her brother Jake, sharing the same fair hair and skin, was tall and wiry like their father. Younger and not as confident, he reminded me a little of Harrison. Jake broke the silence. "You will find who did this to our mom, right?"

I assured him confidently, "We will." I then changed tack. "I wanted to ask you about your mom and your dad and what it was like growing up in your house."

Sarah's tone shifted to one of accusation. "Why? You don't think my dad had anything to do with this, do you?"

"Of course not," I said calmly, and hopefully convincingly. "We're just trying to understand more about your mom and her life. It's typical in this type of investigation to learn as much as we can about the victim."

Their father, who was sitting silently in the corner next to Sarah, tapped her on the shoulder and nodded, giving his approval for them to answer our questions.

I would have preferred to interview the children alone, but they had insisted on their father being present. Perhaps it made them feel more secure.

Sarah nodded, her eyes reflecting a mix of sadness and nostalgia. "We had a great home life. I mean, sometimes Mom was a little strict. It was kind of annoying to have your mom as one of the teachers at your school, but she was pretty cool about it. And after I started college, she'd send me care packages with homemade cookies, and she always made sure we had everything we needed. She cheered us on at our basketball games and made us costumes for Halloween."

Jake chimed in with a soft voice, "She was the best mom."

Jordan hung his head, likely feeling the weight of his children's grief. As Sarah began to cry, Jordan excused himself to get her some water and tissues.

Typically, one of us would've done that for them, but I wanted to take advantage of Jordan's temporary absence.

I said, "Was there anything unusual going on at home? Did you know of any close friends, neighbors, or students she was having any issues with?"

Sarah wiped away her tears and shook her head firmly. "No, never."

"When was the last time you came home from college, Sarah?"

"A few months ago. I just got back from a summer study program in Spain, and then I went directly back to school. I have off-campus housing and wanted to settle in before the quarter started. Mom and Dad were planning to visit me soon." She paused before saying, "I'm studying at UCLA."

"What are you studying?"

"International business." She stopped, as if remembering

something, and said, "They were supposed to visit this weekend."

Her face scrunched up, like she was fighting back tears.

Turning to Jake, I said, "How about you, Jake? You're about to start your second year of college?"

"Yeah."

"When was the last time you visited home?"

A moment passed before he said, "Back in June."

"How long were you home?"

"Just a week. I went back to school early because I'd started a new part-time job, and we're on the semester system. Classes started last week."

"Since you'd been away, had you noticed any changes between your parents, or in your mom? Did she have any new hobbies or friends?"

Jake shook his head, a hint of confusion in his eyes. "No, nothing I can think of, except we were planning a family trip, and Mom and Dad talked about a second honeymoon."

There was nothing to indicate there was any trouble at home. We hadn't found a single person who could crack the image of the Nelsons' perfect family.

Except for Sally and my instincts telling us something was off about Jordan.

Jordan came back into the room, and the children's demeanor shifted, their eyes following their father's movements. Sarah grabbed the tissues Jordan offered and dabbed at the corners of her eyes.

Observing them, it was evident that the Nelson family was devastated, their hearts broken by the loss of Claire, their beloved mother and wife.

It didn't fit.

There was something we were missing.

Claire had either been extremely unlucky and had been the

victim of a random robbery and murder, or she had been betrayed by someone she thought was a friend.

"Is there anything else you can tell me about your mom that might help us find out who did this to her?"

Jake's expression changed, a sudden realization dawning on him. "One thing about Mom, she was always so nice to everybody. Strangers, people on the street, everyone. Maybe she was too nice to someone."

That caught my attention, and I jotted it down in my notebook. "Was it common for your mom to talk to strangers?"

Sarah nodded eagerly. "Oh, yeah, she volunteered at the soup kitchen, and during the holidays, she'd pass out care packages at different encampments around the county."

This new information was helpful. Had Claire become a victim of someone she had met while helping the less fortunate? She certainly wouldn't have been the first person to extend a hand to someone down on their luck, only to have that trust betrayed, paying for it with her life.

And just like that, we had a whole new pool of people to interview.

"This is really helpful. Is there anything else you can tell me?"

They shook their heads, their faces a blend of sorrow and hope. "Please find who did this to Mom," Sarah said, tears brimming in her eyes.

"I will, I promise. Thank you both so much. But if you wouldn't mind, could you give your father and me some time alone? I have a few additional questions."

Jordan looked like he was about to protest, but a firm look from me made him pause, realizing the gravity of the situation. "Kids, it's okay. Let me talk to her. We want to cooperate as much as we can. We need to find out who did this to your mom. Wait out in the hall, I won't be long."

The kids nodded, and Brady escorted them to the hallway, leaving Jordan and me alone.

Jordan Nelson positioned himself directly across from me, his demeanor slightly unsettled. As he sat down, I scrutinized him closely: his face, neck, and overall bearing. Like Brady and Allan had noted, there were no visible cuts on his hands. Observing his gait as he had walked into the room, he displayed no signs of a limp or physical discomfort, suggesting he likely hadn't injured himself in a violent encounter. He was also six feet tall. Claire was only five feet, two inches, which meant he wasn't the killer.

"Thank you for talking with me," I began. "I've been reviewing the case file and discussing it with Deputy Tanner and our research team. There are some details I need you to reconfirm for us. On Monday night, what time did you leave the hardware store?"

"It was about eight o'clock, give or take five or ten minutes."

"And what time did you get home and discover your wife?"

"It took me about ten minutes to get home. When I arrived, I didn't see her car, so I assumed she wasn't there. I went straight up to our room to take a shower, and then I went downstairs to grab something for dinner. When I came down to the kitchen, that's when I found her."

"Were the lights on when you came home?" I asked.

He shook his head.

"Did you expect your wife to be home that night?"

"I did."

"Did you try calling her to see where she was?"

He hesitated. "I didn't."

"Do you realize it was forty minutes between the time you got home and the time you called 911?"

His eyes met mine and, in a monotone voice, he said, "It had been a long day. I must've taken a longer shower than I usually do."

My instincts, honed by years of experience, told me he was hiding something. "Have you submitted your DNA to our team yet?" I knew he hadn't.

"No, I don't believe so."

"Would you be willing to give us a sample to be tested?"

"I don't think that's really necessary, is it?"

His reluctance to provide DNA was puzzling. "Well, in the event that there's more than one contributor from items found at the crime scene, it would be quicker to exclude you, if you give us the DNA now."

"I'm going to reserve my right to not give you my DNA, but if you need to exclude me, we can revisit the topic," he responded coldly.

He stood up, his presence more imposing than before, and I couldn't shake the feeling of unease. "If that's all, I need to get back to my children. Good luck with your investigation."

In a flash his shoulders slumped, and his head hung low, and he exited the conference room.

The abrupt shift from cold and monotonous to that of a seemingly normal grieving husband, was startling.

Every single red flag was now raised.

Brady entered the room and must have noticed the perplexed look on my face. "What's wrong?"

"I'm not sure," I said, "but I'm certainly going to find out."

FOURTEEN

VAL

In Claire's classroom, I caught a glimpse of who she had been. Thirty student desks were meticulously arranged, all facing Claire's. The walls were adorned with quotes from renowned poets like Yeats, Thoreau, Shakespeare, and Taylor Swift. Flowers and cards brought by her students and colleagues decorated her desk. Each one a testament to the affection and respect she garnered.

The principal somberly explained that the entire school was in mourning and therefore thought it best to relocate all of Claire's classes, now being taught by a substitute, to one of the portable classrooms near the football field.

The team had interviewed nearly all of her students and the teachers she had collaborated with, and it was remarkable that they had found nothing useful. There were no reported issues with any student or coworker, with the exception of a few disgruntled students who hadn't agreed with the grades they'd been given on an assignment. But the principal insisted it wasn't unusual and was par for the course when teaching teenagers, and none of the students had done more than request a new grade. There were no signs of a threat from any of the students.

Her performance reviews were consistently positive, and again, not a single person had a bad word to say about her. Was Claire genuinely one of the inherently good people, or was this phenomenon a result of her passing, where out of respect, nobody wanted to speak ill of the dead? If the former were true, it made her death even more tragic.

Brady and Allan walked around scrutinizing the classroom. Allan said, "Well, if you ask me, I don't think it's anyone related to the school."

I thought that was a bit premature. As far as I was concerned, the only person we could rule out was one with a verifiable alibi like Jordan Nelson.

Brady added, "Nobody made the hairs on the back of my neck stand up either."

"What are you thinking? Maybe one of the homeless people she served, someone on the street?"

Allan said, "Maybe. There really aren't that many homeless in Hectorville, but we do have a few encampments. Should we head there next?"

Brady said, "We definitely should question the folks at all of the ones she visited. At this point, the most possible suspects are a complete stranger or a completely random event."

"Or someone she trusted and didn't have any issues with until the day of her death."

They nodded in acknowledgment.

I wished the forensic testing was completed. Jonathan, the lead forensic scientist, had assured me the fingerprints and DNA analysis would be done by Friday. Once the results were in, I hoped it would offer us a clue as to who could have killed Claire. At this point, it was like looking for a needle in a haystack.

I said, "All right, let's go. Skid Row it is."

Just then, Brady stopped in his tracks. His phone was ringing. "It's the sheriff." He answered the call. "Hello? Yes, okay. All right, we'll be there in ten minutes."

What was that about? "What is it?"

"The sheriff wants a meeting."

"About what?"

Brady gave a knowing look. "About Jordan Nelson."

"What about him?"

"I don't know. He said he wants to meet face-to-face."

What did the sheriff want to discuss? I didn't know but I had a nagging feeling that whatever it was, it would not sit well with me.

Shutting my eyes and breathing deeply, I braced myself for the confrontation I knew was coming. My suspicions, unfortunately, were correct. "Sheriff, with all due respect, I disagree. This case isn't closed yet. We shouldn't be handing over the crime scene back to Jordan Nelson," I argued.

He seemed unconvinced and said, "Please, call me Kingston. I've checked with the CSI team, the lab, and the medical examiner. They've taken samples, photographed everything. There's nothing left to do there."

But it wasn't necessarily true. "Kingston, I know that Red Rose County doesn't see a lot of violent crime. But in my experience sometimes there's a need to go back over the crime scene once new information is obtained. We may find we need to take a second look. The CSI team is human, and it's not unusual for a team to miss crucial details, especially before they have a better idea of what they're looking for."

Kingston said, "At this point, I think it's best we return the home to the Nelsons. They're grieving, they need to plan the funeral, and they want to have the wake at the house. We're going to give it to them. If your investigation warrants a second look, we'll revisit the idea of another search."

I couldn't hide my frustration. "You've got to be kidding me. This is ridiculous. You're compromising the entire investigation by giving the house back. It's too soon."

Sheriff Phillips, call me Kingston, tilted his head and said, "Val, we're on the same side. I brought you in because we appreciate your experience, but I have to do what's best for the people of this county. I know for a fact Jordan Nelson is an upstanding member of his community, and we know he did not kill his wife. You told me that yourself. His alibi checks out."

I shifted back in my seat; he had a point. The CSI team had been thorough and it wasn't likely they missed something, but that didn't mean it was impossible. My thoughts drifted to the Nelson children and their grief. Maybe we'd just have to take a chance and give them back their home. "I understand. Is there anything else?"

"No, that's it. Thank you for your cooperation. We appreciate your help and I'm confident you'll find who killed Claire."

Without a word, I nodded and left, Brady following close behind.

"I had no idea he was going to do that, Val," Brady said, as he tried to keep up with me.

But I didn't stop, instead I continued down the hallway, trying to contain my frustration. The sudden realization that a lead investigator meant something different here in Red Rose County—it didn't mean I was in charge. The sheriff was the ultimate decision-maker. Good to know. It didn't matter. My focus was on Claire Nelson and finding her killer.

Outside, inhaling the cool evening air, Brady said, "Are you okay?"

I stopped and stared into his eyes. "I'll be fine." And with a determined stride, I continued toward the parking lot. "Now, come on. Let's head to the encampment and find out who killed Claire Nelson."

Brady nodded. "Yes, ma'am."

That was the *correct* response.

FIFTEEN

VAL

Settled behind the wheel of my car, I realized I didn't know where I was going. "Where's the local encampment in Hectorville?"

Brady gave the slightest smile and said, "There's one off I-5. I'll direct you there."

"Works for me."

Brady said, "I wouldn't worry about the sheriff. He's under a lot of pressure from the community to wrap this up quickly. The Nelsons are well-liked, and nobody wants to believe that one of their own could have done something so heinous. Especially when there's no concrete evidence linking Jordan to the murder. If it turned out there was a connection, it would devastate the town. But all the evidence is pointing elsewhere. The sheriff is just doing what he thinks is best for the Nelsons."

"Are you sure about that?"

"I know it may seem like politics, but Kingston is a good guy. Since I've been working with him, I've never seen him be less than ethical or fair. He's only been in office a few years and I think he's still navigating the waters. Give him a chance. Not to mention, he's got big shoes to fill."

Indeed, my mother had been a formidable sheriff, revered and beloved. Her successor still had much to prove, and aligning with the community's sentiments was likely a good political move, even though I didn't agree with it.

The probability the team had overlooked crucial evidence was a long shot, but it existed. But it didn't matter at that point. We'd just have to keep on investigating. "Do you have much interaction with the encampments?" I asked, changing the subject.

"Every once in a while, we get a disturbance call and go check on them. And periodically we go out there and ensure everything's peaceful."

"How many are there?"

"They seem to be increasing every day. But in Hectorville, there's really only the big one, with about fifty tents."

We still had a few hours of daylight, enough time to question those who might have crossed paths with Claire.

Brady pointed out the way, "Up there on the left." I turned right onto a winding road, with trailhead signs and trees lining the two-lane highway. "Right there," he added.

I nodded, swerving across to park in the lot. Stepping out of my car, I took in the surroundings. It was breathtaking.

"Must be public land?"

"Yep, they're all here legally. We just make sure it stays peaceful. There's some drug use, but as long as no one gets hurt, we don't intervene. And mental health issues? Definitely, so be forewarned, not everyone here is fully stable," Brady cautioned.

"Consider me warned," I replied, having dealt with far more challenging characters in my time.

Dressed in plain clothes, I blended in, while Brady, in his tan deputy sheriff uniform, stood out.

He waved amicably to the first person who poked their head out of a tent.

Around us, several groups were gathered, some sitting in

lawn chairs, engaged in conversation. Brady took the lead, introducing me to the community.

"Welcome to town," said a woman with weathered skin and a suspicious glare.

"Thanks, and what's your name?" I asked the woman.

"My name is Maisie, Maisie Gray."

She was missing several teeth and looked to be around sixty, her thin frame clad in a T-shirt and sweatpants, a pair of Crocs on her feet.

"It's nice to meet you, Maisie. We're here because, I don't know if you've heard, but Claire Nelson was recently killed."

Maisie's expression changed from suspicion to one of shock. "Claire? That nice lady? Oh no, that's terrible," she exclaimed, calling over to two men she referred to as Deacon and Tony, "Deputy Tanner and Ms. Costa said Claire got killed."

Deacon and Tony, eyes wide, hurried over. "What? How did this happen?" they asked in disbelief.

"She was stabbed several times in her home. We're asking around to see if anybody knows anything or if anyone saw anything suspicious when Claire visited."

"Well, we haven't seen Claire in a few months, but who would do such a thing to her? Was it her husband?" a smaller woman, who had been lurking behind Deacon and Tony, asked timidly.

"No, it doesn't look like it. Did you ever see them arguing?"

She shook her head. "No, I just assumed, I guess. Husbands can be violent. Even ones who seem nice on the outside."

It was true and I wondered if it was due to one of those types that she was living in an encampment. "Did Claire usually come here alone?"

"Most of the time, yes. Occasionally, she'd bring someone along, I think one of her kids, a girl. Sarah, maybe that's her name. Blonde and pretty like Claire," Maisie recalled.

"And her husband? Did he ever accompany her?"

"I don't think so. Maybe once, but he stayed in the car. Claire mentioned he was just worried, you know, because we're unhoused," Maisie said, her tone tinged with skepticism.

"But Claire wasn't afraid of you?"

"Oh, heavens no! We would never let anything happen to her. We all loved Claire. She was one of the few who didn't look down on us. She was safe here," Maisie asserted firmly.

"Did any of you ever hear of someone who was mad at Claire or wanted to hurt her."

They all shook their heads.

"Would you be willing to help us ask around? See if anyone knew of anyone who might have wanted to hurt Claire?"

Maisie nodded. "Sure. I'll guide you around. Some folks aren't as willing to talk to new people. But I'll help."

"We appreciate that."

After about an hour of talking to dozens of residents, we encountered a woman, probably in her thirties, with greasy brown hair and pockmarked skin, likely an addict. "Did you know Claire?" I asked.

She shook her head rapidly.

Maisie intervened, and whispered, "Don't pay Laney any mind. She's had a hard time, and the drugs have affected her mind. She's not quite right."

With a nod, I let Maisie know I understood. But the look in Laney's haunted eyes made me want to press harder. "Did you know Claire Nelson? Maybe her daughter Sarah?" I asked her again.

Laney simply repeated, "I don't go near that house. I don't go near the house."

I stepped closer, sensing there might be more to her words. "Do you know something about the Nelsons?"

Laney continued in a trance-like state. "Don't go near the house. I don't go near the house."

Maisie shook her head, a mixture of pity and resolve in her

eyes. "I'll take care of this," she said, and then guided Laney, who was still muttering, back to her tent.

Maisie appeared to be the unofficial leader of the encampment, looking out for all of them. A kind, warm woman who protected those who couldn't protect themselves. Moments later, Maisie reappeared, apologetic. "Laney's lost in the drugs. She doesn't make much sense most days, but she's harmless. I wish we could've been more help. Claire's death is such a tragedy. She was so kind, always coming here with care packages and food, especially around Christmas. She really looked out for us."

"Claire sounds like she was an incredible woman."

"She was. I hope you find who did this."

"Me too."

Thanking her, Brady and I headed back to the car. "Sounds like Claire was highly regarded in this community too."

"It's what I suspected, but it still leaves us with more questions than answers."

Nodding, I climbed into the driver's seat, and called it a day.

SIXTEEN

VAL

Staring at the murder board, I found myself standing a bit too close to Brady. His cologne, a distracting blend of cedar and sandalwood, filled my senses. It had been a while since I had been on a date, not that I needed that in my life right now, especially with a killer on the loose. Not just Claire's, but the one who had captured me and might still be hunting me. Despite the distractions in my life—the Claire Nelson case, my mom's rehabilitation sessions, and my new friends—I couldn't shake off the feeling that it was the Bear who had left that note in my mailbox, congratulating me on the Scarlett Douglas case. And that he wasn't done with me or my family.

"What do you think?" Brady asked, pointing at the open questions on the board.

"I'm hoping the forensics team's analysis will come back with something useful."

"They said today's the day."

Lucy and Allan walked into the war room. Lucy beamed, "TGIF."

"TGIF," I said with a smile. We had plans for a girls' night out—Sally the medical examiner, Lucy the top researcher, and me. Dinner and drinks were on the agenda, but I knew shop talk would inevitably seep in. We were all working on a case together, and depending on the lab's findings, we might have a lot to discuss. Maybe we would be celebrating the closing of the Claire Nelson case.

"What are you guys talking about?" Allan inquired.

"Lucy, were you able to look at similar crimes in the surrounding counties and states?" I asked.

"I was," she said, flipping open her laptop and staring intently at the screen. "There have been a few stabbings and robberies in Utah and Nevada, and one up in Oregon. None in the surrounding counties here in California, but in all four cases, the suspects were apprehended. Each crime had a different perpetrator, all of whom either had a mental health issue or were under the influence of narcotics."

Allan took a seat, crossed his legs, and leaned back. "So, needle in a haystack, huh?"

"It's possible this is just a random robbery. If so, let's hope they're in the system."

"Fingerprints don't usually take this long. It's been four days," Brady pointed out.

"Maybe they're saving it to present all of it together?" I suggested.

The delay likely meant that they hadn't found any matches for the fingerprints at the scene in AFIS, a crucial tool for identifying suspects in crimes, as well as in cases involving unidentified individuals. But my guess was that if there had been a hit on any fingerprints from the scene, we would have heard about it by now.

"It's not instilling any hope that the suspect is in the system."

Brady nodded. "That could explain why they were so brazen about leaving their prints everywhere."

"True. It's an odd case. The only prints were in the kitchen and on the front doorknob. It was like they went in, grabbed some food, her car keys, wallet, bandaged their hand, and walked right out the front door. In broad daylight."

Brady nodded in agreement. "I worked quite a few robberies back in San Francisco, and from my experience that seems like exactly what happened."

"So maybe all they really wanted was a car?" I speculated.

"Or there were two suspects and they needed a second car. Maybe they ditched whatever car they were driving after getting the new one," Allan suggested.

"That's a good point, Allan. We should check for any abandoned or stolen vehicles in the area. They could be swapping them out."

Lucy, ever efficient, responded, "Just give me a little while, I'll check the database."

The atmosphere in the Claire Nelson investigation team was noticeably different compared to the Behavioral Analysis Unit at the FBI. While we did joke around occasionally, everyone was usually more reserved. But today being Friday, the casual vibe was in full effect. Brady, now working on the case full-time, was dressed in plain clothes. Seeing him in jeans and a white button-down shirt was a change; it suited him.

Brady and I sat down, me next to Lucy, Brady next to Allan. "Any plans for the weekend?" I asked Brady casually.

"Probably catching up on paperwork. Since I've been helping out with the Claire Nelson case, it's been piling up."

"That's pretty boring, dude. You need to get out more," Allan teased.

"How about you, Allan?" I asked.

"I'm a family man. Got the wife and kids. Maybe do a hike, go fishing."

"What about you, Brady? Your kids visiting?"

"No, the kids are back at school. It's just me."

Maybe I should suggest we go for lunch. We were friends, after all.

The chatter continued amiably until the sheriff arrived for an update. He wanted weekly briefings on the case due to the immense pressure from the community for a resolution. I couldn't blame him for wanting frequent updates, given the nature of the case.

The atmosphere in the room shifted abruptly as a knock sounded at the door.

Our casual banter ceased, and we all quickly composed ourselves. Lucy stood up to answer the door. "Oh, hey, Jonathan, what's up?" she greeted.

"I've got the results if you're interested."

Interested? We were eagerly awaiting the forensic analysis from Claire Nelson's crime scene. "Come on in," I said, noticing Sally, our medical examiner, trailing behind him. "Hey, Sally," I greeted her.

"Happy Friday," she said cheerfully.

Jonathan, the head lab scientist, was in charge of processing DNA, fingerprints, and trace materials. Despite his casual attire —a T-shirt with a surfboard logo and baggy jeans, not your typical forensic scientist look—he was the expert we were relying on. Red Rose County had its own style, it seemed, and it was growing on me.

Not wanting to wait a second longer, I said, "So, what did you find, Jonathan?"

He tucked his hair behind his ear. "Well, the fingerprints are not in AFIS. The person has never been fingerprinted," he explained.

Allan interjected, "Which means the person has never committed a crime before, or at least, has never been caught."

"So, this is their first crime?" I asked the room.

"Quite a bold indoctrination," Allan commented dryly.

"What else did you find?" I pressed on.

"The dirt and footprints in the laundry room were analyzed for trace evidence, including minerals, to see where they might have come from. We found that the dirt and debris inside the house were consistent with what's in the Nelson's backyard."

Another dead end. "How about DNA?" I asked, hopeful for something more.

Sally chimed in. "We completed the DNA analysis. There were two contributors. One from Claire Nelson, as expected, and a second contributor, like we also expected, based on the blood found on the countertop and mixed with Claire's. It likely means the killer cut themselves during the attack."

None of this was new information, but based on the look in her eyes, she had to have more. Eyeing her, she let a small smile slip before she continued. "And based on the autopsy results, we were able to match the stab wounds on Claire to the missing knife from the block of knives at the Nelsons' home. We believe the missing knife from the block was the murder weapon. We'll need to have it for confirmation, but it's consistent."

We knew what Claire Nelson was killed with and where, but the why and the who remained the big questions. "I'm guessing the DNA wasn't in CODIS?" CODIS, the Combined DNA Index System, is a database used by state and local crime laboratories to store and compare DNA profiles from crime scene evidence and convicted offenders.

Jonathan nodded. "It's not. But it was interesting."

"How so?"

"Well, who do you think killed Claire Nelson?" he asked, a twinkle in his blue eyes. "You're the profiler, right?"

"So far, what I've deduced about our suspect is that they killed Claire Nelson for a specific reason. It wasn't a random act of violence, nor did they seem to derive any pleasure from killing. They needed something, and she got in their way. Right now, it appears they were after car keys, money, and possibly even food. We might be looking at someone who is unhoused or in desperate need of those things." It was my best educated guess, at that point.

"Have you considered what gender the suspect might be?" Sally asked, her eyebrows raised in anticipation.

Feeling a little like the kid who forgot to do their homework, I said, "Not specifically."

She winked, and said, "Based on the height at which the blows struck Claire Nelson, it seems likely the perpetrator was around her height, maybe a little taller or shorter, judging by the angle of the blade and where she was struck. The suspect, the person who killed Claire Nelson, was female. The DNA results confirmed it."

I nodded in agreement. "Yes, the shallowness of the wounds, the positioning... It all points to an inexperienced, female assailant." How had I not deduced that earlier? The killer was a female, who had never committed a crime before, or at least wasn't in the AFIS or CODIS databases.

Brady tipped his head toward me. "Does that fit the profile?"

"Yes, it does."

Teenagers can be temperamental. Jordan Nelson's words echoed in my mind and made me think of a teenage girl killing Claire. But who? A student? A young lover Jordan had manipulated into doing his dirty work?

The words "Nice work" had just left my lips as the door to the room opened and Kingston came in. I said, "Afternoon, Kingston."

"Hi, Val and team. Quite the full house."

"Have a seat, and we'll update you."

The sheriff was pleased with the progress we had made and equally puzzled by the revelation of the killer's gender. Understandably. He thanked us and told us all to have a good weekend.

Maybe he wasn't so bad after all. Considering the killer was female and the Nelsons' daughter had an alibi, the Nelson residence likely wouldn't need to be searched again. Perhaps the lesson I'd learned was that if I was going to work in Red Rose County, I couldn't always go in guns blazing. I would have to exercise some patience and embrace the local politics. It wouldn't be easy, but I could try a softer approach.

SEVENTEEN
THE SECRET ADMIRER

Valerie's transformation was striking. Her hair, usually pulled back into a practical ponytail, cascaded freely down her shoulders, framing her face beautifully. The bold choice of scarlet lipstick contrasting against her olive skin enhanced her natural beauty. It was a refreshing change from her typical work attire of black slacks and a white button-down blouse. Now, she donned a pair of black skinny jeans paired with a flowing blouse that accentuated her figure. I had to admit, I had never seen her so dressed up, so feminine and carefree.

This new look contradicted the many roles she played. An FBI agent, homicide investigator, mother, and caretaker. Since our meeting, I had seen her in various lights, but this was a side of Valerie that was completely new to me. And her friends, they too were stunning in their own way. Were we all destined to meet? The woman with the bright red hair was a bit too bold for my taste, but there was no denying that the woman, who I recognized as the medical examiner, was striking. But I thought a more subdued hair color would suit her. Maybe a soft strawberry blonde.

The blonde with the large glasses had an intellectual, nerdy appeal that many found attractive. The sexy librarian type. There weren't many kinds of women I didn't find attractive. And the young woman was no exception. Who was she? I didn't know her identity but I had seen her going in and out of the sheriff's station.

Observing the trio, chatting and laughing as they scuttled across the parking lot to the restaurant, it was evident they were on a fun night out. I wondered if they were celebrating a victory. Had the sheriff's department caught a break in the Claire Nelson murder case?

I hadn't seen any news about the case being solved, so maybe Valerie was just looking to unwind and enjoy some leisure time. I could understand that desire—everyone needs to let loose occasionally, have fun in their own way.

As they entered the restaurant, their laughter and excitement disappeared with them. Oh, to be a fly on that wall, to witness their interactions and be a part of their world, if only for a moment. I watched Valerie and her friends disappear inside and was hit by a pang of longing. It was good to see her having fun, outside of work and caring for her mother.

"Live it up while you can," I said to myself.

Valerie's world and mine were so different, yet somehow, we were connected. In time, Valerie and I would be together again, and share our own kind of fun—the kind that shapes and defines a lifetime.

EIGHTEEN

VAL

Sitting at a restaurant with white tablecloths surrounded by female friends, I couldn't help but reflect on how my life seemed to be restarting. It had been ages since I had done something as simple and enjoyable as a night out with girlfriends. It felt odd yet fitting to call it a "girls'" night, considering we were all much older now.

Not that I knew exactly how old Lucy and Sally were. My guess was Lucy was in her late thirties, Sally in her early forties, and here I was, approaching forty-six, nudging closer to fifty. But life was far from over; my mother was a testament to that. At seventy, surrounded by her best friends, she was recovering from a stroke and teaching me about the resilience and zest for life at any age.

I had promised to have dinner with Mom every evening, but she said that was a ridiculous idea, especially when I mentioned my plans to dine out with Sally and Lucy. Both were acquaintances of hers from her sheriff days. Julie and Diane, her ever-present companions, were with her now, easing my guilt.

The investigation into Claire's death made me consider my

future in Red Rose County. A new job. New friends. Old friends. Family. It all seemed to fit like a glove.

My house back in Washington, DC, had been vacant since I had moved in with Mom. Harrison would be starting college soon and wasn't likely to be spending much time at home except for the holidays and summer break. He could easily fly to Red Rose County to visit, and I could fly to visit him at school. And once he graduated, his options were limitless. Would he choose California for the tech sector, or perhaps Texas or Washington state? The wealth of opportunities that awaited him made it impossible to predict where my son would end up.

If I sold my house, would that be it? A goodbye to my old life? It was too soon to make such a drastic decision, but the thought had crossed my mind. If I sold my DC home, should I buy my own place in Red Rose County or continue living with Mom? Did I really need that much privacy? My love life was nonexistent at the moment, and any potential partner would likely have their own place for quiet evenings together.

It felt like the first time I had been at such a crossroads since my divorce from Harrison's father. Starting over now, at the age of forty-five, was daunting yet somewhat invigorating. It was a chance to redefine my life, to explore new paths and possibilities. The uncertainty was a little nerve-racking, but the potential for new beginnings was an exciting prospect too. Why didn't I feel more content?

"So, what are you drinking?" Sally asked, breaking the ice as we settled into our seats.

"I'm usually a wine gal. Have you been here before?" I asked, curious about her familiarity with the place.

"A few times, on dates with my new guy," Sally replied, her face lighting up with excitement. It was clear she was eager to tell us about the new man in her life.

"A boyfriend?"

"Well, we've only gone out a few times. He just moved to Red Rose County from Nevada."

From Nevada? An unease suddenly stirred within me. "Oh, what does he do for a living?"

"He works in construction," Sally said, a hint of pride in her voice.

My mind raced—could this be more than a coincidence? "How did you meet?" I asked, trying to remain calm.

"At a bar. I know, lame," she said, chuckling.

Lucy said, "It sounds like you really like him."

"I do. He's sweet. It's early days, but he's really good-looking —tall, dark, and handsome. He's got these big brown eyes that seem to look right into my soul," Sally gushed.

Brown eyes. Not the Bear. The Bear had blue eyes. It was the only feature I knew about him. And I often wondered if I would be able to recognize him based on his eyes and his voice. I hoped I would because it seemed to be the only way I could identify him. He had been outstanding at not leaving any trace evidence at his crime scenes. "Oh, that sounds like it could be promising," I managed to say.

"I think so. I'm just taking it day by day, but I'm a little smitten," Sally admitted, and her cheeks turned rosy.

"That sounds great. How about you, Lucy?"

"Single and ready to mingle."

I smiled and almost laughed. Lucy had a sense of humor that I was beginning to really enjoy. "No prospects?"

"Well... I haven't dated much since I've been in California, but if we're talking about crushes, I may have a teeny-tiny little crush on someone at work."

Our serious girl talk was interrupted by the waitress's arrival. "Hi, ladies, what can I get you to drink?" She was young, probably in her twenties, dressed in black slacks, a white shirt, and an apron—attire that would fit right in at the FBI, minus the apron.

"I'll have your house red."

Lucy grinned. "I'll have a lemon drop."

"And I'll have a cosmopolitan," Sally added with a grin. "I know they're so 2006, but I just love them."

"Coming right up," the waitress said, jotting down our orders and scurrying away.

Lucy leaned in. "Okay, before we start drinking and go into full gossip mode, we've got to talk about what happened today."

I nodded in agreement. "Oh yeah. A female killer. I hadn't considered it, or even thought that it could be a female. But that opens up so many different angles. Like, was Jordan Nelson having an affair? We looked into his background; it didn't seem like it. But maybe he coerced some young, innocent thing into killing his wife for him."

Sally tipped her head toward Lucy. "Could it be the daughter?"

That was another angle that had crossed my mind. Lucy said, "No, it can't be the daughter. First of all, I checked. The second contributor didn't have a familial match to Claire. Second, I checked her flights and confirmed she was still in Los Angeles when her mother was killed."

"When did you do that?" I asked, surprised. "We've been together all day."

"When you went out for lunch with Brady," she replied with a smirk.

"Very sneaky and efficient. Thank you."

"Well, we can now cross her off the suspect list, and eliminate all the men, right?" Sally asked.

"I don't know. I've got this niggling feeling about Jordan," I said. "He said something the first time we met about 'teenagers being temperamental' or something to that effect. Now we learn it's a female. There's something fishy there."

"Perhaps a student of hers," Lucy said. "It might be worth taking a second stab at talking to the students, or at the encampment. You mentioned meeting a female who reacted strangely when you asked questions about Claire, like staying away or something."

Lucy had a great memory. "True," I agreed. "I'll have to re-interview the students at the school and go back to the encampment. Find out if any girls held a grudge or were overly friendly with Jordan."

"Excellent idea." Lucy nodded.

I smiled, feeling a sense of relief to be around people who understood the intricacies of my work but also had a lighter, fun side to them. It was refreshing. "It's the only one, at this point."

"Is working at the sheriff's department very different from working with the FBI?" Sally asked.

"It's a lot more casual. Typically, with the FBI, there's no such thing as a weekend when you're working a case. You're always on call," I explained.

"I guess if you had some leads to track down, the sheriff would probably give you the overtime budget. He's under a lot of pressure," Lucy said.

"What have you heard?"

"People are blaming him for not catching the killer yet. They say it's taking too long," Lucy said.

Shaking my head, I figured the sheriff was under pressure, but to blame him for not catching a killer was ridiculous. I wondered whether I should talk to him on Monday and see if he needed my help dealing with the community. Maybe it would help if the message came from a former FBI agent? I said, "That's not fair. Solving a murder is much more difficult than people realize. It's not like on TV where everything's resolved in thirty minutes. We waited four days for the DNA results, which is actually pretty fast compared to twenty years ago when it could take weeks or months. People just don't understand."

"I'm glad you're part of the team, and I'm glad you

suggested we go out. It's exactly what I needed," Lucy said gratefully.

"Yeah, there aren't a lot of people our age in town who aren't married with kids and putting up a white picket fence," Sally added with a smirk.

"I've noticed. I grew up here."

"That's right," Lucy said with a curious smile.

Our drinks arrived, and we each took a sip, the tension of the case quickly forgotten. "Okay, Lucy, just because we talked shop didn't mean we forgot about you mentioning a little crush on someone at work," I teased, eager to dive into lighter conversation and enjoy our night out.

Lucy's cheeks turned a shade of crimson as the conversation turned to her and I wondered if she regretted telling us. I hoped not, I really believed, for some intangible reason, that we would be good friends. It was like we'd had a near-instant connection.

Pushing her glasses up her nose, she said, "Okay, I'm pretty sure he's single, but I've got a thing for Jonathan."

"Oh, he's cute," Sally agreed, setting down her cosmopolitan. "He's the tall, long-haired, bad-boy type, but really smart, you know, being a scientist and all."

"You should go for it," I said, encouraging her to take a leap of faith.

"Are there rules against that?" Sally asked.

Lucy shrugged. "I mean, we don't really influence each other's cases. He's not my boss, and I'm not his." She paused and tilted her head as if contemplating further. "But it would be so embarrassing to work with someone who knows you have a crush on them but they don't feel the same."

"Yeah, but in life, you've got to take chances," Sally said encouragingly.

I had taken many chances in my life. Some had worked out well, others had led me into perilous situations, like being tied up in a barn by a serial killer. I took another sip of the house red, its fruity and bold flavor a pleasant sensation.

"You're really quiet over there," Sally observed, looking at me curiously.

"Just thinking about all the changes," I replied, my mind flitting between personal and professional concerns.

Lucy took off her glasses and teased, "I don't think it's just that, Val. Maybe you're thinking about someone who works with us too?"

"We're just friends," I said, attempting to brush off the insinuation.

Sally finished her cosmopolitan and set the glass down with conviction. "I don't think so, honey. We can see the way he looks at you. That is not a 'just friends' situation."

"I don't know. Yeah, he's attractive, and yeah, he's single, but with everything going on: my return home, taking care of Mom, the new job, not to mention the serial killer who held me captive..." My voice trailed off as the reality of my situation settled in.

"Do you really think he's coming after you?" Lucy asked, her voice laced with concern.

"I can't shake the feeling that he's not done with me. It's more than just a hunch; it's a deep, instinctual feeling." It wasn't something I could explain with facts or spreadsheets. Maybe he wasn't after me. Maybe it was my own fear that he might be.

"We'll keep a lookout. Like it or not, you're one of us now," Sally said, trying to make light of the situation.

"I appreciate that," I said, feeling a sense of camaraderie that I realized I had been missing for some time. Maybe going it alone wasn't always the best approach. Cut to being held captive by a serial killer. Going it all alone was a really bad idea.

"Now, I am starving. Shall we order food?" Sally asked.

As the conversation continued, I felt a sense of belonging. It had been lonely taking care of Mom on my own, but the Red Rose County Sheriff's Department had some good people. Maybe joining them at least for the foreseeable future wasn't such a bad idea after all. At least until I learned who had killed Claire, and why.

NINETEEN

TALLY

Four days earlier

I gripped the steering wheel so tightly that my knuckles had turned white. Taking a deep breath, I uncurled my fingers and inspected my hands. There was dried blood on my nail beds and underneath my fingernails.

At the first truck stop I found with only a few sixteen wheelers in the lot, I hurried into the bathroom and was disappointed to find there were no paper towels that I could clean myself up with. So I removed my T-shirt and wet it under the faucet to use as a washcloth to scrub off the sticky stuff. It was all over me. My shirt, my shorts, and my shoes. In my hair, on my neck and face—my arms. Scrubbing as fast as I could I tried to look less like I had stepped out of a horror movie and more like a normal person out for a drive.

Working quickly, I removed the rest of my clothing and shoes and washed them with hand soap in the sink. Satisfied with the rushed job, I put on the wet clothes and thanked the heavens for warm weather. After a pit stop to the toilets I ran back to the car and set off again. As I sped down the road, I removed everything but my top, swerving as I pulled off my shorts and shoes.

The clothes only took a few hours to dry in the August heat, and when I pulled over into a forested area I redressed and tried to get some rest. Exhaustion and a lack of nutrients had taken their toll and I thought I would fall asleep instantly. But sleep eluded me, and all I managed to do was toss and turn. The front seat of the sedan was uncomfortable, but I didn't want to risk sleeping in the back and not being able to get away quick enough if someone were to approach me. Even if I were on a fluffy mattress, I doubted I would have slept. Every time I shut my eyes, her image haunted me—her body sprawled on the kitchen floor, eyes wide with surprise. I hadn't expected them to stay that way after she died, but they did. Blood had pooled beneath her and was splattered on the cabinet and tile. It was the most horrific sight I had ever seen, no, strike that—it was *almost* the most horrific thing I had ever seen.

Before it all happened, I was starving, having not eaten in almost two days. After I did it, I immediately raided the refrigerator. I was careful not to eat too much, to avoid making myself sick. I drank from an open container of apple juice before loading up a reusable grocery bag with food and drink from the pantry and refrigerator. A sampling of crackers, bread, packet of sliced cheese, another carton of apple juice, strawberries, and a few other snack foods would have to do for a while.

First rule of survival: food and water. The second was shelter—I had to get out of that house. Her wallet and the keys to her car were easy enough to find. Once they were in my hands, adrenaline and fear pushed me out of that house.

With about a hundred dollars in cash, my resources were limited. Gas for the car was a priority. The food I had would be enough for a while, or at least until I figured out where I would go.

I never imagined I could be capable of something so drastic.

Shame and fear consumed me, along with questions about who I had become. Who was I? Who was she, really?

From the photos on the walls, I knew they had children—a boy and a girl. The enormity of it all was overwhelming. What would they be like without her? Would they stand at her grave, with tears streaming down their faces, telling stories of a caring mother who bandaged scraped knees and soothed upset stomachs? Who was she, really? I knew very little about her, but I knew I had to do everything I could to get as far away from here as possible.

Zooming down the highway, I had no idea where I was headed. Where could I go after taking a life? I was on the run. Was I fugitive? Had anyone seen me leave the house? Had her body been found? Images of her slashed, lifeless body flashed before me and the enormity of what I had done threatened to overwhelm me. I had to get a grip.

I'd seen enough on TV to know about DNA and fingerprints. I knew they would be looking for me. But as far as I knew, I had never been fingerprinted or committed any felonies that required a DNA sample. So, I might be safe and they'd never find out it was me. But could they somehow still figure it out? I wasn't sure, but that wasn't my immediate concern. I needed to plan my next steps.

I was running on empty, my were nerves frayed, my body felt like it was full of lead and my mind was struggling to process what I had done. But I needed to think clearly. As I continued down the highway, I had to make a decision. North or south? Which direction might offer me safety?

There was only one person I knew I could trust. And I had just enough gas to get to her. I hoped she hadn't moved or had someone living with her that I couldn't trust. A quick peek in the mirror confirmed that I looked a mess. My face was pale, my eyes bloodshot, and my hair in total disarray. Not to mention, my hand was still bleeding, not as bad as before, but it needed actual bandages as opposed to the paper towels that I had taken from the house.

With the small house in view, I prayed she was home. Despite the modest size, the house was on a decent-sized lot and there weren't many close neighbors. If I remembered correctly, I could swerve around behind the garage and park there so the car would be hidden from anyone passing the property.

As I eased the car onto the property, fear filled my conscious. What if she wouldn't help me? What if she wasn't home? What if she turned me in? Maybe she didn't need to know everything. I could just say I needed a few days to rest. That should give me enough time to come up with a longer-term plan. Despite my nerves, I had to take a chance because I didn't have any other options. I couldn't keep driving endlessly. I didn't have enough money to keep filling the tank or to feed myself without help. I should've taken her phone, then I could've made phone calls, but I knew phones could be traced and they'd find me right away.

I parked behind the garage, got out of the car and glanced around. Her neighborhood wasn't an uppity place. People weren't likely to ask questions about the new person in town. With mostly run-down homes, passed down from generation to generation, from what I remembered, people here tended to keep to themselves aside from the odd wave as you drove or walked past.

Thankfully, nobody was out and about. I didn't want to risk being seen. Mustering the little courage I had left, I walked up to the house and knocked on the door.

The door cracked open, and her eyes were wide. "Oh my gosh, oh my gosh," was all she said, over and over again, as she wrapped her arms around me and I cried.

She shook her head. "I'm so glad to see you. Oh my gosh, let me look at you." She pulled back and looked me up and down before shaking her head. She said, "Come inside, honey, come inside."

Without hesitation, I hurried inside, and she shut the door behind me. "What can I get you? Are you hungry? You look..."

"Awful," I said through tears. "But I'd love a shower and some fresh bandages if you have any."

She inspected my hand and the blood-soaked towel. Her face crumpled in concern. "I have gauze and tape."

"I'd like to get cleaned up first if that's okay."

Looking deep into my eyes, she said, "Are you sure that's wise?"

"Yes. I need a shower, please."

"Of course. We can get you bandaged up, and we can talk after you get cleaned up. I'm guessing you'll need some fresh clothes?"

I nodded, so grateful for her. She was probably one of the nicest people I'd ever known. Compassionate, loving, kind—one of those rare people in life.

"Do you remember where the bathroom is? I'll bring you some clothes. How about some sweatpants, or I've got shorts too. What do you want?"

"Pants and a sweatshirt if you have it." It was warm outside but inside it was cooler and there seemed to be a chill inside me I couldn't shake.

"Okay, I'll get you a T-shirt too." Before I could agree, she wrapped her arms around me again and squeezed. "I'm so glad to see you."

And I was so happy to see her. There was a time I thought I never would, ever again.

TWENTY

VAL

Armed with a subpoena and the entire Claire Nelson investigation team, we returned to the head office of Hectorville High. The receptionist, an older woman with gray hair styled up in a bun and spectacles dangling from a colorful beaded necklace, stood up as we approached.

"Good morning, Mrs. Klein," I said.

Slightly curious, she answered, "Val, it's good to see you. And I'm sorry, I don't know you, hon."

Lucy replied confidently, "My name is Lucy. I am on the research team, I'm here to help out the investigators."

"Nice to meet you. What can I help you with today?"

I handed her the subpoena. "This is a subpoena for attendance records. We need to know who was absent last Tuesday and into this week."

It had been one of Lucy's great ideas while we were downing our drinks—not too many, of course. I had two glasses of wine, and it felt so good to be warm and relaxed. It was so much fun and it felt like we'd been friends forever, a true bond forming between the three of us, which was surprising and had filled me with gratitude.

"Students from all four years?" Mrs. Klein asked.

"Yes, all students," I confirmed. "As well as teachers. Anyone who called in sick on Tuesday and had a substitute."

The woman's eyes widened. "Of course, it'll take me a few minutes. You're welcome to have a seat."

"We'd also like to re-interview some of the students, once you have provided the list," I added.

She nodded and returned to her desk, picking up the phone, presumably to notify the principal. She glanced up at us, whispering into the phone as if we wouldn't know exactly what she was doing. None of us took a seat; instead, we waited, rather impatiently, which probably didn't ease the nerves of the receptionist.

After hanging up the receiver, she informed us, "It will just be a few minutes. Mrs. Richardson will be out shortly to help you with anything else."

Mrs. Richardson, the principal of the school, soon emerged from a nearby door and shuffled toward us. Early forties, wearing a blazer and leggings, she said, "What can we help you with? Has there been a development in Claire's case?"

"There has," I confirmed.

"Oh?" Mrs. Richardson said, likely hoping for more details.

"We've come here with a subpoena for attendance records."

"Oh, okay. And I'm guessing you're going to want to re-interview some of the staff, maybe some of the students?" Mrs. Richardson inquired.

"Yes, we would."

"Of course. Anything we can do to help find out who did this to Claire. Is there anything I can do while you're waiting for the records?" Mrs. Richardson offered, clearly willing to assist in any way possible.

Her cooperation was a relief, as the investigation was reaching a critical point. The revelation that the perpetrator might be female narrowed our scope of suspects, which was a step in the right direction. "We were hoping to have a voluntary fingerprinting of all the students," I proposed.

"You'll need a warrant or consent from the parents for those under eighteen," Mrs. Richardson said.

Nodding, I acknowledged her concern, "Yes, we understand we can't force it, but this is a voluntary effort. We'd like to get the fingerprints once parental consent has been granted for those under eighteen. Is that something you could assist us with?"

She seemed hesitant. I added, "This is strictly voluntary. It would help us eliminate any potential suspects that are associated with the school. It's completely voluntary."

In California, it was mandatory for teachers and anyone who worked with children to be fingerprinted, so they had already been eliminated as suspects.

"Do you have fingerprint kits?"

"Yes, and we're willing to teach anyone who may be collecting the prints how to do it properly."

Mrs. Richardson nodded. "Okay, I think we can put together an assembly. We'll send an email to the parents tonight and hold the assembly tomorrow. Maybe we can provide prizes or have a raffle to incentivize the students. Would that work?"

"Yes. That's a wonderful idea. Thank you, Mrs. Richardson."

She nodded. "I don't think you'll have much resistance. Everybody loved Claire."

The list of suspects was mostly blank. Jordan Nelson had checked out as being faithful, but we would most definitely take a second look, perhaps we'd uncover a romantic rival, someone who wanted Jordan all to themselves, or a disgruntled student, or someone Claire had worked with at the encampment. We'd be doing the same drill back there.

A few minutes later, the receptionist hurried over with the

attendance records for the students. "These ones here," she pointed to the paper, "were absent on Tuesday."

"Thank you so much. Do you know if they're in school today?"

She pointed to another column on the paper. "Yes, it shows their attendance for today."

I scanned the paper. There were a few students, more than a few, out on Tuesday. But no teachers were out, and none of the staff, so we would be able to talk to the teachers about any of the students that were added to the potential suspects list.

Pointing to the paper, I said, "We'd like to pull this student here, and this one."

Mrs. Richardson nodded. "Yes, right away."

"And if you could also pull their homeroom teachers," I added.

"Of course, just one moment," Mrs. Richardson said, hurrying away to make the arrangements.

Turning back to the group, I saw Lucy had already started to arrange the fingerprint kits.

Meanwhile, I spoke with Brady and Allan, in a hushed tone. "There were three female students who were out of school on Tuesday, and Wednesday, but they've now returned."

"It's too bad we didn't know this information earlier. We could have checked their hands for cuts," Brady noted.

"If there are any, they won't be completely healed by now, but they won't be as noticeable if they've been taking care of it."

As we planned our approach to question the homeroom teachers, as well as the three students who stood out among those absent on Tuesday, the day after the murder, the door cracked open. A young woman with bright blue eyes and hair pulled up in a messy bun peeked in, took one look at us, and stepped back outside.

"We must look intimidating," Allan commented.

I shrugged. "If I was a teen and saw law enforcement standing in the office, I wouldn't come in either."

"That's because you were a bit of a rebel back then," Brady said with a sparkle in his eyes. He was probably remembering some of the shenanigans of our youth. Nothing too serious, just pranks and a few late-night trespasses onto our school grounds, just because we could.

Lucy glanced up with a knowing smile. "I knew it."

A few minutes later, I sat in an empty office with a young woman, named Jenny Cargill. "Thank you for speaking with me, Jenny."

"Sure, what can I do to help you?"

"As I explained earlier, we're investigating the death of your teacher, Mrs. Nelson."

She nodded.

"The attendance records show that you were absent on Monday, Tuesday, and Wednesday last week. Can you explain why?" Jenny was pale with dark rings under her eyes, a sign that this lead might be a dead end. "I had Covid," she explained.

"How are you feeling now?"

"I'm better, testing negative, so that's something. I'm getting most of my energy back, but not completely."

"Are you getting plenty of rest?"

"I'm trying, but it's my junior year, and my course load is pretty heavy."

My maternal instincts took over, and I found myself more concerned for the sick child than with finding the killer of Claire Nelson, at least for the moment. "Well, I hope you start to feel better. Thank you for coming in."

Jenny asked if she could return to class, which I allowed, planning to verify her story with her parents.

Returning to the reception area, I found Brady and Allan looking just as empty-handed. "Anyone interesting?"

"Two kids with Covid," Brady reported.

"Make that a third," I added.

"So, it wasn't anyone who was absent that day. Is it possible the killer was coldhearted enough to kill her in a frenzy and then come to school on Tuesday?" Allan asked.

"I doubt it. This person was likely desperate, unhinged. They wouldn't have come to school the next day." I couldn't be entirely sure, but I was fairly certain. "Anything from the teachers?" I asked.

They all shook their heads. Brady said, "Same as last time, nobody knew of any students with a serious grudge against Mrs. Nelson. She was beloved."

"Okay, let's set up the principal with all the kits and instructions for fingerprints from the students."

I didn't want to admit that I had little hope that anybody at the school was involved, but it was a necessary step. We would be kicking ourselves if we didn't rule them out properly and later found out we were wrong and the killer had been walking the halls of the high school once graced by Claire.

TWENTY-ONE

VAL

Brady drove us over to the encampment. As there were no more than fifty residents, we didn't need the whole team for this visit. Part of me wondered if bringing Lucy along would have seemed less intimidating than just Brady and myself. On the way, Brady said, "How's your mom doing?"

"She's doing well. She was actually able to bathe herself for the first time and she's so very happy about that."

"That's good to hear. It's hard to think of her as anything but tough and capable of just about anything."

That was true. It had been difficult to see her so weak after the stroke, but the progress she had made was a testament to how strong-willed she really was. "I know, it's so unlike her. But she's regaining her strength and pushing hard in physical therapy. Julie says she's pushing a little too hard."

"It wouldn't be Elizabeth if she wasn't," Brady said with a smile.

It was nice to have someone close to me that knew Mom. My thoughts drifted to the teasing, or not teasing, from Sally and Lucy. They were convinced there were sparks between Brady and me, and maybe I felt them a little, but with everything I had been through over the past few months, I didn't think I could start a relationship. My therapist told me it would likely be a while before I could have a meaningful relationship, and I think if Brady and I crossed that line, there would be no going back.

"So, how likely do you think the folks at the encampment will give us their fingerprints?" I asked, shifting the topic back to our investigation.

"Maybe fifty-fifty. A lot of those people do not trust law enforcement."

"Even with your charm?"

"You think I have charm?" He asked with a flirtatious smile. There it was, something I couldn't avoid even if I tried.

"I know you've got it in you," I said playfully.

"All right, I'll lay it on thick and see who takes a bite."

We parked, and within moments, Maisie, the unofficial leader of the encampment, emerged from her tent.

We greeted her with friendly smiles. "Maisie, how are you doing?"

"Can't complain. What can we help you with today?" she asked.

I took the lead. "We're still investigating Claire Nelson's death. We've learned some new information about our suspect, but they're not in any of our databases—not fingerprints, not DNA. We've already gone by the school where Claire worked to get fingerprints from all the students. We were hoping to do the same here. Could you help us convince some of the residents to give us their fingerprints?"

Maisie tilted her head, looking at Brady and then at me. "Okay, I'll see what I can do to help. I'll encourage the residents, but don't hold your breath," Maisie said, a hint of skepticism in her tone.

We understood the challenge ahead. The residents of the encampment had their reasons for mistrust, especially toward law enforcement. Maisie, with her first-hand experience and trust from the community, would be our best ally in the effort.

"Not to mention, some of them may already be in your system," she added.

I had considered that. It was common knowledge that it could be difficult for someone with a criminal record to find employment, which could then lead to homelessness.

As Maisie walked over to the first tent, she paused and looked back at us. "I didn't even offer up mine, did I?" she asked.

I responded with a simple "No."

"I'll give it to you, then. I did nothing wrong. I didn't hurt Claire," Maisie declared.

I was inclined to believe her. We flipped on some gloves and prepared her finger while Brady held out the fingerprint card. With a successful print secured, we slid it into the envelope and continued. "You're going to put that in a database to see if I've committed any crimes, right?" Maisie asked.

"Just to see if you killed Claire," I clarified.

"Okay."

Next, we approached another tent. A woman we met during our last visit emerged. "What is it now? Did you find out who killed Claire?" she asked.

"No, they haven't yet, Darlene. They're trying to get finger-prints to match up to Claire's killer. Trying to rule us all out," Maisie explained. And I was grateful for her help.

"So, the person you got prints from aren't in the system?" Darlene asked.

"They're not," I confirmed.

"A first-timer, huh? Well, I'll give you my fingerprints, but I'm gonna be honest with you, they're already in the system, so you can rule me out," she said in a huff.

"Do you mind if we take down your details? Your name, do you have a driver's license or identification card?" I asked.

"Sure, I've got ID."

We noted down her details and thanked her for her cooperation.

Maisie said, "That's two so far."

We continued on, with about seventy-five percent of the residents complying with our request. For those who didn't, I made a note of their names and descriptions, in case we could construct a profile from the DNA evidence we did have, like possible hair color, eye color, and race.

As we approached another resident, I said to Maisie, "I definitely want her prints."

"She may consent, but I'm not sure if she's in the right mind to do so," Maisie cautioned.

"We'd really appreciate it," I said, feeling a sense of urgency. The one person's prints I really wanted were Laney's. She was the only resident of the encampment that gave me pause. I saw fear in her eyes when she spoke of Claire Nelson and when she warned us to stay away from the house. I wished she were lucid enough to explain her ramblings.

Maisie approached Laney with caution, raising her hand to have her step back so that she could speak to Laney alone. She said something that caused Laney's eyes to grow wide, and then she nodded in agreement.

Maisie beckoned us over, her tone reassuring. "Now, Laney, this is Val and this is Brady. They're cops, but they're the good ones. They're trying to find out what happened to Claire, and they're going to take your fingerprints."

Laney's eyes widened, and she nodded ever so slightly, indicating her understanding. This response made me wonder about her earlier warning to stay away from the house. As I inked her finger, she was visibly skittish.

It was plausible that Laney, perhaps in the midst of a psychotic break, had gone after Claire. Maybe Claire had tried to help her, brought her home to clean her up and give her something to eat, and all hell had broken loose. Once we'd finished, I took the opportunity to say, "Thank you so much, Laney. I have a couple of other questions too."

Laney stood there staring at me, clearly unnerved. I asked gently, "Have you ever been to Claire's house or been in her car?"

She placed her hands on her head, agitatedly repeating, "I don't go to the house. I don't go to the house." Clearly, she was deeply troubled and did not want to discuss Claire or their interactions.

"Did you like Claire?" I probed further.

Her eyes wide with distress, she repeated, "Don't go near the house."

Maisie, understanding the situation, shrugged and escorted Laney back to her tent. Mentioning Claire Nelson had triggered this response, but why?

When Maisie returned, she said, "If there's anything else I can do to help, just come on by. You know where to find me," she said with a smile, her missing teeth adding a charming characteristic to an already charming individual.

"I appreciate that. We're just trying to find out who did this, who killed Claire."

"I know you are, and I want to help as much as I can. Just let me know if there's anything else I can do," Maisie offered earnestly.

We thanked her and headed back to the station, eager to process the fingerprints as soon as possible. The encounter with Laney had added a layer of complexity to our investigation. Her reactions, her fear, and her repeated warnings not to go to the house—all these elements formed a puzzle and I couldn't shake the feeling there was more to Laney than met the eye.

TWENTY-TWO

TALLY

Wrapped snugly in flannel pajamas and a cozy bathrobe, I paused to look in the mirror. There was some color in my cheeks, and I looked a little more like myself. Bernie had applied Neosporin diligently and made sure my bandages were clean and fresh, like she had done when I was a child. She had suggested I go to the hospital, thinking I might need stitches, but I refused. The thought of divulging what had happened, even to the doctors, was something I wasn't ready to face.

Bernie didn't press me for details, which I deeply appreciated. Yet, I knew her patience wouldn't last forever. She deserved an explanation.

How had I cut my hand? Why wouldn't I go to the hospital or to the police? She hadn't asked but I knew she must be wondering. Trusting someone was never easy for me, but Bernie had proven to be the exception. Even so, I wasn't ready to talk about it.

When I first met Bernie, I was living in a group home after my mom had succumbed to her heroin addiction. With no job to sustain her habit, she had resorted to unsavory means. Her addiction spiraled so out of control that she neglected to care for or feed me. Neighbors and teachers noticed, and the next thing I knew Child Protective Services was at our door, and I was dropped into the system.

I had only hazy memories of life before the group home. Fleeting images of my parents together, before my father's overdose that shattered everything. Despite his addiction, he was the stable one, always leaving the house in a three-piece suit, briefcase in hand. Before he died, each day he would step through the door and be greeted by dinner on the stove, and me doing my homework in the living room. He managed to maintain the facade of normalcy despite his addiction. When I was growing up, I had no idea he was a heroin addict; he was always kind and even-tempered, from what I could see. It wasn't until his overdose that I understood how destructive drugs could be. They had killed my father and ripped apart our stable home.

The details of his death were murky, but I remembered my mother's broken promises of vengeance against those who'd supplied him with drugs. It was very confusing at the time. Her descent into despair was fast and our lives crumbled as the life insurance money ran out. I wasn't an easy child either, moody and obstinate. Looking back, I could see how my behavior added to her burdens. If only I had known, I might have tried harder to be a better daughter, or at least tried to ease her pain.

Life in the group home was the opposite of my previous life. The people who ran the place weren't bad people, but the kids I shared my space with came from backgrounds that were unlike mine. Most had been born into families of addicts and criminals, and a rough childhood was all they knew. It made them tougher and harsher than I had become, having only experienced a few years of adversity.

Life in the group home had been a brutal lesson in survival. The few foster homes I'd been in had been worse. Although the caretakers were strict, they didn't pose any real threat compared to my fellow wards of the state. Horrors I swore I'd escape from one day. And then there she was. A glimmer of hope.

Bernie, a new foster parent had agreed to take me in when I was just twelve. The year I spent with her was like a dream compared to the group home. Bernie was more than a guardian; she was a mentor and a friend. She taught me the simple joys of baking cookies and the warmth of home-cooked meals. Living with her, a single woman who preferred the company of dogs and innocent children to the harshness of the world, was a sanctuary. She confided in me about her own past as a foster child, explaining her deep desire to give something back and make a difference.

Being placed with Bernie felt like I'd won the lottery. For the first time since my father's death, I felt safe. I was still a damaged, scared child, but Bernie's home was a safe haven. However, this peace was short-lived. My mother, having achieved sobriety, reclaimed me. Despite my happiness at seeing her well, a nagging feeling in the pit of my stomach warned me that it was only temporary, and when all was said and done, I would have lost my spot at Bernie's and would end up back in the group home. When I left Bernie's home, I felt like I was stepping into a calm that before long would turn into a storm.

Sure enough, my mother's sobriety lasted less than a year, and I found myself back in the group home, facing the same kids who had mocked my earlier claim of never coming back. Walking back through the doors of the group home felt like a defeat, like I'd broken my word. Bernie, meanwhile, had taken in another child and couldn't offer me a place. Knowing I only had a few years left in the system, I grew tougher, more resilient, knowing I didn't have long there.

Part of me knew I had survived because of Bernie. Even though she couldn't take me in, we had kept in contact through the years, and she had thrown me a lifeline. She provided me with a cell phone and regularly checked in on me. Bernie was the only person who genuinely cared about me.

When I learned that she would soon have an open spot, I couldn't wait to go home. But of course, that was also when the universe decided it had other plans for me. My luck ran out and evil took over.

Now, back in the only safe place I'd ever known, I realized it was time to come clean. She deserved to know the truth about where I'd been and what I'd endured. It was a daunting thought, but Bernie's unwavering support gave me the courage to finally share my story with her. My only hope was that she wouldn't turn me in.

TWENTY-THREE

VAL

It was strange being on the other side of the interrogation, especially when the interrogators were my mother and her two best friends, Julie and Diane. It had been a week and a half since Claire Nelson's death, and to date, the only thing we had determined was that her killer was female. Her husband, seemingly uninvolved, at least physically, was still a person of interest. I didn't have any concrete evidence against him, but there was something unsettling in his eyes that I had seen before, and this made me uncomfortable and suspicious.

"But what about all the fingerprints you got from the high school? Did you learn anything there?" my mother asked.

We hadn't, and it was upsetting, disappointing even. Nearly every student had agreed to be fingerprinted, albeit with disclaimers restricting their use solely in the Claire Nelson murder investigation. They weren't added to any databases.

The team had worked tirelessly over the past forty-eight hours to screen every single fingerprint from the students and compare them to the killer's, but we were practically back to square one, or maybe square two now that we knew the killer's gender. However, narrowing down the suspect to half the population wasn't really much to go on.

There was nothing to incriminate Claire's husband. We couldn't find any evidence of him seeing another woman, a woman who might have viewed Claire as a romantic rival and eliminated her. But even if there had been a romantic rival, why would they take her car, her keys, her wallet?

"There weren't any matches. It wasn't any of the students at the high school, or the teachers, or the staff."

"It's pretty amazing that the community agreed to the fingerprinting. I would've expected some resistance," Julie said.

Diane countered, "I'm not surprised. Claire was beloved. Everybody wanted to help."

Mom said, "It was a testament to the community's love for her."

Was anyone that saintlike, though? Had something in Claire's past come back to haunt her?

Diane didn't let up. "Have you been looking for suspects elsewhere? I know that Claire did a lot of volunteer work with the homeless."

Unfortunately, unless one of the people who Claire encountered in her volunteer work had moved on from Red Rose County and had never committed a crime before, that was a dead end too.

It was unusual for a first-time offender to commit such a heinous crime, but it wasn't unheard of. I was beginning to feel like I was losing my touch. It had been ten days since Claire's death, and we had absolutely no answers for her family or the community. I explained to my trio of investigators, "We tested fingerprints and did background checks on everyone at the encampment, as well as fingerprinting anyone who had encountered her at the soup kitchen. No matches."

"So, a random killing?" my mom asked, her eyes shining

with interest. I knew she enjoyed discussing the case, considering her entire life's work had been in law enforcement.

"It's possible, but my experience is telling me it's not likely. I'm wondering if it was someone from her past that we haven't identified yet. Maybe someone outside of Red Rose County."

Mom nodded. "Go with that instinct, Val. You've got good instincts. Don't ignore them."

Julie, the more vocal of the bunch said, "When are you going to be able to release the body? I heard from Jordan that he couldn't hold the funeral yet. The town, the county, is grieving. We need to be able to pay our respects."

I couldn't keep anything from these ladies. "We've collected all the evidence we can. They'll be releasing her body soon so Jordan can have the funeral."

Julie picked up the empty dinner dishes from the table and said, "It's about time."

My mom chided gently, "Be nice, Julie. Police work is a lot harder than you can imagine."

Julie set the dishes in the sink and said, "I know, I'm sorry. It's just... She was one of us, a good one. You know, some people you kind of tolerate, but Claire was a sweetheart. It's a real loss for the county, for the school."

"I understand," I said. I also understood that it wasn't only bad people who were victims of violence. Random violence and senseless acts of evil weren't limited to those who "deserved" it, if anyone ever did. "We're going to widen our search and look for some people who may have moved on from the encampments. But they're hard to find because, well, they don't exactly leave a forwarding address before they hit the road."

"It's a tough case, Val," my mom sympathized.

"It is." I couldn't help but feel disheartened that the first case I had worked on since leaving the FBI was proving so difficult to solve. Had my trauma dulled my investigation skills? At the very least it had me doubting my own instincts.

Aside from leaving bloody prints in the kitchen, which had only confirmed the killer's gender, whoever had killed Claire had been careful. Her car, stolen from the scene, hadn't been picked up on any traffic cams. The killer must have either hidden it or gotten rid of it somehow. This led me to wonder whether this could have been a hit. Had Jordan hired someone? Maybe a handyman, someone that Jordan told Claire would come by the house to fix something. That person could have been hired to kill her, taking the car and wallet to make it look like a robbery.

"I have a question for you, ladies," I said, drawing the attention of all three seniors. I had asked this before, but considering Sally and Lucy had a different opinion of Jordan Nelson than everyone else, I thought I'd ask again. "You're sure Jordan would never ever cheat on Claire, never hurt her?" We hadn't found any financial motive; they were both set financially, and there weren't large life insurance policies on Claire. We hadn't established any reason for Jordan to want to get rid of his wife. The only thing we had left was that maybe he wanted a fresh start, maybe there was a new life waiting for him with or without a new woman.

"I have a pretty high opinion of Jordan and Claire, but you're right, you never know. Maybe he did have an affair, and he hid it well from the rest of us," my mom said thoughtfully.

Julie and Diane nodded in agreement. Julie added, "It's true. Sometimes the nicest guys in the world still have affairs. Well, maybe not the nicest in the whole world, but those you thought were the nicest and just weren't capable of it. But I also know sometimes men lead with parts of their bodies that aren't inside their skulls."

"So, you're saying it's possible?" I said, seeking confirmation.

"Anything is possible, Val. We don't know Jordan *that* well.

I mean, maybe he has a woman in another town or something like that?" Diane speculated.

As we pondered this possibility, my phone buzzed. It was nearly nine o'clock at night; why would the sheriff's station be calling me? "It's work," I said, excusing myself to answer the call.

"Hey, this is Val."

"Hi, Val, this is Brady. We need you to come down to the station."

"Why?"

"Somebody broke into Jordan Nelson's house, and he's saying it was you."

What? "That's ridiculous. When was I supposed to have done that?"

"Earlier this evening."

I was astounded. "This is outrageous. I'm literally sitting here with my mom, Julie, and Diane. We've just finished dinner, and now we're about to have tea. Before that, I'd been with you all day."

"The sheriff wants you down here. Can you make it?"

I shook my head in disbelief and responded, "I'll be there in fifteen minutes."

Ending the call, I explained what had just happened. Mom echoed my sentiment. "That's ridiculous."

"Why would he think it was you?" Julie asked, her eyebrows raised in confusion.

"Who knows? Maybe because I'm the only one who is suspicious of him."

Diane said, "Well, if someone did break into his house, maybe they know who killed Claire."

That was a good point. Maybe this new development would provide us with some new clues. "I've got to go down to the station to be questioned by the sheriff. I'll see you ladies later."

My mom gave me a knowing look as she said, "Be careful."

"I will." With that, I headed out, my mind racing with all kinds of scenarios—why was I being blamed for the break-in?

As I arrived at the sheriff's station, Brady met me at the entrance. I waved and asked, "What's the latest?"

"Jordan thinks it was you who broke into his house. Apparently, you left some sort of note."

Weird. "Well, I didn't."

"Yeah, I know. We all know you wouldn't break into his house, but it sounds like somebody did."

"Well, let's go learn more," I suggested, eager to clear up this misunderstanding.

Inside, I spotted the sheriff, his face flushed as if filled with anger at the situation we now found ourselves in. "Hi, Kingston."

"Hey, Val, thanks for coming down."

"For the record, I did not break into Jordan's home, or anyone else's for that matter."

He let out a breath. "He thinks you're out to get him, for whatever reason."

"For whatever reason?" I asked incredulously.

The sheriff walked toward his office, and we followed. He continued, "I don't know, Val. Let's get your formal statement tonight and file it away. Who knows, maybe whoever broke into his house had something to do with Claire's death and it will help with the investigation."

That would be one positive outcome from this situation. But I had to admit my dislike for Jordan had intensified. I don't know what it was—it was a vibe I couldn't shake.

Before we could enter the sheriff's office, Jordan stormed toward us, his face red and his eyes wild. "You broke into my house! You had no right to come inside my home without my permission. I should sue the entire sheriff's department for this." He was beside himself.

I stepped back, maintaining my composure. "Jordan, I didn't break into your house. I'm sorry if somebody did, but it wasn't me."

The tension in the air was palpable. It was clear that this case was taking a turn, one that was becoming personal and increasingly complicated.

Jordan exclaimed, "You're the only one who thinks I had something to do with my wife's death, which I didn't. I know you keep asking around about me! When will you move on from your little witch hunt and find the real killer? Not only that, but you also haven't released her body yet, so I can't arrange the funeral. My kids are grieving, and now someone broke into my house. Don't you think it's time you did your job properly!"

Brady stepped in, positioning himself between us. I moved aside, determined to meet Jordan's gaze. "I did not break into your house. But I'd like to understand why you think I did," I asserted calmly. Despite my racing heart, I felt proud of myself for staying even-tempered.

He reached into his shoulder bag and pulled out a piece of paper. "This. This is why." He handed me a note card. Typed on it were the words:

I know what you did.

My heart nearly stopped.

I couldn't speak. I had frozen.

"Val, what is it?" Brady asked, noticing my reaction.

Looking at the sheriff, I said, "We should process this for fingerprints, touch DNA, anything that might tell us who left this note." Turning back to Jordan, I asked, "Where did you find the note?"

"On my kitchen countertop." His calm demeanor and his grieving-husband act had disappeared, replaced with a mix of worry and rage.

"Did you find it, or did one of your kids?"

"Thankfully, it was me. It would have completely freaked out the children."

"Where are the kids now?"

"They're out for pizza. I was supposed to meet them. I just dropped by the house to take a shower before going out, and I found it right there on the kitchen counter."

"And you asked your kids about it?"

"They hadn't been home, but I called them at the restaurant and neither of them left the note."

The sheriff spoke up. "Do you really think we should process it?"

"Absolutely."

"Okay, well, we'll process the note. And we'll send over the CSI team to collect fingerprints and other evidence at the house. Is that okay with you, Jordan?"

"Yeah. I want to know who broke into my house."

I muttered, "Good idea" and excused myself, hurrying down the hallway to the women's restroom. Inside, I splashed my face with water as I tried to compose myself. The mascara ran down my face, but that was the least of my worries.

The note could be a crucial piece of evidence. Not only in Claire's case, but I needed to compare it to the one I had received previously, following the Scarlett Douglas case. Why would someone break into Jordan's home, especially now, and more importantly, what did they know that Jordan had done?

After taking some deep breaths, my heart rate steadied. I cleaned up my face and stepped out, where Brady was waiting.

"Are you okay?" he asked.

"That note looked identical to the one I found in my mailbox after we'd solved the Scarlett Douglas case. I think it's from the same person."

"But why would they leave a note at Jordan's house?"

I shook my head. "I don't know, Brady, but I don't like this one bit."

"We need to compare the two notes, the card stock, the ink from the typewriter or printer. We can send them to the FBI. I have photos, so we can visually compare the details and see if we might have a bigger problem."

Brady placed his hand on my shoulder, a gesture meant to comfort, but my mind was a whirlwind of thoughts. Nothing could calm me until I knew the truth. Was it possible that the original note hadn't been from the Bear after all? Could it be someone in town? Or was the Bear tracking my investigations, and me, or just observing from afar and having someone else do his dirty work? Was it possible the Bear had an accomplice?

The possibilities were dizzying. Whoever left the note at the Nelsons had to know I'd see it. Was the message really for me? Was it a warning, were they mocking us, or was it a clue for our investigation?

TWENTY-FIVE

VAL

"Thanks, Kieran, I appreciate it." I ended the call and turned to Lucy. "They're going to send me the information as soon as possible about the card stock and ink so our lab can compare the two."

"Do you really think it was the Bear?" Lucy asked, clearly concerned.

"I had been really sure until now. But now I don't know. All I know is the two notes look very similar. The same type of card stock, and the same font. Whoever sent me the note and left it in my mother's mailbox is the same person who left a note in Jordan Nelson's house. It's weird." And I was having a difficult time getting my head around it. Had I been wrong about everything? Had I lost my touch?

"Do you think the message was really intended for you?"

It had crossed my mind. "Maybe."

"Well, if the notes are from the same person who left a message for you before, maybe they're following your cases. Maybe they're doing some weird, twisted thing where they think they're helping you," Lucy suggested.

But would the Bear really do that? From everything I'd learned about him, I doubted he'd be following my investigations. Unless, after capturing somebody in law enforcement, he'd changed his MO, and he'd become fascinated by me and my profession. But if he had broken into Jordan Nelson's house, that meant he was close. How close, exactly?

"Maybe we'll know for sure once we get the information from the FBI and analyze the note that was left at the Nelson residence," I said, trying to keep a level head amid the swirling theories.

Just then Brady and Allan entered the war room. "Hey," they greeted in unison.

"How's it going?" Brady asked.

"No news on the note," I said and explained what I had just told Lucy.

"So, what do we do now?" Allan asked.

I explained. "The sheriff told Brady and me that he is concerned about Jordan. He's obviously coming unglued. He's having security installed at his home, so if anything else happens, he'll be able to get it on video. Which could help us. But for now, we have to work with what we already have."

"But haven't we processed all the evidence collected from the scene?" Brady asked.

"Not entirely. We have DNA. They caught the Golden State Killer after decades by doing genetic genealogy. I was thinking we could submit the sample and do the genealogy thing? It might take a little while, but our killer might be related to someone who has submitted their DNA to a database to map their family tree or they're related to a felon."

The room filled with a new energy, one of hope that we might finally get a lead.

Lucy eyed me, skeptically. "We can work with Parabon Labs; they're number one in genetic genealogy for forensic use.

But it's really expensive, and it could take weeks, if not months, to track it down to a single subject. Then we'd have to get their DNA to confirm that it's our perpetrator, if we can find her."

I sat down, feeling a little deflated. "But we haven't been able to find the car or any trace of the person who killed Claire, so maybe it's worth a shot." It might not work out, but it was a last resort. A little surprised by Lucy's pessimism, I said, "Lucy, do you have any idea how much the genetic genealogy costs?"

"No, but I think it's quite a bit."

Trying to renew the group's enthusiasm, I said, "Maybe we could figure out how much it's going to be. We've already mapped the DNA, so they just have to find a match for it in their databases. Hopefully, it won't be a long, drawn-out search for family members of Claire's killer."

Lucy nodded. "I can do that. I'll look into the cost and what we need to do to submit the samples, or see if there are any other labs that have cropped up since the popularity of genetic genealogy."

"Perfect. It's similar to how we were able to identify some of the victims in the Scarlett Douglas case, right? I think it could help," I reminded her. Although for that case, we didn't need to have a full mapping since it was her father's DNA, a close relation, that was matched to Scarlett's kidney donor.

A knock on the door interrupted our planning, drawing our attention to Jonathan, the head scientist from the forensics lab, as he entered. I glanced at Lucy, noticing her reaction. She had been crushing on him and had told me they had had dinner the previous night, which she thought had gone really well.

"What can we do for you, Jonathan?" I asked, curious about his sudden appearance.

"Well, I was talking to Lucy yesterday about how the killer could have been living in one of the encampments. It got me thinking."

"Oh?" I asked.

"On a hunch, I took a second look." There was a hint of excitement in his voice.

Lucy gasped. "Did you find the identity of the person who killed Claire?"

Jonathan smiled confidently. "I believe I did."

TWENTY-SIX

VAL

The room sat in stunned silence as we processed Jonathan's revelation.

"How did you find the identity of Claire's killer? Where did you look?" I asked.

"Well, after speaking with Lucy and hearing how you guys were looking into the encampment angle, that maybe a homeless person had killed Claire. Well, I thought about who usually ends up in the encampments and then I thought what if it was a runaway. And maybe somebody reported that person missing, but it was recent, over the past few months or shortly after Claire's death. It can take anywhere from a couple of weeks to several months to get a missing person's DNA profiled and uploaded into NamUs and, consequently, CODIS. It had been a week since the initial search in CODIS, so I ran a second search and I got a hit. The DNA had been uploaded only a few days ago," Jonathan explained.

NamUs, the National Missing and Unidentified Persons System, is a national central repository and resource center for missing persons, often used to match DNA of Jane and John

Does, as well as missing persons with unidentified remains. The NamUs organization submitted all of its DNA into CODIS.

It took a lot to stun me at this point in my career, but Jonathan had done it. I wouldn't have thought to rerun the DNA. "Well done, Jonathan."

He smiled.

"Well, then. Who is it? Who is the killer?" I asked, impatiently.

"Can I plug in my laptop?" Jonathan asked.

"Of course." We all hurried to assist him, eager to learn the identity of Claire's killer. The projector whirred to life, and the screen dropped down.

Jonathan clicked a few buttons and stepped back, revealing the profile of Talitha Blackwood, a seventeen-year-old girl who had been missing for two and a half months from the group home she was living in.

A missing person, or a runaway from a group home, was our suspect. Staring into the eyes of Talitha Blackwood, displayed on the screen, I didn't see a killer. She had mousy dirty-blonde hair down to her shoulders, an uneasy smile, and haunted brown eyes.

"What's her story?" I asked, trying to understand how or why she would have killed Claire.

"She's been in the foster system off and on since she was eleven years old. It was a turbulent time for her. She was sent to a group home after her father died and her mother nearly OD'd. After a while she was placed in a few foster homes, some that went very badly and some that were quite good, until she was taken out by her mother when she sobered up, only to be swiftly returned when her mom relapsed," Jonathan explained.

"Who reported her missing?"

"The group home. Her mom died a year ago, overdose."

"Was there an investigation after the missing persons report was filed?" I asked.

Jonathan shrugged. "You'll have to request the file from the Modesto Police Department, see what they found out about her disappearance."

"Thank you, Jonathan, nice work."

"I do what I can," he said with an easy smile.

Glancing over at Lucy, I could see how much she liked him. She was smitten with him and impressed by his initiative, which had ultimately led to a break in the case.

The revelation of Talitha Blackwood as a suspect in Claire's murder opened a slew of new questions about Claire's death. Who was Talitha and how had she crossed paths with Claire? What was her motive for killing her?

TWENTY-SEVEN

TALLY

Clutching my mug of tea, I watched as the expression on Bernie's face transformed from sympathy to horror, and then to restraint. It had been almost a week since I had showed up on her doorstep, looking so messed up. Bernie hadn't asked any questions at first. She told me she knew I would tell her what had happened to me when I was ready. I didn't know much about Bernie's past, or what had turned her into the saintlike human being she had become, but I knew she'd been in foster care, so she understood what I'd been through. But telling her the truth about how and why I ended up at her house, begging for her help, was a test to see how much I could trust her.

And I had done it. I had told her everything, and she hadn't said a word in response.

Fear crept through my body as I wondered if she would turn me in. I feared that I had gone too far, that I was so rotten I couldn't be brought back to being a normal, decent human being. Had I ever been normal? Or had I always been broken? I wanted to be whole again, like I was when I was little, but I wondered if that was even remotely possible.

And now, the one person in this unfriendly world that I trusted completely saw me differently.

Finally, after what seemed like an eternity, Bernie placed her hands on the table and said, "What do you plan to do?"

"I don't know. I just drove here thinking you were the only person I could trust. I don't have a plan beyond that."

"You've been through so much in your young life. It breaks my heart," she said softly.

"Do you think I'm a terrible person?" I asked, my voice trembling.

I wondered if I was. Maybe I had finally turned into one of those horrible kids I had met who only looked out for themselves and did whatever it took to survive.

Shaking her head, she said, "No, honey, of course not. I just... I think maybe we should go to the police."

My heart sank. "I can't. I can't go to the police."

"I think you need to. You are a survivor and I think you can survive this too. It's the right thing to do."

I *thought* she understood. Why would she think I should go to the police? Had I made a terrible mistake coming here? She had fed me, clothed me, and was trying to heal my physical wounds. To suggest going to the police didn't make sense to me. "They won't find me. I think I can just hide out, let it blow over," I said, though even as the words left my mouth, I knew how absurd they sounded. Murder doesn't just blow over.

Bernie raised her eyebrows. "I think you need to go to the police. Even if you don't, they will find you eventually."

As she continued to speak, I watched her lips move, and for the third time in my life, I felt my world crumbling into rubble. It was over, all over.

TWENTY-EIGHT

VAL

The name Talitha Blackwood went through my mind on repeat as I stared at the murder board. It was brilliant of Jonathan to think of rechecking CODIS. It gave us the identity of Claire's killer and although that was a huge breakthrough, we still needed answers to a lot of questions. The first, and most important, was how had Talitha and Claire crossed paths, and second, why had Talitha killed Claire? Did Talitha have mental health issues?

Thinking back to the murder scene, an inexperienced killer, who took food and drink from the refrigerator after the attack and then ran off with the victim's car and wallet, definitely fit with a desperate, possibly mentally ill, homeless teenager who needed food and money. But if that was the case, why hadn't she ransacked the house to find more cash or items she could sell? We were missing something. Talitha wanted to kill Claire for a specific reason, but I doubted it was for her car and some orange juice.

Assuming that Talitha had run away from her group home, which wasn't all that unusual, it was most likely that she had met Claire at one of the encampments or soup kitchens where Claire volunteered.

We had questioned people at both the encampment and the soup kitchen. Everyone insisted they knew nothing about Claire Nelson's death nor could they think of anyone who might have wanted to hurt her. But that didn't mean they hadn't known Talitha. The killing had seemed frantic. Talitha had needed something and Claire had got in her way. But what was it?

It was possible Talitha knew Jordan or one of the Nelson children. She was around Jake's age—maybe she was his girl-friend and had met Claire that way. Or, worse, maybe she had been having an affair with Jordan? Stranger things had happened. If Talitha was desperate enough, she would have been malleable to a person like Jordan, who could have manipu-lated her into killing Claire. It wouldn't be the first instance of an older man linked to a teenage love, who then went on to kill the wife in order to have the man all to herself.

Something didn't add up. The timeline. Talitha Blackwood had gone missing from Modesto two and a half months ago. The Nelson children had been away at college two and a half months ago. So unless they had met her before she had left the group home, it was unlikely Talitha knew them. And how had Talitha arrived at the Nelson house the day of the killing? There was definitely more to the story. We needed to know more about Talitha. Like *everything*.

Lucy, as if reading my mind, said, "I'll call over to Modesto PD to get everything they have on the case."

"Can't we pull up the electronic files?"

"Yes, but the officer assigned may have some unique insight. I'll be back." Lucy hurried out of the war room, presumably to contact the Modesto Police Department.

Jonathan approached and asked, "Is there anything else you need before I go?"

"No, this has been extremely helpful. Thank you again."

"All in a day's work. I'll see ya. Good luck with the case and let me know if you need anything else from me." And with a wave, he exited the room.

Meanwhile, Brady and Allan were deep in conversation.

"What are you guys thinking?" I asked.

Brady said, "Well, whoever killed Claire had to have a reason, right?"

"Of course. I think the only way to find out what that reason was is to learn everything we can about Talitha Blackwood. Hopefully, Modesto PD will have some leads on what happened to her." Their skeptical looks prompted me to ask, "What?"

"Do you really think Modesto PD, with their crime rates, went looking for a kid in the system who didn't show up at her group home?" Allan asked.

"Are you saying you don't think this was investigated at all?"

"That's right," he replied confidently, "I bet you a beer that not a single thing other than a record of the report was done."

"It's a missing teen, a child," I argued, disheartened by their cynicism.

"Welcome to underfunded police departments. Tight budgets mean resources go to the worst, most violent cases, and those with the highest probability of recovering the missing person. Missing wards of the state? Not so much," he explained somberly.

"But someone submitted her DNA to NamUs."

Allan shrugged.

Lucy returned, her expression grim. "I just got off the phone with Modesto PD. The intake officer on Talitha Blackwood's missing persons report didn't have any insight."

"None at all?"

She shook her head. "We can pull up the electronic file on my computer. Spoiler: they didn't do much."

Glancing over at Brady and Allan, they gave me a "told you so" look. At the FBI, we didn't typically get notifications of local missing persons unless there was suspicion of interstate kidnapping. How many missing persons were there that nobody was looking for? Young people just written off as runaways? Probably far too many.

Lucy manned the computer keyboard and turned on the projector. "Read it and weep, for real," she said.

After a few minutes of scanning the tiny summary, I said, "They didn't check her cell phone records, social media accounts, or her financials, but they labeled her as a runaway. Yet, according to the group home, she left all of her belongings behind except her cell phone and purse. And the one person who talked to her before she left said she was going to the grocery store." Letting that sink in, I said, "Foster kids don't leave all their belongings behind if they're planning to run away. Something happened to this girl. But what?"

Brady looked at me and voiced his thoughts. "Maybe she wasn't really going to the grocery store. Maybe she was meeting someone, a boyfriend or someone promising her something that was too good to be true and it went sideways. And she ended up north with no way of getting back. We should re-interview the encampment and soup kitchen to see if anyone recognizes her."

It was a good theory. "Good idea."

Lucy said, "I'll put in a request for her cell phone records right away, and her banking records. Cell phone data can take a bit longer, but banking records we should get pretty fast. And I'll scan through the socials."

"All right, let's prepare for that. We'll print out her photo and revisit the encampments, soup kitchen, and the school to see if anyone has seen Talitha Blackwood. We don't need to say she's a suspect in the murder. We just want to get confirmation that someone encountered her. She had to be staying somewhere in Red Rose County to have met Claire. Someone had to have seen Talitha. We need to find that person."

TWENTY-NINE

VAL

Holding an eight-by-ten photo of Talitha Blackwood, Brady and I approached Maisie's tent. She greeted us with a wave, her demeanor warm yet inquisitive. Meanwhile, Allan and Lucy had ventured to another encampment nearby, broadening our search for any leads on Talitha. We were determined to leave no stone unturned.

"Deputy Tanner, Ms. Costa. You're becoming regulars around here," Maisie remarked with a hint of humor.

I nodded. "Yes, there have been some developments in the Claire Nelson murder case."

"Did you find out who did it?" Maisie asked, her brows raised.

"We think so. We're following a lead on a young woman who may be connected to the murder," I explained, mindful of the legal nuances that required us to presume innocence until proven guilty.

"And you think she was here?"

After we briefed her on Talitha Blackwood's missing person case and our suspicions about her involvement in Claire's murder, Maisie's expression changed. Her eyes widened as she glanced at the photo I was holding. "I don't think she's been around here, but she does look familiar, doesn't she?"

"Does she?" I asked, surprised by her reaction.

Maisie nodded, urging us to follow her.

We passed familiar faces, some of whom we had spoken to during previous visits. To my surprise, Maisie led us to Laney's tent. Maisie called out, "Come on, Laney, come out. We've got a few questions for you."

Laney emerged, her eyes wide and alert.

It was then I understood Maisie's earlier comment. Talitha Blackwood bore a striking resemblance to Laney, though Laney was about ten years older. "I see what you mean, Maisie," I said.

"They do look really similar, though obviously not the same. Laney is a bit older," Maisie pointed out.

"What are you talking about?" Laney asked, her voice unusually lucid compared to our previous encounters.

"We're looking for a young woman who went missing," I said, handing her Talitha's photo. Laney's reaction was immediate—she recognized her.

"Have you seen this girl?" Brady asked.

Laney's response was cryptic yet charged with emotion. "Don't go near the house," she repeated several times, a statement that seemed to trigger something deep within her. What did she mean by this?

"Have you ever seen this woman?" I pressed, looking into her eyes. For a brief moment, I saw a glimpse of someone not just triggered, but deeply traumatized. There was a story hidden behind those eyes, one too painful for her to share openly. What had happened to Laney?

"Not her. I didn't see her," Laney finally replied, her words careful, handing the photo back to me.

The way she phrased her response sparked a new question. "Have you seen someone who looks like her?" I asked, hoping to decipher her cryptic message.

Laney's reply was just as enigmatic. "Not her. I haven't seen her," she said, leaving us none the wiser.

Exchanging a glance with Brady, I couldn't shake the feeling that Laney was dealing with a major trauma. As a detective, not a psychiatrist, delving into her psyche wasn't my expertise, but it was clear that Claire's death had triggered something inside of Laney. Perhaps Laney had witnessed a brutal crime herself, one that had driven her to hide out in the encampment, away from the rest of society.

I tried to hold her attention. "We think she killed Claire Nelson," I said, watching Laney closely. Her reaction was unexpected—a slow nod and the faintest hint of a smile.

It was unsettling. "Did you not like Claire?"

Her body jerked as if the question had struck a nerve. Without a word, Laney retreated into her tent and zipped it shut, cutting off any further conversation.

Mark that as one person who didn't have a glowing review of Claire Nelson. Were there others?

Turning to Maisie, I said, "Have you heard Laney talk about Claire before?"

Maisie shook her head, her expression mirroring our surprise. "No, but I can see why you might ask that."

With Maisie's permission, we proceeded to ask other residents about Talitha, but after an hour of inquiries, Brady and I returned to his SUV empty-handed. "What do you make of that?" Brady asked, starting the engine.

"They haven't seen her, but Laney... There's something more to her," I said. "Her reaction to our questions was unusual. And her fingerprints came back clean, right?"

Brady nodded. "Yep, there's no record of her being committed or committing any crimes. She's not in the system."

"Trauma, then," I speculated. "Maybe something in her past, possibly involving her mother, or strong female who was once in her life. Talking about Claire's murder seems to send her into a tizzy." There was something about Laney I couldn't shake. What had caused her to react so strongly to Claire Nelson's murder and then made her smile when I told her I thought Talitha killed her? It was so disconcerting.

"We'll keep that in mind. Once we find Talitha, who knows? Maybe Laney did see her and just doesn't want to tell us."

It was possible. If Laney had known Talitha, perhaps she didn't want to get her in trouble. "True. Thanks for coming with me. I probably could have gone alone, but it's nice to have company."

"No problem. And you're not so bad to be around," he said with a playful smile.

Forcing my own smile down, I said, "Thanks. Well, I hope we get something useful from the soup kitchen," I said, trying to deflect from the feelings that were starting to sprout, and to direct the focus back to the investigation, where it belonged.

THIRTY

VAL

After I set my things on the kitchen floor, I glanced up at the three ladies, who seemed to always be gathered in the kitchen. It made sense, considering it allowed them to sit next to my mom, who could just roll right up to the dining table. Julie waved at me with a bottle of wine in her hand, and I nodded, placing my hands together as if praying to her. "That's exactly what I need," I said.

"Long day, honey?" Mom asked.

"It was a long day, and quite the day."

"Any leads on Claire's killer?" Julie asked. "Let me get you a glass of wine first, and you can tell us everything. Dinner's in the oven. I'm assuming you're hungry."

"Yes, thank you."

I could really get used to this. Julie and Diane, Mom's best friends, were always at the house since I had started working on the Claire Nelson case, and I was always greeted with wine and home-cooked food. It was so nice to be among people with optimistic attitudes that verged on the glass always being half full.

Seated across from my mom, I gratefully accepted a generous glass of red wine from Julie.

"Okay, tell us everything that happened today," Julie said, pulling up a chair, Diane following suit.

As much as I enjoyed witnessing every aspect of their strong female friendship, they were just as enthralled at my law enforcement job. "We discovered the identity of Claire's killer."

The three women gasped.

"You're kidding! Who is it?" Mom asked.

"You have to keep this between us."

Diane winked at me. "What happens at the kitchen table stays at the kitchen table."

The other two nodded.

Holding back a chuckle, I said, "Well, it's strange. The killer is a seventeen-year-old girl who was reported missing two and a half months ago from Modesto."

"Well, that's strange. Is it somebody who was at the encampment or at the soup kitchen where Claire worked? Or maybe even one of the students? That's peculiar," my mother said.

"It is unusual. We reviewed the missing person report and learned she had been living in a group home when she went missing but she had left all her belongings behind, except for her purse and cell phone."

My mother sighed. "Let me guess, there was absolutely no investigation whatsoever."

"You got it in one," I said dryly.

Julie chimed in. "But you guys are going to change that, right?"

"Yes, and not just because she's a murder suspect. Her disappearance should have been investigated. But even if the police had acted right away, the group home hadn't reported her missing until one of her previous foster moms called to see if they'd heard from her. Apparently, she was very close with the foster mom and they spoke every day, but when she hadn't called in two days that's when the foster mom got in touch."

"Maybe she got into drugs, or she's living in an encampment. Have you checked?" Julie asked.

"Yes, the entire team checked all of the encampments in the county and at the soup kitchen. So far, nobody recognized her. We just got the girl's financials back. Her bank accounts haven't been touched and Lucy couldn't find any active social media accounts for her." No movement on the bank accounts was telling, but no social media accounts was odd for a teenager. Perhaps Talitha's social media accounts weren't under her real name.

"What about cell phone records?" Mom asked.

It was as if I had two investigative teams: one at the office and another at home.

Sitting around the dining table, they offered me flowing wine and home-cooked dinners. It wasn't a bad trade-off. "We're still waiting on cell phone records. Lucy put in a request today. Sometimes cell phone records are trickier to get, despite the warrant," I explained.

"That's so bizarre. Why do you think this missing person might have killed Claire? Does the girl have a violent background?" Julie asked.

"No, no criminal arrests, no violent behavior reported by the group home, or any of her foster families either."

"And her parents?" Mom asked.

"Her father died when she was ten, and her mother died about a year ago."

"Awful," Diane commented.

"What about the break-in at the Nelsons' house and the note that was left there? Have you heard back from Kieran yet?" Mom asked.

I hadn't heard yet if the note left at the Nelsons, claiming they knew what he did, and the note placed in my mother's mailbox after the Scarlett Douglas case were connected by the card stock or ink. But my gut told me it was from the same person. The photograph showed they were visually too similar to be a coincidence. But who had sent them? I had been so sure it was the Bear, but it was hard to imagine the Bear—a notorious serial killer—breaking into the Nelson home and leaving a note. Or maybe I just didn't want to think he would. Because if it had been him that meant he was right here in Red Rose County and that was the worst possible scenario. But then who else could it have been?

"Not yet, but I think it's from the same person," I said eventually.

Mom eyed me. "I would think so too. Makes me think it's a local. Do you?"

"Maybe." If the notes were from a local, why had they inserted themselves in two of my investigations? I tried to think of anyone from my younger years that could be the culprit, but I came up blank. That didn't mean I didn't have a stalker or someone who had been fixated on me. Like I didn't have enough fears to fill my nightmares. A nameless stalker/fan *and* the Bear could be after me?

"And the scene was processed after the break-in at the Nelsons, and they didn't find any trace evidence or fingerprints. So no luck there."

Which meant the person who broke in had worn gloves.

Julie sat back, crossed her arms, and said, "You know, all these peculiar things started happening when you came home, Val."

"Are you saying this is all my fault?" I asked, half amused and half offended.

"No, but it makes me think you were brought home for a reason. This town needs you, we need you, and your mom needs you," Julie said.

Finishing off my glass of wine, I contemplated her words. "Maybe."

"Any idea what you'll do after you solve the case? You've

kind of solved it because you know the who and the how, but the why seems like it'll be the most interesting part of the case," Diane said.

"I think so too. As for my plans after the case, I'm not sure yet. I really haven't made any plans. I will obviously stay as long as Mom needs me."

Julie set her glass down and peered at me. "Mothers always need their daughters."

"Well, I guess it's something I'll have to think about once the case is over and Mom gets better," I concluded.

Mom looked into my eyes and said, "You don't have to stay here for me. If you want to go back to DC, to the FBI, I'll be okay, you know."

That was Mom for you, always independent, not wanting to accept help from anybody. But as I sat there with two women who felt like aunties, and my mom, and thinking about my new friends from work, Brady, and the cases I was working on, I wondered what I would be going back to in DC. An empty house with Harrison off at MIT, a nonexistent love life, no job, and my only friends on the East Coast would be busy working all the time, like I used to. It didn't seem like I had much to go back to. "I appreciate that, Mom. But since I've been home, I don't regret leaving the FBI and I'm beginning to feel like I'm where I should be."

Mom's eyes lit up. "Well, you know you are welcome to stay as long as you like."

I nodded.

Diane said, "Let's get that dinner out of the oven. We need to keep your energy up. You've got to find that missing girl who killed Claire. I, for one, would like to know why she did it and make sure she doesn't do something like that ever again."

I was quite determined to figure that out too.

THIRTY-ONE

TALLY

Bernie apologized profusely, her voice heavy with concern. She had been fighting for me, trying to find out what had happened to me when I had stopped calling her every day. She confessed that her concern for my well-being had driven her to act since the police weren't doing anything to find me. She even went to the group home to inspect my things and my room before submitting my toothbrush for DNA analysis to be added to the NamUs system, hoping someone would find me. Her actions showed she cared for me, making her the only one who seemed genuinely concerned about where I ended up.

However, this concern for me now posed a threat to my freedom. Her efforts to find me would lead the police right to her doorstep. Bernie interrupted my thoughts. "If you go to the police, I'll stand by you, no matter what. I think you need to go to the police. I don't want this to end really badly for you."

How could it not end badly for me? Her words stayed with me, but all I could think about was how badly it would end for me. There was no happy ending, no rainbow—only dark, stormy clouds. Bernie was the sole ray of sunshine in my life, yet even her love couldn't shut out the darkness that I was trapped in.

"I'm not ready for that right now. It just seems like too much," I whispered.

Bernie said, "I understand what you've been through is awful, but I think you'll be surprised. It won't be as bad as you think."

Despite her good intentions, it was clear she had failed to grasp the enormity of what I had done. She didn't know the horror of it, the blood everywhere, and the most disturbing of all, the gurgle of that dying woman. A part of me had died at that moment, making me a different person. I was forever changed, no longer able to return to the person I was before. Could Bernie not see that?

It was reassuring she'd stand by me, but I wasn't ready to go to jail. Would it be worse than the group home? Probably. I didn't want to find out but I couldn't see a way out. "I'll think about it. I just need more time. Is that okay?"

The truth was sooner or later they would come for me. My days were numbered and I wanted to savor my final moments or hours or days I had left with Bernie.

"Of course. I'll be here for you through it all," Bernie said, her commitment unwavering.

Right then, I realized Bernie was the one constant in my life —the one person who had never betrayed me, had never left me, nor wanted something from me. She was the only person in this whole world who cared about me, and it nearly destroyed me to think I'd disappointed her.

THIRTY-TWO

VAL

Huddled around the coffee maker, I listened intently as Lucy told me about her big date with Jonathan.

"I don't know, Val, it's just not like any other date I've been on. I didn't expect to have so many feelings and emotions."

She had just told me all about their lovely date over the weekend, which they had spent out on the lake, kayaking and having a picnic lunch on one of the small islands. It sounded romantic, and I had to admit I was a bit jealous.

"Has he asked you on another date?"

She nodded enthusiastically. "I think this could really be something, Val. You and I haven't known each other that long, but I think you kind of get that I'm not like a gushy, girly girl, and I'm not usually boy-crazy or anything like that. But there's something about Jonathan—that smile and the way he tucks his hair behind his ear when he's talking, and he's always using his hands when he talks. Have you noticed that?"

I nodded and smiled. "I have. He's a cutie."

"I know, right?"

Lowering my voice, I said, "Did you kiss?"

Her cheeks turned crimson. "Yeah... oh, man, Val, I think I've got it bad."

We stopped talking as Brady approached.

"Good morning, ladies." He eyed us, and said, "Sorry, am I interrupting something?"

A week had passed, and I hadn't called Brady to see if he wanted to grab lunch or dinner, or kayak on the lake. But he also hadn't reached out to me. Was he waiting for me to extend our friendship, or was there another reason he didn't want to hang out with me? I didn't know, and I wasn't ready to explore that question yet. Maybe I never would be. Maybe it was better we stayed good friends. I didn't have many of those and if things didn't end well, I'd lose exactly one third of my friends in Red Rose County.

"Lucy was just telling me about her weekend," I said casually.

"Yeah, it was a nice weekend. How about you, Brady? Did you do anything exciting this past weekend?" Lucy asked, hiding her excitement at her new love interest.

"My daughter and her friend visited for the weekend. The three of us went hiking and watched movies. It was fun and it was good to see Paige."

Was that why he hadn't called? Maybe we were just colleagues, work friends, nothing more. When he looked at me, I didn't know, maybe it was just Sally and Lucy getting in my head, thinking he had a crush on me. Crushes at forty-five years old? I shook away the thoughts and said, "That's great."

"How about Harrison, is he back from his trip yet?" he asked.

"Right now, he's on a flight back to DC. Then in two weeks, he starts up at MIT and will be moving into the dorms."

Lucy said, "It's crazy to think you're old enough to have a son in college."

Despite our fun ladies' night out, we hadn't disclosed our

ages. "Oh, I am plenty old enough. Brady has a kid in college too. Isn't that right? We're both old folks."

"That's right," Brady responded, smiling.

I spotted Allan heading down the hall, and I took it as my cue. It was time to actually get to work.

"How about you, Val? What did you do this weekend?" he asked as I started leading us toward the war room.

"I hung out with Mom and all her friends who visit constantly. At first, I thought it would be a bit crowded, but they always bring baked goods, there's always home-cooked meals, and unlike my mom, they seem to have an endless supply of wine."

"Sounds like it's turning into a sorority house over there!" Brady joked.

"Kind of, it's actually really nice." It had made me realize how much I missed having close girlfriends.

"Girl power," Lucy said with a wink. "Speaking of, I didn't get a chance to tell you—the cell records are back for Talitha Blackwood. Who wants to have a cell phone record review party?"

Lucy was like a ray of sunshine, always upbeat, getting us to look at things as half full, just like Mom's friends. Stepping inside the drab war room, I said, "Let's get to it."

Allan had arrived just before we did.

He glanced up from his phone. "Hello, fine folks, how are you doing this morning?"

"Great. How are you doing, Allan?"

"Pretty good. I saw the three of you huddled together. You got something?"

"We have cell phone records."

Brady joked, "That means us old folks need to pull out our readers."

I laughed, wishing I wasn't part of that "needing readers" gang, but I was.

With laptops on the table, we opened them up and began divvying up the records. With lines and lines of tiny text and numerals on the screen, the room fell silent as we forged ahead with the painstaking task.

A few minutes later, Lucy said, "Okay, I know we need to go through every single record because we're going to want to interview the people she called, but I think this is kind of strange."

"What is it?" I asked.

"The last ping on her cell phone was two and a half months ago. Do you want to guess where it was?"

"Red Rose County?"

"Hectorville, more specifically. The cell tower it pinged from was right on the Hectorville-Redford border," Lucy clarified.

Not that we hadn't known she was here, but the fact that she came here and stopped using her cell phone meant it either died, she lost it, or she destroyed it for some reason.

Brady tilted his head, as if he'd caught an idea. "If it's true that her cell phone stopped pinging two and a half months ago in Hectorville, it means she had to have been in Hectorville for the last two and a half months. Where was she? We went to the encampments, the soup kitchen—where could she have been? Somebody had to have seen her."

"Exactly. Let's keep sifting through the records to see if there are any local numbers. Maybe she knew someone in town and was going to stay with them."

There were nods of agreement as we lowered our heads and returned to our task.

THIRTY-THREE

VAL

An hour into our meticulous examination of Talitha Blackwood's cell phone records, the room was filled with a quiet intensity. When I came to several interesting phone numbers, I printed hard copies and began highlighting the most significant ones. Brady sat next to me, and lay four highlighters in pink, blue, yellow, and green on the table. "In case you want to color-code," he explained.

I smiled and met his gaze. "I would love to color-code, thank you." It was a good idea, as it would make it easier to distinguish between different numbers. "In the section I have, there's a number that she called every single day for at least the last month before she went missing."

Lucy nodded. "Is it—" she said, rattling off the number.

"Yep, that's the one. How about you, Allan, Brady? Have you found that number too? Or any other recurring numbers we should be looking at?"

"Yep, same as you two," Allan confirmed. "Seems like the other calls are mostly where she worked, the group home, and a few randoms."

"Well, for this number, let's print it and highlight yellow.

Use the other colors for any other numbers that we should take a closer look at."

"Yes, ma'am," Brady said, winking at me.

Was he flirting in the war room or just being supportive? I forced my thoughts back to the case. I thought the number Talitha called every day must have been the foster mom she had been close with. "Let's find out who that phone number belongs to. It might be the foster mom that alerted the group home when she hadn't heard from Talitha for two days. Maybe she's still in contact with Talitha, maybe she knows where she is or where she's been."

"I'll get right on it," Lucy said, already tapping away at the keyboard.

"I think we're getting close, Val," Brady remarked.

"I think so too. We know who killed Claire, we know how she killed her, we just don't know why. I have a feeling, based on my profile, she had a good reason, and that's the most troubling thing about all of this."

Brady said, "We talked to everyone, and nobody had a single bad thing to say about Claire. I just don't see why she would have killed her."

"But we can't forget Laney's reaction to hearing Claire's name and that she'd been killed by Talitha. I don't think Laney liked Claire. Why?"

"Who's Laney?" Lucy asked.

"She lives at the encampment. She seemed almost happy that Talitha had killed Claire. It was odd."

Brady shrugged. "I don't know, Val. Laney seems more than a little unstable. I don't know how much stock we can put in her reaction. Everyone else loved Claire."

Not everyone. Talitha Blackwood had stabbed her to death. "I have a feeling the only way we're going to find out why Talitha killed Claire is if we can find and talk to Talitha ourselves. Assuming she'll admit it, but I think if we find her, she will tell us. We have a mountain of physical evidence against her."

"True. Maybe she had a psychotic breakdown," Brady suggested.

That was my top theory. A brainstorm session of all the reasons why someone might kill another person wouldn't be helpful. We needed to find Talitha Blackwood. She was a kid, after all. If we could get a location on her, we could bring her in. She might not be cooperative at first, but eventually, I thought we would be able to break her.

Glancing down at the photo of Talitha Blackwood, her haunted eyes and stoic features spoke volumes. This girl had lived through trauma. Had she somehow felt threatened by Claire? Whether it was real or perceived didn't matter to the person who felt that way.

Lucy broke the silence. "Okay, I've got it. Bernadette Dickerson, Tracy, California."

Brady nodded. "That's kind of a remote area."

"You're familiar with it?" I asked.

"It's far east of the Bay Area, outside of San Francisco, maybe an hour and a half. A lot of farmland. If she's hiding out, it'd be a good place."

"Let's give her a call and see if she's heard from Talitha."

"Would you like to do the honors?"

"I'd be honored to do the honor. Thank you," I said as I pressed the numbers on my cell phone.

THIRTY-FOUR

TALLY

The scent of pancakes filled the air, a comforting aroma in Bernie's kitchen. She had always been too good to me, a symbol of kindness in an unkind and unfair world. As I savored the delicious breakfast, a troubling thought lingered in my mind. My time was running out. The choices before me had gone from bad to worse. Go on the run or turn myself in. Bernie had sworn to stand by me, but I had fears far greater than arrest that I wasn't ready to face.

"These are great, Bernie. Thank you so much for breakfast," I said, trying to hide my inner turmoil.

"It's nice to have somebody to cook for again."

"I sure do appreciate it. If I haven't told you this before, you're the best foster mom I've ever had, and honestly, the best friend I've ever had. I won't forget that."

Bernie gave me a reassuring smile. "Of course, you won't, because I'm in your life for good. I consider you family. I only had you here for a year, but in my heart, you'll always be my daughter. Like I told you before, I will stand by your side."

Her words were cut short by the buzzing of her cell phone on the kitchen counter. "Who could that be?" she wondered aloud, tilting her head in curiosity. Hesitantly, she picked up the phone. "Hello?" Bernie nodded and said. "Yes, this is she." A pause, followed by, "Oh, hello, Ms. Costa." Bernie's eyes met mine, before she said, "You're an investigator from Red Rose County?"

My heart skipped a beat, and in that instant, I knew my time was up. I had to leave, and fast. My funds were running low and my gas tank was nearly empty, but I had to make a break for it. I stood up, ready to leave. I couldn't ask Bernie to lie, and I knew she could get in serious trouble if they found out she was hiding me.

Bernie pointed at the pantry, and I nodded in understanding. She was telling me to grab food and be on my way, so she wouldn't have to lie. The last thing I wanted was to make her complicit in my crimes. I hurried to the pantry, grabbed a box of granola bars, and made my way to the door. My hand clasped Claire's keys.

After a moment's hesitation, I stepped out the front door, rushing toward the car hidden behind Bernie's house. It was only a matter of time before they found me and the car. Should I remove the license plate? Would that make it more conspicuous?

I had to go somewhere, but where? I could disappear for a little while, but then what? Should I turn myself in, as Bernie had advised? Maybe it was time. Was I brave enough to face it all, though?

THIRTY-FIVE

VAL

Standing in the corner of the room, I said, "Yes, Ms. Dickerson, I'm calling about Talitha Blackwood."

"You're calling about Tally?"

Tally. Tally didn't sound like a cold-blooded killer. "Is Tally what she prefers to be called?"

"Yes, Tally is the only name she'll respond to."

"Then yes, I'm calling about Tally. We are investigating her disappearance."

"Tally went missing from Modesto, so why is the sheriff's department calling from Northern California?"

"We're calling because we believe that Tally may have gotten into some trouble here in Red Rose County. We would really like to speak with her," I said, choosing my words carefully.

"I see. What kind of trouble do you believe she got into?" Bernie asked, her voice filled with apprehension.

I wasn't sure how much to tell Bernie or if she already knew what Tally had done. "We believe she may be involved in a homicide."

"All I know about Tally is that if she killed somebody, she had a really, really good reason."

I was surprised at Bernie's response, and it made me think she knew what Tally had done. Not only that, but I would bet that Bernie was on Team Tally and would try to protect her. I also thought Bernie might be the key to finding her. "I tend to agree with you, Ms. Dickerson."

"Please, call me Bernie."

"Bernie, I am a former FBI agent, part of the Behavioral Analysis Unit. Based on the crime scene, I do believe Tally had a very good reason for killing this particular woman. I just have no idea what that reason is, and I'm really hoping to talk to Tally so that she can explain what happened."

"Tally's not here," Bernie stated.

"Have you spoken with her in the last two and a half months?"

"I hadn't heard from her for about two and a half months, but she did contact me about a week or so ago."

"So, you have talked to her?"

"I have."

"Do you know where she is right now?"

There was a moment of hesitation. "I don't know where she is right now," Bernie said, but her tone made me think she either knew or had a very good idea of Tally's whereabouts.

"Bernie, have you seen Tally in the last week?"

After a pause, she sighed and said, "I have."

"Did she tell you what happened?" My curiosity was piqued, and I glanced around the room. All eyes were on me.

"Yes."

I nodded at the room. "Can you tell me what she told you?"

"Ms. Costa, that isn't my story to tell. But, I'll have you know, I have encouraged her to go to the police. However, I'm afraid she doesn't have much trust in law enforcement. I'm sure you can understand."

"Being a kid in the system is tough. I don't know personally, but I have seen what it can do to a person."

"Well, then, let me tell you, as someone who survived the system, there were very few friendly faces along the way. I don't blame her for being afraid to come forward. But let me tell you something else, Ms. Costa. Tally has had a rough go of things. She is not a bad person. She has a big heart that's been stomped on one too many times. She's a good person, and she had a good reason for her actions."

"Do you have any idea what that reason might be?" I asked again.

"Like I said, it's not my story to tell, and it would be hearsay anyhow. But here's my advice to you, former FBI Agent Costa. Talk to the woman's husband. The man that woman was married to. Talk to him, find out what he did."

The line went dead.

A bolt of electricity shot through my body.

I knew it. Maybe I hadn't lost my intuition after all. There was far more to Jordan Nelson than the people of this county realized. Those eyes—eyes don't lie. I had seen it enough times. I had a really bad feeling that he wasn't just bad, he might just be the worst of the worst.

THIRTY-SIX

VAL

With the phone call concluded, a flurry of thoughts and theories raced through my mind. The pieces of evidence, like dirty footprints by the back door, the ransacked kitchen, and the need for a car and keys, began to form a clearer picture. It was just a hunch, but if I was right—we needed to act fast.

"What is it, Val? What did she tell you?" Lucy asked.

After sharing everything that Bernadette Dickerson had said, I laid out my plan. "We need to keep an eye on Jordan Nelson. We need to search his house again, talk to his employees, and find out where he was two and a half months ago. I want to know all his movements since then. He's hiding something, and he's key to this."

"Whoa, whoa, whoa," Allan interjected, his hands up in the air as he leaned back in his chair. "You're saying you want to launch a full offensive against Jordan Nelson, the grieving husband? Based on what exactly?"

"According to my profile and Bernie—someone who was close to Tally, not Talitha—she's a good person and only killed Claire for a very good reason. She wouldn't tell me why, but she knows the story. She told me to look into Jordan Nelson, the husband. The husband caused this, and I think he knew exactly who killed his wife. That's why there was a forty-minute gap between when he got home and when he called 911. I want to know what he did in that time. Did he clean up the scene? Was he looking for Tally? Did he know Tally? I want every single detail of Jordan Nelson's life over the last three months, and I want someone on him now. Watch his movements, see where he goes, who he talks to. We're missing a major piece of this murder puzzle, and he is it. Between Tally and him, there's something there."

Brady cautioned, "I don't know, Val. A woman, who is likely harboring a killer, saying to look into the husband isn't exactly evidence."

The similarity in appearance between Talitha and Laney, and their lack of "love for Claire," which had been in the back of my mind, had made its way to the front of my thoughts. Jordan's involvement was the only scenario that fit. Shaking my head, I said, "We have no other leads. We need to look deeper into Jordan."

"Something like that will have to be approved by the sheriff. And I'm not sure I can sell it. But you're the lead and could give it a shot."

Shocked at his lack of trust in my instincts or willingness to defend the direction I thought we should take the case made me angry—or hurt. Or a mix of the two. So much for Brady having my back.

Lucy said, "Background checks and interviews don't need approval."

At least one person on the team trusted my leadership. I said, "Actually, you know, I need some hardware from a hardware store." With the community having ruled out Jordan Nelson, we hadn't visited his place of work or checked his work schedule, if he had one.

"Anyone want to come with me?" I asked.

Brady said, "I'll come with you." As he got up, he added, "But just so you're aware, Val, you're going to ruffle a few feathers by going after Jordan."

So be it. "If I'm right, and if Tally had a good reason for killing Claire Nelson, then this isn't just about Claire Nelson's murder or about Tally. We could be looking at more victims that we just haven't found yet."

"What do you mean 'other victims'? The only victim is Claire Nelson," Allan retorted.

"Claire is the only one we know of."

Allan shook his head. "I think you might be off base here, and I'm not willing to risk my badge over it."

But then it clicked—the statement from Jordan Nelson about temperamental teenagers. "That's it! That's what he was talking about. He was talking about Tally," I said out loud.

"What are you talking about?" Brady said.

"The first time I met Jordan Nelson, he said that 'teenagers can be temperamental.' Tally is a teenager. He has always known who killed his wife, and I want to know why he didn't tell us. He's hiding something. And if you don't have it in you to talk to the sheriff, no worries because I have no problem with it, because I'm a professional with good instincts."

Brady said, "Okay, everybody calm down. Allan, I understand your concerns. Jordan is a respected member of our community, but if Val is right and he knew who killed his wife, that means he's hiding something else too. And if it's something really bad, we don't want to be the ones who looked the other way when more victims pop up."

Allan shrugged. "If everyone else is in, I'll go with it."

Trying hard not to put Allan on my list of spineless detectives, I looked away so he wouldn't see what I really thought of him.

Brady said, "Okay, Val, let's go talk to the sheriff and tell him what you suspect."

With a nod of agreement from everyone, we all headed toward the sheriff's office.

THIRTY-SEVEN

VAL

Staring intently at Sheriff Phillips, who was on a call, I stood patiently until he had finished. He didn't make us wait long. It was an uncommon sight, the sheriff being approached urgently by four members of our team, all waiting to discuss a pressing matter. He hung up the receiver, his gaze meeting ours.

"Well, by the looks of it, I'm guessing there's been a development in the Claire Nelson case," the sheriff said. "Thank goodness, I was just on the phone with Jordan Nelson. They've set the funeral for Friday. C'mon in."

Kingston was a decent man. Surely, he'd agree with our approach. "We got an ID on the second contributor at Claire Nelson's crime scene."

"Well done, team. Who was it?" Kingston asked.

Brady said, "A teenager named Tally Blackwood. But we think the case is a bit more complicated than just identifying the killer."

"Oh?"

We described the details surrounding Tally and expressed our concern that there might be a connection with Jordan

Nelson, justifying further investigation into him. "We think he may have known all along who killed his wife."

Kingston furrowed his brow. "Are you sure? It sounds like you have no evidence to support this theory whatsoever. Now you want to put a surveillance team on him and go through his employment records, travel records, credit card statements? The man is grieving."

I stepped forward, hands on my hips, determined. "With all due respect, Kingston, it may be that he is absolutely devastated that his wife has been murdered. But I think he's always known who killed her. That's why he waited forty minutes to call 911. Why did he cover it up? It might be that he wasn't covering up the crime of his wife's death, rather he was covering up a crime of his own. All we're asking for are warrants for his cell phone and work schedule. We also want a surveillance team to watch where he's going, what he's doing, and who he's doing it with."

"That's all you're asking for?" Kingston asked, brows raised.

"We can act discreetly."

"It's difficult to be discreet when he's self-employed. He owns the hardware store where he works," Kingston pointed out.

"All we need to know is what days he was working and when he wasn't. We can ask some of his employees."

"I don't know," Kingston said, hesitant. "You seem to have some probable cause for the warrants, though. I can't deny that. I'll approve the warrant submission for cell phone records, but I'm not sure about questioning him about his work schedule. He's grieving. Plus, the kids are still in town. They're distraught, not to mention the break-in at his house."

"Kingston, I really do think this might be bigger than just Claire Nelson's murder," I persisted, looking him in the eye. "You saw what Brady and I were able to accomplish on the Scarlett Douglas case. The things we uncovered, sir. I've been doing this a long time. I'm telling you, there's more to this."

The sheriff leaned back, a look of contemplation crossing his face. "What exactly do you think Jordan did to this young woman that she would resort to killing his wife?"

"Those are some of the details we haven't figured out yet, but it must have been pretty bad. We need to re-search the home. I'd like a warrant."

"Let's just take this one step at a time. You'll get your warrant for the cell phone and employment records. If then you can prove that there is an inkling of evidence or circumstantial evidence that connects him to this Tally Blackwood, then we will execute a search warrant for his house. Until then, work with what you've got."

I glanced around the room. "Is the hardware store still open?"

Brady said, "It should be."

Good. We'd head there next. But before that, we had another ask. I said, "We also need a favor from the Tracy Police Department. We'd like to get Tally into custody. She did murder Claire Nelson. Until we understand why, she should be under arrest. We have reason to believe she's in the Tracy area."

Kingston nodded. "I can put in a call, unless anyone has a contact there."

"Brady, do you know anyone?" I asked.

"I do. I can call, see if they can send someone out to Bernie's house, and be on the lookout for Tally and for Claire's car."

"All right, nice work, team. Let me know what happens with Jordan Nelson. And please, be discreet. His two children and he are grieving, and they're valued members of our community. Wrap up any questioning you have before the funeral. There'll be absolutely no interviewing suspects there," the sheriff instructed.

That was a green enough light for me. "Thanks, Sheriff." And then I turned to the team. "All right, let's go."

Walking out of the sheriff's office, Lucy said, "I'll work with

Allan to get the warrants written up and approved and get those records rolling."

"Brady and I will hit the hardware store."

A series of nods and then Brady and I headed toward the parking lot to make sure we made it to the hardware store before it closed.

THIRTY-EIGHT

THE SECRET ADMIRER

Deputy Tanner parked his SUV in front of the hardware store. In the passenger seat was the most spectacular specimen I had ever encountered, I thought to myself, well done, Valerie. I knew why she was there. It was as if we were forever linked. Two minds merging into one.

Like me, she was adeptly putting the pieces together, much like I had started to do. But I had a beautiful picture in my mind. Valerie would too—in time. If she was re-interviewing Jordan, then I suspected it wouldn't be long now.

She climbed out of the SUV, Deputy Tanner right behind her. They spoke with their heads close together outside the hardware store. They had known one another a long time, but there was a certain look in his eyes, one that suggested he admired her, perhaps more than just professionally. And who could blame him?

Valerie, in slacks that complemented her figure. Her lips and her long, elegant neck. She seemed to have gained a bit of weight—maybe just two or three pounds. It suited her, giving her a softer appearance. I quite liked it. I thought she could add a few more.

Exchanging a confident smile with the deputy, they made their way into the hardware store. I wondered if she would be asking Jordan about his whereabouts on specific dates and times. What did she already know? I had faith she would figure it out. But oh, how electrifying to be able to discuss it with her.

Now she was out of sight, my mind wandered to our time together.

And how it would be when we were together again.

All in good time.

Until then, I wanted her to know how much I respected and cared for her.

A gift.

A gesture.

There was one present I knew she would love. It was something unique, and I sincerely hoped she would appreciate it.

THIRTY-NINE

VAL

A chill ran down my spine as I stepped inside the hardware store. Was it the air-conditioning set too high, or was it something else stirring within me? As I hesitated, I bumped into Brady.

"Are you okay?" he asked.

I glanced up at him. "Just fine, thanks," I said, and continued inside. It was my first time in this particular hardware store. In our town of Rosedale, two towns over, we had our own. This one was impressively stocked—gardening tools lined one wall, and ceramic pots were neatly arranged on a shelf to the left. And there were about four aisles lined with shelves. It was quiet with no overhead music.

The sight of the tools made me consider if I would ever take up gardening if I stayed in Red Rose County. It could be a new hobby for me. My mom loved working in her garden. Maybe she'd like it if I joined her. It was supposedly a relaxing activity. That was something I could benefit from according to my therapist.

Arriving at the counter, I was surprised to see the Nelson

children standing next to a man in his twenties that I didn't recognize. He must be an employee.

Brady said, "Hi, Sarah. Hi, Jake."

"Hi, Deputy. Do you want us to get our dad?" Sarah, the older sibling, asked.

"Not yet."

I stepped up to the unidentified man. "Hi, I'm Valerie Costa. I'm working with the sheriff's department. Do you work here?"

His hair was thin and fell just to his shoulders. He wore a baseball cap backward. "Yes, my name is Darrell."

"How long have you worked here, Darrell?"

"Since high school, so like ten years."

I nodded. "That's quite a while. You can call me Val, and this is Deputy Tanner."

"Call me Brady."

"Nice to meet you. What can I help you with?" Darrell asked.

"We'd like to ask you a few questions, but first we need to speak with Sarah and Jake. Is that okay?"

"For sure. Just let me know when you need me."

"Of course."

Good. Jordan had an employee who was likely to tell me everything I wanted to know with the right prodding.

I looked over to Sarah and Jake. "We'd like to talk to each of you individually, if that's okay?" I wanted to requestion the kids about what type of father Jordan was when he wasn't lurking there in the corner. In the first interview, he had been right there. How honest had the kids been?

"Sarah, I'd like to talk to you for a moment alone. Brady, why don't you speak with Jake?" I saw uncertainty in Sarah's eyes. "Is that okay, Sarah? It'll be just for a moment. We can just step aside right here in the store."

Sarah hesitated then said, "Okay."

Brady spoke to Jake as I ushered Sarah to the corner. "How are you holding up?"

"Okay, I guess. I can't believe she's gone."

"I'm so sorry for your loss."

She nodded.

"I wanted to talk to you because we have made some developments in your mother's case."

"You have? Like what?"

"We know the identity of her killer."

Sarah gasped. "Who was it? Who did this?"

"It was a young woman named Tally. Do you know anyone by that name?"

Sarah shook her head. "Was she one of Mom's students?"

"No."

"Was she one of the homeless she tried to help?"

"We're still trying to figure that out." From my bag I pulled out the photo of Tally and showed it to Sarah. "Have you ever seen this woman before?"

She stared at the photo. "That's who killed her?"

"Did you know her?"

She shook her head again.

"Had you ever seen her before?"

"No. Never. Why did she kill my mom?"

That was what I was trying to find out. "We're not sure yet."

"You haven't asked her?"

"We haven't been able to locate her yet."

Sarah's face scrunched up. "She kind of looks like me."

Tally did have light hair and fair skin like Sarah. "We're going to find her and figure out why she hurt your mom. I promise you."

She looked away, and I placed the photo back in my bag.

"I have a few more questions for you."

After a sniffle, she turned to look at me.

"I know I asked you this before, but growing up, did your parents seem happy together?"

"They seemed like it. Why?"

I couldn't answer that just yet. "Did your father travel a lot?"

"No, not really. Maybe a few overnights for work."

For work?

"What was he like growing up? Was he strict? Did he yell a lot?"

"No, I mean, Mom pretty much laid down the law. Dad was always fun, taking us hiking or fishing. Because he worked in town, he always came to all of our sporting events. He even took me to the father-daughter dance when I was in elementary school. I couldn't have asked for a better dad," Sarah said sadly.

Her portrayal of Jordan didn't match up with what I suspected he might have done. Could I have been wrong, or was he skilled at compartmentalizing his life? "It sounds like he's a good dad."

"He is. I can't believe anyone ever thought he could hurt my mom."

"We don't believe he hurt your mom," I assured her.

"Good."

"Thank you so much, Sarah," I said, grateful for her honesty yet puzzled by her account of Jordan's parenting and the suspicion I had of her father. I moved a few paces over to Brady, who had just finished his conversation with Jake. Giving Jake a reassuring pat on the shoulder, he walked toward me.

All eyes in the store seemed to be on us.

"Do you want me to get my dad now?" Sarah asked.

"Yes, please," I replied.

As Sarah went to the back to fetch her father, Brady leaned over and whispered to me, "Jake says Jordan was the best dad ever. And he has never seen Tally before."

I turned and whispered back, "It was the same with Sarah."

We both shrugged, a mutual understanding of the complexity of the situation. Just then, Jordan emerged, his expression one of surprise. "What can I do for you? Have you figured out who broke into my house yet?" he asked.

"Not yet," I said, feeling the hairs on the back of my neck prick up as he eyed me with those dark, beady eyes.

Brady took the lead. "We'd like to speak with you. We have some new developments in your wife's case."

Jordan remained motionless for a moment, studying us both. "Is that so?"

"It is," I affirmed.

Sarah interjected, "They found out who killed Mom."

Jordan's gaze shifted to his daughter, then slowly back to us.

I said, "We'd like to speak with you privately, Jordan."

Without a word, Jordan lifted the counter, joined us, and led us outside the store. "You have identified a suspect," he stated rather than asked.

"We have. It's a teenager, a young girl, actually."

"Do you have her in custody?" he asked without much emotion.

I chose my words carefully, aware he might have been interested in the girl's whereabouts for less than noble reasons. "We were able to confirm her identity through DNA. But we haven't actually located her yet." I wasn't about to disclose our progress in tracking her.

"Oh, that's such great news. Hopefully, you can get her off the streets so she doesn't hurt anybody else."

"Yes, that's exactly why we want to get her off the streets," I agreed.

In every case I had worked, the family of the victim asked for the identity of the person who had killed their loved one. Not Jordan. Because he already knew. All I had to do was prove it.

Brady raised the photo of Tally. "Have you ever seen this girl before?"

Jordan glanced at the photo for a moment, and said, "No."

Everything inside me screamed that he was lying. *Another thing to prove.*

Brady broached the more sensitive topic. "Jordan, we'd like to request your employment records to see the days you were working and match them up with some dates relating to our killer."

"What do you mean?" Jordan asked, immediately on the defensive.

"Well, we want to see if there was any possibility you had encountered the girl before Claire's death," Brady explained.

"I told you I hadn't."

Brady said, "It's possible you had, but perhaps you weren't aware of it."

Jordan stepped back. "You know, I don't really keep track of my own employment," he said coolly.

"How about your employees' attendance?" I prodded.

"Sure, for tax purposes, we keep records of the hours they work." He hesitated for a moment before saying, "Don't you need a warrant for that type of information?"

Brady and I exchanged glances, and for the first time, I saw in Brady's eyes an understanding of why I had been suspicious of Jordan's behavior.

"Yes, of course, we would need a warrant to access your employment records officially," I said. "And it's coming. But we don't need a warrant to interview your employees. And to be honest, Jordan, I'm a little surprised you're not being more forthcoming. We're investigating your wife's murder. Why wouldn't you just give us the records?"

Jordan's quickly replied, "I have no problem with that. I just don't see how it has any relevance to my wife's murder. I'm grieving. I lost my wife, my partner of more than thirty years. My children lost their mother. Have you no shame?"

As we stood there, I could sense we were getting to him. Looking directly into his eyes, I replied, "Do you?"

He shook his head, clearly agitated, and walked back into the hardware store. Brady and I watched him go. Turning to me, Brady said, "He said he had no problem with us looking at the records and talking to his employees."

"That's right," I said. "Let's get those records and then talk to Darrell."

The situation at the hardware store had escalated faster than I had anticipated. Jordan's reactions were a mix of grief, defensiveness, and now a hint of anger. His reluctance to cooperate fully, despite protesting his innocence, spoke volumes. We were rattling him, and that was exactly what I had intended.

FORTY

VAL

Thirty minutes later, with Brady sitting next to me, I was surrounded by piles of attendance records and work schedules from the hardware store. From the stacks, I pulled out the records for the week Tally Blackwood went missing but quickly realized it wouldn't be a bad idea to make copies of all the records in the event we needed to match up Jordan's time with other events in connection to Claire's death.

"What do you think?" Brady asked, scanning the records.

"What he told us was true. He doesn't record his working hours. He only keeps track of his employees' schedules. And from what I can tell, it looks like Darrell is his only employee. At least according to the schedule."

"Do you have the week Tally went missing?"

"Yeah, and for the week of Claire's death. In both instances, Darrell was working," I said, tracing my finger along the dates on the schedule.

"Do you have enough to interview Darrell?"

Nodding, I said, "I think so. We have the time Jordan left the hardware store on the day of Claire's death from the surveillance cameras, but I'd like to know his demeanor that day. And the weeks and months leading up to it. Darrell worked that day, so he may be able to provide insight. Let's make copies of all of these and then go talk to him."

As we emerged from the back room, carrying the stacks of records, we waited for Darrell to finish helping a customer. The Nelson kids and Jordan were near the counter, speaking in hushed tones. I was surprised Jordan hadn't sent them home, but then again, since the break-in, maybe he wanted to keep them close. He did seem protective, with an arm around each of his children, their heads bowed.

Despite not being Jordan Nelson's biggest fan, I approached slowly to give them a heads-up. "We're just going to speak with Darrell, and then we'll be out of your hair."

"Thanks," Jordan replied curtly.

Sarah eyed me suspiciously. "Dad, why are they still here? What are they looking for? They said they found out who killed Mom."

"Oh, honey, they're just dotting the i's and crossing the t's. Just making sure that the person who killed her hadn't worked at the store. They're trying to figure out why she killed her. Isn't that right, Ms. Costa?" Jordan said, looking at me somewhat threateningly.

It wasn't lost on me how quickly he could create a reason for our continued presence. "Your father's right. We are very interested in learning why this young woman killed your mother," I said, giving Jordan a look that conveyed I would uncover whatever it was he was hiding. Then, I turned and headed back toward Brady.

After Darrell had finished serving the customer and wished him a nice day, he turned to us. "Is there something I can help you with?" he asked.

"Yes, do you mind if we have a few minutes of your time?"

He glanced over at Jordan, who said, "I'll take the register. Don't worry, Darrell."

"Sure," Darrell agreed.

"Let's step outside," I suggested.

He nodded and followed us out of the store.

At a bench, we paused briefly to let a few passersby on the sidewalk continue on their way. The town was quiet, and with only a few folks milling around it was quintessential Main Street, USA. At seven o'clock in the evening, the sun was up, but most people were likely at home having dinner or at one of the few restaurants in town *not* worrying about solving a murder. Or maybe they were at home, locked away, worried that whoever killed Claire would come after them next.

Standing on the sidewalk, with no one else around, I turned to Darrell and said, "We have a few questions for you about your time here at the hardware store."

"Is this about Claire's murder?" he asked, as he fidgeted with the buttons on his shirt.

"It is. We're trying to get a picture of what life was like for Claire and Jordan before she was killed. We've been reviewing the work schedules here at the hardware store, and it looks like you've worked here five days a week for the last ten years."

He nodded quickly. "That's right."

"Since you've known the Nelsons for so long, we'd like to get your take on a few things."

"Sure."

"What's it been like for you working at the hardware store? Is Jordan a good boss? Have you ever had any problems with him?" I asked.

"No, he's a great boss," he said matter-of-factly.

"Have you ever had any disciplinary issues?"

He shook his head. "None. I'm always on time, and if I'm sick, I call to let him know. He's always very understanding. It's a great job, honestly."

From his soft demeanor, I was inclined to believe him. "Do you live here in town?"

"I do. I'm still at my parents' house. I'm an aspiring artist, and well, this job helps pay the bills as I work on my collection," Darrell explained.

"What kind of art do you create?"

"Mostly watercolors. I'm starting to get into oils too. Luckily, the hardware store carries all the materials, so I get a discount, which is pretty cool."

"That is lucky."

His eyes lit up, and I could tell he was staring to relax. "Were you friends with Jordan and his wife? Did you see them at picnics or barbecues, or were you ever invited to their house?"

He shook his head. "No, but I saw them around at community stuff. I mean, they're a lot older than me, around my parents' age."

Pulling out the work schedule for the week Tally Blackwood went missing, I pointed and said, "You were working that week."

"Yes."

"Do you remember if Jordan was here with you?"

"Hmm," Darrell pondered. "Let me think about it."

"Take your time. Why don't we have a seat?"

We sat, and Brady remained standing.

"Can I see those schedules?" Darrell asked.

"Sure."

I handed the stack to him, and after he reviewed them, he said, "Yeah, that makes sense. Okay," he added, as if piecing together the answer to whatever question he had.

"What is it?"

"Well, there were a couple of days that week that Jordan wasn't here. Once a quarter, Mr. Nelson goes to meet our suppliers. That week was his quarterly visit."

I turned my head to glance up at Brady, who gave me a knowing look. "Do you know which suppliers he regularly visits and if there's a record of those visits?"

"I'm not sure. You'd have to ask Jordan. But usually, he drives there. I don't think he flies to any of the suppliers."

"And how long is he usually away for?"

"Well, sometimes a few days."

"How can you tell he was gone on those days?" I would be surprised if Darrell had that great a memory.

He smiled gently. "Well, as you can see from this schedule, I'm closing. Usually, I'm off at seven, but on the nights I close, my schedule ends at eight thirty. I only close when Jordan's not here."

I studied Darrell, grateful for his insight. "So, all the days that you closed, which show you working until eight thirty, are the days that Jordan was not at the store?"

"Yes." Darrell paused. "Is that helpful?"

"It's very helpful, Darrell," I said, before shifting the focus to the week Claire was murdered. From the schedule, Darrell hadn't closed that week, so that meant Jordan was in town. "Do you recall, over the last few weeks before Mrs. Nelson's murder, if there was anything off with Jordan? If he was acting unusual, more on edge, anything like that?"

"No, not that I recall. Honestly, he's a pretty even-keel kind of guy. Pretty much friendly to everyone. He's usually pretty chill, like one of those Zen people, you know? I don't know if he does yoga or not, but he's kind of like one of those types."

Interesting. "Well, thank you very much for speaking with us, Darrell. You've been a great help."

"Sure, anytime," he replied and walked back into the store.

Brady's phone rang.

"I'll go tell Jordan we're done," I said.

"All right, let me answer this. I'll meet you back at the car."

Stepping back inside the store, I immediately felt uneasy. Jordan's eyes followed me the entire walk down the aisle to the counter. "We're done for now, so we'll be going. I hope you have a good night," I said.

The Nelson children simply stared at me, and I received a slight tilt of the head from Jordan. As I turned to leave, I could feel Jordan's eyes on me, tracking my every move. If nothing else, Jordan Nelson was guilty of being a big old creep in good-guy's clothing.

FORTY-ONE

VAL

Brady ended the call, a peculiar expression on his face.

"Everything okay?" I asked.

"Yeah, that was Paige. She's thinking about coming to visit again," he said.

"Well, that'll be nice," I said, a little jealous I wouldn't be seeing my son for another week. Although we texted twice a day, I missed him.

"Yeah, but I'm wondering if I should tell her another weekend might be better. I might not be home. If they find Tally, we might be hitting the road to pick her up and bring her back to Red Rose County."

"Or we'll just have to solve the case before the weekend," I said optimistically. Plus, I needed the case wrapped up so that when I headed off to the East Coast to move Harrison into the dorms I wouldn't feel like I was deserting the team.

"Good idea. I'll call Lucy and see where they're at with the warrants on Jordan's cell records," Brady said, pulling out his phone again. "Hey, Lucy, it's Brady." He nodded. "Okay, great. Thanks."

Putting his phone back in his pocket, he said, "The warrants are signed and submitted to the cell phone company."

"That's step one."

"It's something." Brady eyed me and said, "I'm starved. Do you want to grab a burger from Drake's?"

"Is it any good?" I asked, buying myself time to consider the proposition.

"They've got great beers on tap," Brady recalled.

"And wine?"

"Lots of wine," he confirmed.

I needed to get out of my head. Brady and I were friends. Friends and coworkers grab burgers after work. "Sounds good. Let me check in with Mom."

"Oh yeah, I forgot you promised to have dinner with her every night. That's good of you," Brady said.

"It's usually dinner with Mom and her friends, where they spend the entire dinner interrogating me about the case."

"Those ladies are fierce," he said, with a smile and a twinkle in his eyes.

"You're telling me. I can call on the way. Chances are she's fine."

As we drove to Drake's, I called home.

"Hi, honey, are you going to be late for dinner?" she asked.

"Actually, Brady and I were thinking of grabbing a burger and a beer. It's been a long day."

"Okay, no problem. Julie, Diane, and Margie are here too."

"Quite the party, huh?"

"It is. So don't hurry home on my behalf," she said.

"Okay, Mom."

"Tell Brady I said hi. Have fun tonight. You deserve it, Val," she said, her voice fading into a whisper to inform her friends that I was having dinner with Brady.

I hung up, smiling at the thought of being their main source of entertainment. "Mom says hi," I told Brady.

"How's she doing?" he asked.

"She's doing well, getting stronger every day."

"That's great," he said and we continued to make small talk until we arrived at Drake's.

We chose a tall table near the bar. A server with long brown hair and wide eyes approached us. "Hey, Brady, you having your usual?" she asked.

"Yep, and whatever she wants. Have you met Val?"

The woman shook her head. "I'm Brenda."

"I'm Val. Brady and I went to high school together and now work at the sheriff's department."

"Oh, you're Sheriff Costa's daughter, the FBI agent, right?"

"That's right," I said with a smile.

"Well, welcome home. What can I get you?" she asked.

"I'll have whatever red wine you've got and a cheeseburger with a side of tater tots."

She confirmed Brady's order and said, "Coming right up," before hurrying away.

"So, this is your hangout?" I teased Brady with a smile as we settled in.

"They might know me here. They've got a good burger, good prices, and they always have the game on," he admitted.

"Your friend Brenda seems to like you a lot." I eyed him. "She seems nice."

"She is. But not like that, Val. She's a little young."

"I suppose," I said with a shrug. Changing the subject, I said, "So, how are the kids?"

"Paige is doing well. She's got senioritis and can't wait to graduate, even though school only started two weeks ago."

"Yeah, Harrison's on the plane as we speak," I said, glancing at my wristwatch. "Actually, he should have just landed. He starts at MIT next week. We originally planned for his dad and I to move him into his dorm together."

"We can cover the case, Val, and watch over your mom if you need to go," Brady offered.

I appreciated his gesture. The case was important, but Harrison's milestone was a moment I couldn't miss. "I appreciate it. Actually, do you mind if I give Harrison a quick call to make sure he got back okay?"

"Go."

"Thanks," I said, stepping outside near the host stand. My body was practically tingling with the vibes from Brady and the anticipation of hearing Harrison's voice.

He answered right away. "Hi, Mom."

"Hi, honey. Did you get in okay?"

"Yep."

I heard him yawn. "Is your dad there yet?"

"Yep, I'm already in the car on the way back to Dad's."

"Okay, well, I just wanted to call to say I love you."

"Love you too, Mom. I'll call you tomorrow after I get some sleep."

With warmth filling my chest, I ended the call and returned to Brady. "It went well and he's on his way home," I said as my glass of wine was placed on the table.

Brady raised an eyebrow. "Harrison seems like a good kid."

"He is. I can't wait to see him," I shared, taking a sip of my wine.

"I bet. I'm sure he'll be happy to see you too. They act cool, but you know they still want us to be there for those big moments in their life," Brady said.

I stared into Brady's eyes, surprised by his insight. "When did you get so wise?"

"I can be wise, Val," he replied, half defensive, half joking.

"I guess years will do that to you. Speaking of getting up

there, your birthday's next month, right? Forty-six?" I said, remembering his birthday was the month before my own.

"Yep, and if I recall, yours is in November."

Our conversation shifted comfortably between old times and kid antics. It was a welcome respite from the intensity of the investigation. It was moments like these that reminded me of the importance of balancing the demands of work with the need to embrace life outside of hunting criminals.

"True. I guess we're both getting old now," I said with a light chuckle.

As we looked into each other's eyes there was a fleeting moment where it felt like there was something more, a connection deeper than friendship. But before I could explore that thought further, Brady's phone buzzed, shattering the moment.

Answering the call, he nodded as he listened. After a few moments, he said, "We'll be right there."

As Brenda, our server, set down our food, Brady said to her, "Can we get these to go?"

"Of course." Brenda took the meals away.

He turned to me, his expression serious. "There's a fire at the Nelson residence."

"How big of a fire?" I asked, my mind racing.

"Big flames. A neighbor called it in."

As we prepared to leave, my mind was filled with questions. Was this Jordan trying to cover up evidence through arson? Who else would have a motive to burn down the Nelson home? It was too much of a coincidence, too suspicious.

FORTY-TWO

VAL

We heard the sirens before we reached the Nelson home. The sun had set, but the flashing lights were visible in the distance. As we reached the private driveway, we parked and, flashlights in hand, Brady and I hurried down the gravel path. It was about a quarter-mile walk, during which we could see two fire trucks and multiple police cars, their lights flickering in the darkness. Lights had already been set up, facing the home, which seemed to still be standing. The wraparound porch was empty but intact. The smoke hung thick in the air, but there were no visible flames. They must have already contained the fire.

A rather large bald man, dressed in a dark suit with a fire chief emblem, was speaking to a few officers. As we approached, he turned to us.

"Hi, there. Can we help you?"

Brady said, "I'm Deputy Tanner, and this is Valerie Costa."

He nodded in recognition. "I'm Inspector Chisholm. You two are working the Claire Nelson murder case, correct?"

His gaze was intense, and we both nodded vigorously. "What's the story here? Is the structure itself damaged?" I asked.

"A bit to the back of the house. It seems like whoever set the fire, which is now out, did it in the backyard. It's peculiar."

"Have you found the point of origin?"

"No, my guys are still making sure the smoldering is out and that the surrounding forest doesn't catch fire. It'll be a few minutes before we can walk around and see exactly how and where the fire was set, but it seems intentional."

"Are the Nelsons here?" Brady asked.

"No, but they've been notified," he replied. "Do you think this could be connected to Claire's murder? Whoever killed Claire also wanted to burn down their house?"

It seemed highly unlikely Tally was in town and setting fires. "It's not likely the killer. We have identified a suspect and we have people looking for her as we speak. But that doesn't mean the fire isn't related to Claire's death."

The fire inspector gave me a puzzled look. Understandably. But I didn't really want to get into my suspicions when that was all they were at that point.

"Her?" he said.

I nodded.

"Wow, that is surprising. Any idea why Mrs. Nelson was killed?"

"No, that's what we're trying to figure out."

Brady said, "It's awfully strange someone set fire to the house, or the grounds anyway."

"It is," I agreed and turned to Inspector Chisholm. "We'd like to walk around the grounds as soon as it's safe to do so."

He nodded. "No problem. But right now, I need you to hang back, and I'll let you know when it's clear for you to walk through."

"I appreciate it," I said, pondering why someone would set fire to the back of the Nelson residence.

Brady said, "How long do you think it'll be before you learn the origin of the fire and possibly the details around the start?"

"Maybe a few hours. Nobody heard any loud explosions; they just saw the smoke and the fire and called it in."

"How long ago did your team get here?" I asked, trying to piece together the timeline.

"About twenty minutes ago. We were able to get out here pretty fast and thankfully were able to contain it pretty quickly."

"That is lucky," I agreed, scanning the scene before us. There didn't appear to be anyone out of place.

As we contemplated the different scenarios, a truck came down the drive and stopped. The driver exited the vehicle. It was Jordan Nelson, followed by Sarah and Jake.

What a tragic scene for them—their mother had been murdered, and now their home had been set on fire. Jordan approached us hesitantly, as if he didn't want to talk to us but felt obliged to.

"What happened?" he asked, his voice laced with anxiety.

Brady said, "They're still trying to understand what happened. But it looks like the fire was set at the rear of the home. They're asking that nobody goes near the back until they can ensure it's safe to walk around and that there aren't any embers that could spark and set fire to the forest."

The Nelson residence was nestled within a forest, just like all the other homes in the area. The backyard, filled with large trees, could easily catch fire that could potentially spread to neighboring properties and the rest of the national forest.

"The inspector said that there is only minimal damage to the back of the home," I added.

"Did they say how it happened? Or when the fire started?" Jordan asked.

"Not yet."

"And are we allowed to go inside?" Sarah asked.

"I don't believe so, but here's the fire inspector now," Brady pointed out.

"Inspector Chisholm, this is Jordan Nelson and his two children, Sarah and Jake. They live here," Brady said.

The inspector nodded and said, "I'm sorry this is how your evening's ending up. We've got everything contained, so it's safe to go back in the home. There's some damage to the back of the house. My guys are going to stick around for a bit and try to figure out how this happened."

"Thank you. Just let us know when you're done," Jordan said before he ushered his children toward the house.

Jordan didn't seem to know what had happened. His questions—"How did that happen?" "When did it happen?"—indicated genuine ignorance, leading me to believe he wasn't responsible for the fire.

The inspector turned to us. "Do you want to walk it with us?"

"Absolutely."

We followed the inspector into the backyard. What had once been a beautiful patio with tables and chairs was now charred and shreds of what it used to be. In the distance, I thought I caught sight of something on the ground. I hurried over, Brady and the inspector close behind. Pointing my flashlight, I said, "What is that?"

Brady said, "Looks like a hatch or door of some kind."

Momentarily speechless, I said, "Have you seen something like this before?"

Inspector Chisholm said, "Yeah, actually. Back in the sixties, everyone was big on fallout shelters. It's likely left over from that era. I wonder if the Nelsons even knew it was here."

Every part of my being, and every bit of experience I had as a law enforcement agent, told me Jordan Nelson absolutely knew about it. I knelt down and saw a brand-new padlock securing it. "Can we open it up?"

Brady said, "We'd need a warrant."

"Well, I think we should get one."

Just then, I heard the crunching of burned grass and saw Jordan Nelson heading our way. "What's going on over here?" he asked.

"We found a hatch, presumably leading to an old fallout shelter."

He stood quietly, as if stunned.

"Do you mind if we open it up?"

"Is it pertinent to determining the origin of the fire?"

Inspector Chisholm narrowed his gaze and said, "No, not likely."

"Then yes, I do mind, and no, you can't," he said.

With my flashlight on Jordan, I asked, "Why not?"

"I don't have to explain myself to you. Now, if you have nothing to do with the fire investigation, I'll have to ask you to leave."

The fire inspector gave me a quizzical look. Was Jordan Nelson finally revealing his true self?

Brady said, "I'll call in that warrant."

"Thanks, Brady."

What exactly was Nelson hiding in the old fallout shelter? Was he a neurotic prepper who didn't want us to see his stash, or was it something more sinister?

FORTY-THREE

VAL

Inspector Chisholm looked visibly taken aback by Jordan Nelson's response to our request to inspect the bomb shelter. He tilted his head at me, then said to Jordan, "Mr. Nelson, my investigators need to stay on the scene until we determine the cause of the fire."

Jordan gave me what I could only describe as a death stare. "Yes, of course," he said, before turning and heading back inside.

My mind was abuzz with possibilities of what could be inside that fallout shelter.

Brady hurried over. "They're expediting the warrant."

With widened eyes, I said, "Do you see it now?"

Brady said, "I do."

Finally.

"See what?" Inspector Chisholm asked.

"Jordan's hiding something."

He nodded. "I'd say so."

"Did you tell the sheriff what we found?"

Brady said, "He was the first one I called. He's the one pushing it through. He said he's surprised by Jordan's behavior, considering this is still an open murder investigation, and this is the crime scene. He agreed it's odd that he won't let us look inside." Brady eyed us, and then said, "The sheriff also said he hoped we come up with something worth putting the Nelsons through this."

"I hope I'm not right too," I said pensively.

Inspector Chisholm rubbed his shiny bald head. "Maybe the two of you should go back to the station until you get that warrant, to avoid any unnecessary drama."

"You'll watch it until we get back?"

I certainly didn't want Jordan having access to the bomb shelter before we could take a look.

"Of course."

"We'll head out then. You'll call and let us know if you find anything?"

"I will."

Brady and I walked briskly back to the car, hopped in, and headed back to the station.

FORTY-FOUR

VAL

Two hours later, we knocked on the Nelsons' front door ready to serve the warrant to Jordan. The house was dark, and there was no answer. We jogged around to the back to where the fire inspector and his crew were still inspecting the grounds. I waved to Inspector Chisholm. "Have you seen the Nelsons?"

"They left shortly after you did."

Where did they go? A hotel? Was it too much for the kids to stay in a home that had been broken into and set alight, and where their mother had been murdered? I would have thought so. It was surprising Jordan had brought them back at all after the murder and the break-in.

"We have the warrant."

"It's all yours."

With a nod and a smile, I said, "Let's get that open. Brady, call the CSI team."

"Are you sure we need them? It's late. We don't want them to come out if they're not needed."

Unfortunately, my gut was saying we needed them and that it was going to be a long night. "Call them. We'll need them."

"Okay," he said, although I could tell he wasn't entirely

convinced. But I was. A secret bunker he didn't want us to see. A girl who had killed Claire and fled. Dirty footprints at the back door.

"Inspector, do you have a bolt cutter?"

"We do."

"Can we borrow it?"

"Of course." The inspector jogged over to his truck while Brady was on the phone.

Adrenaline rushed through my body as I contemplated what we might find inside the underground room. I also wondered where the Nelsons had gone at this late hour and how desperately I wanted to know Jordan's exact location. My instincts were telling me Jordan's secrets were about to be revealed, which meant he could be on the run.

The inspector returned with bolt cutters, and Brady explained that the forensics team was en route. Pointing my flashlight on the hatch, the inspector inched closer to the charred padlock and cut it open. He stepped back. "It's all yours."

Brady handed me a pair of latex gloves and offered to hold my flashlight. I slipped on the gloves and lifted the hatch.

Shining a light down into the darkness, I could see stairs leading down. Before I could step down, the inspector called over to one of his crew, "Get the floodlights over here."

"Thanks." I wasn't opposed to gritting the flashlight in my teeth, but hands-free would be safer, and I preferred the bright light the floodlights would provide.

He nodded.

His crew hustled over, lights bouncing in the darkness. They set up the lights, and the open hatch was illuminated.

With bated breath, I turned and descended the steps into the shelter. On the ground floor, I found a switch on the wall at the bottom of the stairs and flipped it on, lighting up the entire space.

To the right, there was a sofa, a coffee table, a television, and cabinets with padlocks on them. Other than the padlocked cabinets it didn't seem that unusual.

I turned around and gasped.

There was a mattress on the floor, the cinderblock wall fitted with metal restraints. My heart raced as I imagined the horrors that must have occurred there. Had Claire known about this? What about the kids? I stepped closer to the mattress and examined the wall more closely. There were dried splatters of a darkish, brownish-reddish material. A portable toilet was concealed by a shower curtain.

I called up to the team, "Can you bring those bolt cutters down here?"

The sound of the stairs creaking under his steps broke the eerie silence.

"I've got them. What did you find?" Brady asked as he descended.

"I think I found what Jordan was hiding."

Brady looked around, his expression one of disbelief. "What do you need the bolt cutters for?"

"The cabinets." I pivoted back toward to the cabinets, and Brady cut the padlocks on each one.

Carefully, I opened the door of the first cabinet and immediately understood why Jordan Nelson hadn't wanted us to know about this space.

The cabinet was stacked with labeled video tapes, and I dreaded to think what might be on them. It would all be bagged and tagged and brought back for processing. I pointed at the tapes, and Brady shook his head in disbelief.

In the next cabinet, a Polaroid camera and piles of envelopes. Not particularly wanting to see what they contained, I picked up the first envelope and pulled out a stack of photos.

I shut my eyes and took a deep breath. A dozen photos of

women restrained, gagged, and bruised, their eyes filled with terror.

It was enough. I slid the photos back into the envelope and placed it back in the cabinet with the others.

Another cabinet contained magazines depicting bondage and S&M, and below them were what could only be described as tools of Jordan's sick, twisted rage—whips, handcuffs, a ball gag.

Brady, who had been watching in silence over my shoulder, said, "I'm gonna get some air," and hurried out of the shelter.

Until we had processed the scene and were able to confirm the items' authenticity, and that the women in the photos were not consenting, Jordan would be a free man. And if they *hadn't* been consenting adults, Jordan was a monster. A man living two lives.

FORTY-FIVE
VAL

Surviving on caffeine and sugar from the vending machine, we continued to sift through the horrific evidence we'd collected in the bunker on Jordan Nelson's property. To the team, I said, "We need to find something, anything, to get a warrant for his arrest."

The sheriff's department's research and investigative teams, anyone who had answered their phone in the middle of the night, had come in the wee hours of the morning to help review the evidence. The images were disturbing, and difficult to get through, especially for those who weren't used to it. Even for the seasoned, the sheer volume of images was overwhelming.

Brady, for one, had taken several breaks, and was put in charge of logistics, getting the sheriff down to the station as well as working with the district attorney to bring him up to speed and ready to get a warrant approved as soon as we found something useful.

We needed to make sure Jordan Nelson didn't get a chance to run, if he hadn't already.

The women in the photographs, all with sandy-blonde hair and brown eyes, were likely in their teens to early twenties and it could be argued that they were consenting adults. But highly unlikely. We needed only one indisputably underage, or clear evidence he had abducted one of the women and we could arrest Jordan and present him with a shiny set of handcuffs.

Worried he'd run, my nerves were frayed knowing we were up against the clock. In the dungeon, it looked like there was blood splatter on the walls, as well as other biological materials. We needed to prove it belonged to a missing person or be able to identify the contributor in order to question them about what had happened down there. For all we knew, Jordan could claim it had been him and his wife using it as a love shack or sex room.

Of course, I didn't believe that to be true. The more I looked at those awful photos of young women chained up, and their dead eyes, the more I wondered.

Did Claire Nelson know about her husband's hobby? Had she partaken in their abductions?

If yes, it could explain why Tally had killed her.

But we needed proof. We really needed to find Tally and ask her what happened.

Lucy lowered the screen on her laptop and sat back. "Did you see a lot of this kind of thing at the FBI?" she asked.

"Unfortunately, yes," I replied, shaking my head. The memories of past cases briefly filled my thoughts.

"How did you do it? I mean, when I was with the NYPD I saw my share of gruesome scenes and horrible acts against children, young women, and young boys, but there's so many... and to do it day after day, it just seems like it would eat you up."

"The job is certainly not for everyone. I like to think of it this way: if we don't do it, if we don't stop these people, who will? But not everybody has the constitution for it. I had to learn to detach myself from it, because if I didn't, there's no way I could do this job day in and day out," I explained.

Lucy nodded. "Have you called Tally's foster mom? Maybe explain what we found?"

Brady was supposed to be calling Tracy PD to see if they'd had any sighting of Tally, but Lucy was right. It was a good idea to reach out to Bernie, and try to get Tally to talk to us, assuming they were still in contact. "If our theory about Jordan is correct, that he's been abducting and torturing women, and Tally was a victim, it's possible Tally killed Claire to get free. She could claim self-defense," I said. It fit the profile of Claire's killer. Someone desperate. Desperate for her life. And Claire was standing in her way.

Lucy said, "After all she's been through, if we're right, she shouldn't go to jail. But the only way we can keep her out of jail is if we can prove it was self-defense. We need to find a picture or video of her to prove she was a victim."

"Exactly, so let's keep looking." I raised my voice, and said, "If any of you find a picture of Tally Blackwood, let me know. She's underage. She could be the ticket." And if we could prove self-defense for Tally, we could call her foster mom and get her to convince Tally that if she came in, she wouldn't go to jail.

Nods throughout the room.

With the rest of the team sifting through the photographs, I returned to my screen, watching the video alongside the others. The video coverage was intense, and I found myself looking away briefly or fast-forwarding when it wasn't who we were looking for. He had recorded everything. But he wasn't in any of the videos. Until we could match up the videos to a video camera and prove they belonged to him, he could claim he bought the videos online. That was why he was still out there, and no warrant had been issued.

The next image popped up.

A new girl, older.

I gasped.

Just then, Brady walked in. "Tracy PD has no sightings of Tally or Claire's vehicle," he announced.

I heard him but didn't respond and waved him over. "Who does she look like?"

He squinted at the screen. He stepped back, brows raised. "Is that Laney?"

"It sure does look like her. Let's pick her up, bring her in. She could be a witness."

Lucy said, "What's going on? What did you guys find?"

Allan, curious, popped over and saw the image.

"This woman, this is Laney. She lives in the encampment in Hectorville. We've spoken with her a few times. She's not totally coherent, but when we showed her a picture of Claire and then Talitha, she kept muttering, 'Don't go near the house,' and she seemed to be glad Claire was dead. I think she was held captive and somehow got out too." Staring at the clock on the wall, it was just after three in the morning. "Let's go pick her up."

Nobody would sleep until we had Jordan in custody. Not to mention, Laney could be in danger. Jordan may have assumed she wouldn't be a problem, but he might have changed his mind now. My hope was she would tell us what had happened to her, but I worried she might not be of sound mind enough for it to all make sense.

FORTY-SIX

VAL

Inside the station's only cozy conference room sat Maisie and Laney, both clutching hot cups of coffee. Their presence was a testament to their courage and the trust they had placed in us. I was grateful they had agreed to come down to the station to tell us what had happened to Laney. Of course, Laney hadn't wanted to leave without Maisie, and Maisie, being the mother figure in the encampment, had agreed to help Laney tell her story.

On the other side of the glass, the sheriff, the district attorney, Brady, and Allan were watching, while inside with Lucy and myself, we hoped that a feminine presence might be comforting, considering a man had terrorized Laney and presumably put her in her current mental state.

After introductions to Maisie and Laney, for the recording, I said, "Thank you both for coming down here. We're hoping that not only can we help Laney but also other women we think may have been abducted and held captive."

Laney's pale brown eyes widened. "Is he here?"

In a folder in front of me sat a photograph of Jordan Nelson, Claire Nelson, and their residence, along with photos of the backyard. They weren't great because they had been taken at night, but it was something. I was prepared to show the photos to Laney if she needed to verify details of her abduction and captivity. "Are you referring to Jordan Nelson?" I asked gently.

I slid out the picture of Jordan and pushed it across the table to Laney and Maisie. Laney looked down at the photo, her body shivering. I pointed to it and asked, "Did this man hurt you?"

She nodded.

"Can you tell me how you first met him?"

She looked around the room as if worried he might be watching, then whispered, "He took me."

I glanced up at the window to signal the sheriff and the district attorney that her testimony, being recorded on video and audio, would be enough. "How old are you, Laney?"

"Twenty-one."

She looked closer to thirty. Trauma and rough living had aged her considerably. "How old were you when he took you?"

She looked away. "Fifteen."

Feeling nauseous, I said, "Where were you when he took you? How did he take you?"

She turned her head away as if to avoid the photo of Jordan. I quickly slipped it back into the folder. "I've put the photo away. You don't have to ever look at him again," I assured her, but also thinking of the possible court proceedings. I hoped Jordan Nelson would take a plea once we had enough evidence against him. If not, he was a fool because he was going away, likely for life.

She turned back and looked at me and Lucy. "I was waiting at the bus stop, going to work. I worked at the McDonald's on International Boulevard."

She turned away again, and Maisie embraced her. I gave the two a moment before asking, "What city were you in?"

Laney peeked her head over and looked at me. "Oakland."

"You're doing really great, Laney. With your information

and testimony, we're going to be able to arrest him and put him in jail so he can't take anybody else."

She sat back, and Maisie held her close.

Laney stared blankly at the wall, before murmuring, "He seemed so nice, but he wasn't."

We waited patiently, giving her the space and time she might need to share more. After a considerable silence, I gently probed, "How did you escape? Did he take you somewhere?"

Her eyes widened, haunted. "Don't go near the house," she repeated.

I cautiously slid out the photo of the Nelsons' house, the backyard, and the hatch. "Did he take you here?"

She nodded vigorously. "Don't go near the house, don't go near the house."

Conscious the photos were terrifying Laney, I quickly put them away. "How did you get away?" I asked.

She darted her eyes around the conference room, as if either trying to remember or her mind had wandered off. "She was there," Laney finally said.

"She was there? She helped you?" I asked for clarification.

Laney shook her head. "He didn't lock it. There was no lock. I tried to escape." She shut her eyes. "But he caught me. He said, 'Don't go near the house' over and over as he... punished me."

I waited for her to explain how she escaped. It sounded like a harrowing first attempt at escape.

"But the last time, I got out, and I saw her. And she saw me. He didn't pay any attention. He just looked away when she said, 'Who's that?' He said he didn't know, so I ran. I ran away and didn't stop until my legs gave out." Laney broke down.

Had Claire believed Jordan when he said he didn't know the young woman running from their backyard?

I leaned closer to Lucy and whispered for her to arrange for a psychiatrist to come in. Laney needed help. Telling her story was just one part of the process to heal. Victims often needed intensive therapy to be able to live a normal life, which Laney had not been able to do. It was painfully obvious. "Where did you go, Laney?"

She glanced up. "I ran until I found Maisie."

Maisie nodded, as if she remembered the meeting. Laney had been at the encampment the whole time.

"How long were you with him?"

She said quietly, "Three years," before turning back to Maisie.

My heart nearly broke for her. And for all the other girls Jordan had taken. When Laney was a little calmer, I looked at her and Maisie and said, "You did a great job. Because of you, he's not going to be able to do this to anybody else, okay?"

"He's bad, so bad," Laney murmured, turning away and nestling back into Maisie.

Maisie stroked her hair, and for a moment, I believed in saints, and that Maisie was one of them. She cared for all the vulnerable souls that came to her, protecting them as best she could.

"We can arrange to have a place for you to stay if you don't want to go back to the encampment. Perhaps a psychologist or therapist for someone to talk to, or help you reconnect with your family?" I suggested, trying to offer Laney support and a path to recovery.

"Shame, only shame," she whispered.

It was a common response among victims of sexual violence or kidnapping. It underscored the importance of having someone to talk to, to understand that what happened wasn't their fault, that they could live a normal life again. Even if they worked really hard at recovery, they were forever changed, and the support was crucial. There would be more questions for Laney, but for now we had what we needed to get Jordan.

"We'll leave you for a few minutes. Can we get you anything?"

Maisie shook her head as she continued to comfort Laney.

Outside the room, I said to Lucy, "Let's call Bernie and try to get Tally to talk to us."

If my gut was telling me anything, it was that Bernie was in contact with Tally and could pass on the message. Looking over at the team, including the sheriff and DA, I said, "Is that enough for a warrant for Jordan?"

The DA nodded. "It's enough for me."

The sheriff shook his head and said, "I still can't believe it. But yes. Absolutely. Nice work, team."

FORTY-SEVEN

TALLY

A knock on the bedroom door jolted me awake. Despite the fitful sleep, the sound was jarring.

"Tally."

I shuffled over and opened the door. Bernie stood there, phone in hand.

"What is it?"

"There's someone on the phone. I think you should talk to them."

Was it the police? They must know I was with Bernie. "Who is it?"

She covered the receiver of her phone with her hand and whispered, "It's an investigator from Red Rose County. She said they discovered the bunker and there's another witness. They confirmed that the man kidnapped and kept her hostage. They have an arrest warrant for him. They want you to come in to help make sure he never gets out of jail."

But what about my situation? I had killed Claire. Would I end up in jail too?

As if reading my mind, Bernie said, "She says that she's

already spoken with the district attorney, and they believe you acted in self-defense."

"Do you believe her?" There was no one I trusted more than Bernie. If she thought I should talk to this investigator, then I would. I had been contemplating turning myself in, but I had a difficult time believing I wouldn't be in trouble.

"Honey, I think it's time, and I will stand by you every step of the way. You have my word," she reassured me.

"Can I get a drink of water?" I asked, my throat suddenly dry.

Bernie nodded and ushered me down the stairs into the kitchen. She kept the phone to her ear, speaking softly, "Just a moment, Ms. Costa."

Despite being more than capable of getting a glass from the cupboard, Bernie did it for me, filling it to the brim. I took a long sip of water, not realizing how thirsty I had been. Without another word, I nodded, and Bernie handed me the phone. I was ready to face whatever came next.

"Hello."

"Is this Talitha Blackwood?" the voice on the other end asked.

"This is Tally."

"Tally, my name is Valerie Costa, but you can call me Val. I'm an investigator with the Red Rose County Sheriff's Department. We've discovered some information about Jordan Nelson, and we believe he kidnapped you and kept you hostage."

"He did terrible things," I said, a shiver running down my spine.

"We believe you. We have a lot of evidence against him. We're going to make sure he goes to jail and never gets out."

He needed to be put away forever.

She kept talking. "But we need your help to make sure he stays there. We've met another young woman who went through what we think may have happened to you. She's here with us and told us her story. We need as many stories as possible to ensure he gets the longest term possible."

"But I... I did something bad to get away," I confessed.

"Do you want to tell me about that? Why you hurt Mrs. Nelson?"

"I'm not sure," I admitted, feeling a surge of fear. "I'm afraid of going to jail."

"Tally, I know you don't know me, but I used to work with the FBI. I specialized in finding missing persons and tracking down really bad people. Jordan is one of the worst I've seen. I've dealt with other cases similar to yours, where a young woman had to kill her captor to escape. That is self-defense. I'll make sure you don't see the inside of a jail."

I looked over at Bernie. She gave me an encouraging nod. "What do I need to do?"

"We need you to come down to the station and give a statement. We can come and get you, I'll personally drive you, if you prefer."

I glanced at Bernie and then lowered the phone. "They want me to come in. They said they'd come and get me."

Bernie responded firmly, "I can take you. I told you I'll be with you every step of the way, Tally. We're going to get through this."

I raised the receiver back up to my ear. "Bernie said she'll drive me to the station. Are you sure I'm going to be okay?"

"You have my word."

"Okay, Bernie will take me."

I ended the call, and Bernie embraced me. I cried, not sure if it was relief or sadness, or perhaps the realization that it was all coming to an end and I actually had a chance at starting over. Would I get to stay with Bernie? What would starting over look like? Would the police keep their word or were they lying?

FORTY-EIGHT

VAL

After an APB was put out on Jordan and his vehicle, we received a hit. We had found Jordan Nelson. It was nearly 5 a.m. when Brady and I raced to the Hectorville Hotel, where the suspect's car had been spotted. It was still dark, but the streetlights cast a glow over the hotel's parking lot and the building itself—a large structure with several hundred rooms.

As we hoped for an element of surprise, several cars waited in anticipation while we entered the lobby. The night clerk, a man with dark brown hair and a tan complexion, greeted us. "Can I help you?"

Brady, without hesitation, flashed his badge and said, "We need to know what room Jordan Nelson is staying in."

The clerk hesitated. "I think I'm supposed to see a search warrant for that."

Brady replied, "Sir, Jordan Nelson is a violent predator. Please, tell us what room he's in. We have a warrant for his arrest."

The clerk relented and consulted his computer. "Room 402. I can take you there. I have a key," he said, moving quickly to lead the way.

Brady said, "I'll get the tactical team and meet you up there."

"Okay. Sir, come with me."

He nodded, and we headed toward the elevator. Inside, the clerk asked, "Did he kill his wife?"

"No. Worse. Far worse," I replied.

The clerk gave me a puzzled look but asked no further questions. The elevator pinged upon reaching the fourth floor, and as we stepped out, the clerk said, "Do you want me to stay until your partner joins you?"

"Yes, please, stay. I'll need you to knock on the door, say that you're room service, and open the door if there's no response. We'll wait for the team."

He nodded nervously.

Moments later, the next elevator arrived, and Brady emerged with six officers in full gear. We approached the room with caution, using hand signals to coordinate our movements.

I motioned to the clerk. He knocked on the door, announcing, "Room service."

I nodded at him in approval. The door opened, and he quickly stepped aside, revealing Jake Nelson, Jordan's son. Behind him stood Sarah.

"Uh? How can we help you?" Sarah asked.

"We need to speak with your father."

"He's not here."

"When was the last time you saw him?" Brady interjected.

"It's been hours. He said he had to run an errand and gave us money for pizza, but he never came back. He's not answering his cell phone," Jake said, clearly worried.

Jordan Nelson was on the run.

I said, "Would you both please step outside? We need our team to search the room."

"Okay," they replied, huddling close together as they moved into the hallway. Their eyes widened in alarm as they watched the team, guns drawn, enter the room to search for their father.

"Why did you and your father leave the house?" I asked.

"It seemed like a good idea after the fire and the break-in. He thought we weren't safe there," Sarah explained.

"And you haven't seen him for hours?"

"No, I'm really worried. Why are you here? What do you think he's done? He didn't hurt my mom."

"We don't think he did either," I reassured them.

"I don't understand what's going on," Sarah cried.

At that moment, Brady exited the room and announced, "All clear."

I waved him over. "They say he left a few hours ago."

Brady looked at the kids. "Where was he going?"

Sarah, with tears in her eyes, said, "To run a few errands."

"How did he leave? His truck's in the parking lot."

Jake said, "He took my car. It's a Honda Civic."

"Do you have the license plate number?" Brady asked.

"Not off the top of my head," Jake said.

Brady nodded, stepped back, and began making calls on his cell phone, likely to get the registration and put out an APB for the car Jordan Nelson was now driving.

"You said you've tried calling his cell phone and he's not answering?" I asked.

"Yes, and he's not answering. I don't understand what's going on. There's no way he did anything wrong. He's the best dad ever."

The best dad ever kidnapped and tortured young women. "That may be true, but I'm afraid he's also done some truly terrible things."

"What do you mean?" Sarah asked, bewildered.

"Let's step back into the room. There are some things I need to tell you."

Sarah and Jake exchanged glances. Sarah said, "Okay."

In the hotel room, I asked them to sit down. This would be rough, but his children needed to be warned. Desperate people did awful things, and I didn't want Jordan hurting his children to avoid them knowing about his secrets. I'd seen it before and I wouldn't let it happen again, not on my watch.

They sat, holding hands. It was as if they knew that whatever I was going to tell them would be bad.

I took a deep breath. "What I'm about to tell you is going to be very difficult to hear."

Sarah nodded.

"We have an arrest warrant for your father."

Sarah and Jake shook their heads in disbelief, instinctively defending their father.

"Listen carefully. I'm telling you this because I'm afraid you're no longer safe and I need you to understand why."

More nods.

"We have evidence and witnesses that your father has committed some terrible crimes. There's an old fallout shelter on your property, with a hatch in the backyard leading down to a bunker. That's where he's been keeping young women and torturing, photographing, and even videotaping them. Unfortunately, in these cases, once the perpetrator's crimes have been discovered, it can put their family and children in danger. Is there someone we can call for you? An aunt, uncle, grandparents you can stay with? You shouldn't be alone right now."

Their world was shattering, and I could see the confusion and pain in their eyes as they grappled with the horrifying reality of their father's secret life.

Jake scratched his head, his voice filled with disbelief. "This can't be true, there's just no way," he muttered, struggling to reconcile the image of his father with the monstrous acts he was accused of. I knew I needed to calm them down and ensure their safety. Despite their father's actions, these two were innocent and vulnerable.

"Do you have a relative you can stay with?" I asked again.

Sarah, staring blankly ahead, said, "Our mom's sister, Auntie Janet, and Uncle Tim."

I wondered if she was in shock. "Do you want me to call them for you? Do you have a phone number?"

Sarah shook her head. "I can call her. She's in my phone."

"If you like, once you get hold of her, I can either stay with you until they come to pick you up or I can drive you to them, okay? I'm going to step outside and speak to Deputy Tanner. I'll be right back."

Sarah nodded mechanically, then turned her attention back to her phone to call her aunt. As she explained the situation, tears streamed down her face. Jordan Nelson's actions had destroyed the lives of not only his victims, but also his own family.

Outside the room, I briefed Brady on the situation. "They're calling a relative. I've told them about the arrest warrant for their father and what he's suspected of doing. I want to make sure they're safe and with people who love them."

"It's rough, especially with their mother's funeral just a few days away. Poor kids."

"I know. I can't help but see Harrison's face in Jake's."

Brady shook his head. "It's tragic."

"Did you get the license plate info?" I asked, trying to not dwell too much on the situation and focus instead on apprehending our suspect.

"Lucy found the DMV records. There's an APB out for Jake's car and Jordan Nelson," Brady said.

"Good. We also need Jordan Nelson's face on every news station, social media—everywhere."

"I'll call our media contact."

We needed to locate him as soon as possible.

FORTY-NINE

VAL

I stepped quietly through the front door so as not to wake my mother. It was early, and I had come home only to take a shower, change my clothes, and maybe grab some proper food before heading back to the station. But when I walked into the kitchen and found Julie and my mom enjoying their morning coffee, I realized stealth mode was unnecessary. I should have known they'd be up.

"Morning, ladies," I greeted them.

"My goodness, you've had a long night," Mom observed.

"Yeah, I'm just home to change clothes and have a shower. Thank you for staying over, Julie."

"Anytime, dear, anytime."

Mom said, "We saw the news."

"Is it true? Did he really do those terrible things to those girls?" Julie asked in disbelief.

"Yes, and now we really need to find him."

"Do you have evidence? I mean, why do you think he did these things?" Julie asked, trying to make sense of it all.

Taking a deep breath, I explained, "We found a bunker filled with evidence, and we have witnesses. I need to get cleaned up because one of them is coming into the station today."

"Oh, when you say a witness, like one of his victims?" Julie pressed.

"Yes, one that got away." I decided not to divulge any details about her being the person who killed Claire Nelson. The latest breaking news had already shocked them enough.

"All right, well, I'm gonna head upstairs and take a shower."

"There's coffee, and I can make you breakfast if you're hungry?" Julie offered kindly.

As my stomach growled, Julie smiled. "Eggs, toast, and fruit coming right up. Breakfast will be ready when you come back downstairs."

I smiled back, feeling a wave of gratitude. "Thank you, Julie. I appreciate it."

"Now go, go. I know you don't have a lot of time."

In the bathroom, I stripped down and stepped into the steaming hot shower. Closing my eyes, I savored every hot bead of water dripping down my face and back. I was tired, but my adrenaline was still pumping.

As I rinsed and lathered, my thoughts drifted to my mom and how fortunate she was to have her friend Julie. We were all lucky to have her in our lives. I cherished being there for Mom while also doing a job I loved. If Mom hadn't had the community support she had, I would've had to completely sideline my career.

My thoughts turned back to the case in hand. There were still so many unanswered questions. Hopefully, Tally Blackwood, who was coming in later that day, would shed some light on what had happened to her.

We needed more details. Like did Claire know what Jordan was up to, and why had Tally felt she had to kill her to escape? Had Claire attacked her first? I had made a promise to Tally. She wouldn't go to prison, as I was fairly certain she had acted in self-defense, but I, and the DA, needed to hear it from Tally.

I turned off the water and stepped out of the shower. I dressed quickly, dried my hair, and pulled it back into a ponytail. Glancing in the mirror, I hardly recognized myself—not the professional law enforcement agent I was used to seeing. I shook my head, brushed my hair out, and dried it fully. A touch of lip gloss, and I was ready to return to work.

As I pounded down the stairs, the aromas of toast, butter, and freshly brewed coffee filled the air. Julie, ever the hero, had prepared a full breakfast.

It struck me then, perhaps more profoundly than it had in years, how many good people there were in the world. After so many years with the FBI, where the bad guys seemed to outnumber the good, it was a refreshing change to be in Red Rose County. Here, people like Jordan Nelson were the exception, not the rule. Instead, there were lots of people like Maisie and Julie who only wanted to help others, but asked for nothing in return. These good people deserved to live free of monsters like Jordan Nelson.

I hadn't realized how ravenous I was as I wolfed down my breakfast and knocked back my coffee. Thanking Julie and promising my mom that I would give her a full update soon, I hugged them both. It felt like I had two moms now.

With a wave, I headed back to the station to interview Talitha Blackwood, Claire Nelson's attacker and Jordan Nelson's victim.

FIFTY

VAL

When I arrived, Tally hadn't yet shown up. I sat in the conference room with Lucy and Sally, awaiting her arrival.

"What do you think she'll be like?" Lucy asked.

"Traumatized, terrified," I said, thinking about what Tally must have endured.

"Understandable. I hope they go easy on her, especially after the horrors uncovered at the Nelson property. But did Claire know? Did she really keep her husband's secret? Did she participate?" Sally asked.

"I don't know, but I'd like to find out exactly what her role in all of this was," I said, the questions swirling in my mind.

Just then, Brady trotted in. "She's here," he announced, signaling the beginning of what promised to be a revealing and perhaps unsettling interview.

I quickly stood up and hurried out of the room to meet Tally Blackwood in reception.

She appeared like the frightened yet brave young woman she was. Her brown eyes held a haunted look. Beside her was a woman I presumed to be Bernie, around fifty-five, fit, her gray hair pulled back into a ponytail. She exuded a sense of warmth despite the situation.

"Hi, my name is Val. We spoke on the phone," I greeted them, offering a handshake. Bernie smiled weakly.

"This is one of the other investigators on the case, Deputy Brady Tanner."

"Do I have to talk to him too?" Tally asked, slightly apprehensive.

I gave Brady a look that said I would handle this, but he could observe through the two-way mirror.

"You can just talk to me, it's okay. Let me show you to a room where we can talk. Can I get you anything? Coffee, soda, a snack? You must be tired from the drive."

Tally shook her head, and Bernie, putting an arm around her, declined as well. "No, we're fine."

I knew they might need water or something later, and Brady and the team, including the sheriff and DA, would be on the other side of the room listening to the interview and on standby for requests.

Inside the interview room, Bernie and Tally sat side by side, and I took a seat opposite them. "Thank you for coming in," I began. "I'd like you to know that we will be videotaping and recording this session, and I want to make sure you understand your rights."

"Is she under arrest?" Bernie asked, immediately protective.

"No, this is an informal questioning, but it is being record-ed," I clarified.

"It's okay," Tally whispered.

"Tally, the reason we need to talk to you is, as I believe I mentioned on the phone, because we suspect Jordan Nelson of kidnapping, torture, and assault."

She nodded.

"We'd like to understand the details of your abduction, the time you were held prisoner by Jordan, and your escape. Could you tell us what happened? I know this is difficult, and I want you to take as much time as you need. But know that what you're doing will help us get him off the streets for good."

"Have you caught him yet? Is he in jail?" she asked quietly.

"No, but his face is on every news station, and there's an all-points bulletin throughout the state and surrounding states for any sighting of him. He'll be brought in," I reassured her.

She looked nervously at Bernie.

"He can't get you in here. Everybody knows who he is now and what he's done. Once we catch him, he'll never be free ever again."

"And you're sure you'll catch him?" Tally asked, her voice trembling slightly.

"Absolutely," I said.

She nodded, taking a deep breath, seemingly gathering the strength to recount her harrowing ordeal.

As Tally began to tell her story, Bernie reached out to hold her hand. "I was on my way to the bus stop to meet a friend," Tally started.

"What friend?" I asked, gently.

"This guy named Dan that I met online. It was a dating app," she explained. "I was headed toward the bus stop when this truck pulled up. At first, he asked for directions, but I got a real weird vibe from him. You know, like when your stomach's telling you to run."

Intuition. "I do."

"So, I started to hurry toward the bus stop. But then, he hopped out of the truck, told me not to be afraid, and put something over my mouth. I struggled, but he was too strong. He put me in the back of the truck that had a camper on it. Soon I was out. He must've done something to make me fall asleep, and the next thing I knew, when I woke up, I was in that place, the bunker. I don't know how long I'd been out for."

"Did he hurt you?"

"Not at that point. It was just that thing he put over my face, like a rag. It smelled bad."

Chloroform. Jordan Nelson's guise as a hardware store owner was a perfect cover for a serial killer—all the tools he needed were at his fingertips, and nobody would question it. "Please, go on," I urged.

"Well, when I woke up in the bunker, I was on a mattress on the floor. My right wrist..." she raised her hand, revealing scars and healing wounds, "had a cuff on it, and I was chained to the cement wall. I screamed and screamed, but nobody heard me, and nobody was there. It was dark. I realized it was no use. Eventually, I just lay there quietly. I think I drifted off to sleep for a bit, but then there was a bright light, and there he stood."

Her breathing grew rapid, and I felt terrible that she was having to relive the moment she had first encountered that monster. The ordeal she described was beyond nightmarish, a stark reminder of the evil that Jordan Nelson represented. We were not only dealing with a criminal but a predator who had shattered the lives of his victims in unimaginable ways. Tally's testimony was crucial, not just for our case, but for bringing some semblance of justice to the horrors she had endured.

"He had this smile," Tally continued, her voice trembling, "and he told me his name was Jordan and that we were going to be really good friends. But I could tell by the look of the room... it wasn't even clean. And he had taken off all my clothes except for a pair of underwear. They weren't even mine. He must've removed my underwear and put on a fresh pair. I screamed and screamed, and he rushed toward me, put his hand over my mouth, and told me to be quiet, or he'd kill me." She paused, visibly shaken.

I glanced over at the window, signaling for someone to bring in some water. Lucy entered a moment later with two bottles. After thanking her, she left, and I waited as Tally unscrewed the cap and took a sip.

"Take your time," I encouraged her gently.

"Well, the first time, he just... After I had stopped screaming and realized it was no use, I figured maybe if I could get on his good side, he might eventually let me go if he trusted me. So, at first, he just had me pose for pictures. But then, he wanted more. Disgusting, vile things. It happened pretty quick, and then he brought me some toast and a bottle of water." She glanced at her current bottle, shook her head, and continued, "That was day one. And he came, once a day, every day, for two months. He didn't always... you know. Sometimes he just liked to smack me around, do things to me. It was better than when he could perform. He gave me food, and if I acted like I didn't like him or it, he'd beat me. I tried to do everything he wanted. Day after day, the sound of him approaching, unlocking the lock, opening the door, coming down the stairs, rustling around in the cabinets, sitting on the couch, watching TV, not even saying a word to me... It was so weird. Then he'd turn off the TV and come over to do whatever vile things he felt like doing that day. He'd give me food—nothing fancy, but the more I complied, the better the food. Once, I even got a hamburger, cookies... And then he'd leave, climb the stairs, close the hatch, lock the padlock. The first time I heard him not lock the padlock, I took my chance. But he caught me, dragged me back down, and beat me. He didn't visit me for three days after that. Then one day, it was different."

Tally's story was heart-wrenching, a testament to her endurance and the brutal cruelty that Jordan Nelson was capable of. Her detailed recounting painted a vivid and horrifying picture of her captivity and abuse.

Tally's narrative took an unexpected turn. "One day there were footsteps... coming toward the door, then away, then back again, and coming down the stairs. But it was different. The sounds were different. And that's the first time I met Claire Nelson."

I couldn't hide my shock. Claire Nelson had known.

"I begged her to help me, to free me. She just stood there, staring at me like she was in another world. She left me there, relocked everything, and left," Tally recounted, her voice tinged with disbelief.

"She didn't say anything to you?"

Tally shook her head. "No. At first, I wondered if she was another victim, but she was older, and she seemed shocked. I couldn't believe it when she left."

"Did she ever come back?"

"Yes, she did. She came back, every few days. She never said anything even though I told her what he had done to me. That I needed her help. I pleaded. She never did anything to help. But the last time she came by, she didn't put the lock back on. By that point, I had figured out how to get the cuff off my wrist. I had lost a lot of weight so the cuff easily slipped off, and I ran to the house. I went in through the back door, still in just my underwear, and barefoot. I put on a pair of Crocs by the back door that I found, and snuck upstairs to find some clothes. Once I'd found something to wear, I made my way to the kitchen to get something to eat. I hadn't eaten in two days. That was when I saw her in the kitchen."

Tally paused and took a few deep breaths. "She looked surprised. And she asked me what I was doing. I told her I needed help. Part of me thought she had left the bunker unlocked on purpose. I thought maybe she wanted to help me." Tally shook her head. "But she said I had to go back. I refused. She told me she couldn't let me leave."

"Did she say why?"

"She said I would ruin everything. And that she couldn't have the police taking her husband. Her kids couldn't know. She said it would kill them. She started to cry. Can you believe that? I'd been beaten and raped and she was crying?"

It was unimaginable. "I'm so sorry that happened to you."

"I told her I wasn't the first. And she said she knew but that she had to protect her family." Tally shook her head again. "She was almost as sick as him for letting him get away with it."

I was inclined to agree. "And then what happened?"

"I told her I was leaving, and that's when she grabbed the knife. We struggled but I got it away from her when she cut her finger pretty bad. She still fought me but then I stabbed and stabbed until she stopped moving." Tears streaked Tally's face. "When I saw she was dead, I grabbed food, car keys, and her wallet. And the weirdest part? I was so terrified by what I had done, but more horrifying were the photographs on the wall. He had kids, a daughter. How could he do what he did to a girl who was nearly the same age as his own daughter? And how had a woman allowed it to happen? She was willing to kill me to keep her seemingly perfect life intact. Even so, I honestly hadn't meant to kill her. I'm so sorry." Tally broke down into sobs, and Bernie comforted her.

My heart broke for Tally. Even after everything that she had endured, she still felt bad for killing Claire, despite Claire's unwillingness to help and her attempt to hurt or kill her. Tally's account of what had happened fit with the wounds on Claire and the details found at the crime scene. It had definitely been self-defense.

A knock on the door signaled that the district attorney's office had enough information.

"Thank you for telling us what happened," I said softly. "I need to go speak with the district attorney and discuss the case. Can I get you anything?"

Bernie shook her head, and I left the room. The horror of what Tally had gone through, the revelation about Claire Nelson's involvement, and the unspeakable acts committed by Jordan Nelson weighed heavily on me. I would never get used to hearing victim statements, the terrible things monsters did for their own sick, twisted pleasure. The case against Jordan Nelson was building, but the emotional toll it was taking on everyone involved, especially the victims, was immeasurable. *We needed to find him.*

FIFTY-ONE

VAL

The vibration of my cell phone on the nightstand abruptly woke me from a fitful night's sleep. Wiping the sweat from my forehead, I glanced at the screen. It was Kieran. Did he finally have details about the note that had been left inside the Nelson residence? It would be a welcome distraction from the nightmares I'd been having where I was chained to the wall in a bunker. In these scenes, my captor wore a mask and had piercing blue eyes like the Bear, a mixture of the horrors suffered by the victims of both Jordan and the Bear. But I was also a survivor, just like Tally, just like Laney. How many others were there?

"Hello," I answered groggily.

"Hey, Val, did I wake you?"

"It's fine," I replied, trying to shake off the remnants of my dream.

"I saw the news."

"Yeah, he's still on the loose. We've got everybody looking for him, and his face is everywhere. This guy is a real sicko, Kieran." That was saying a lot considering our line of work.

"That's what the news says. You just let us know if you need the feds for anything. We've got your back."

"I appreciate that, Kieran. Any news on the note that was left at the Nelson residence?"

"Yeah, we sent it over to Red Rose County, and I spoke to their lab technician. It's a different card stock, different ink, but visually, it's almost identical. Your note is likely the same as the one that was put in your mother's mailbox."

That I had already deduced. "Yep. I either have a fan or a serial killer after me."

"Maybe a mix of both?"

That was comforting. "What do you mean?"

"You know better than I do. When a perp changes their MO, it's often because they've become fixated on one of the captives who got away."

"Do you think the Bear is watching me, and following my investigation?"

"Well, has anything peculiar happened? Have you had any good luck recently?"

I was about to dismissively say no, but I paused, flipping on the light to give it a moment's thought. And then I deflated. *Yes.* "There was a fire at the Nelson residence. That's how we discovered the bunker."

"You may have an admirer, Val. Keep us posted and let us know if you need backup. If that's what this is, you could be in a dangerous situation."

The fire had seemed odd at the time, almost as if it had led us straight to the bunker. But it could have been a coincidence. Maybe Kieran was just being overprotective. Or it was all connected. The notes. The break-in and the fire at the Nelsons. *The fire.* It was difficult to ignore.

"How's your mom?" he asked, lightening the mood.

"She's doing really well. Her friends have been keeping her company while I work the case, and she's getting stronger every day."

"She walking yet?"

"No, but she goes to physical therapy three days a week and is making progress. She's determined to walk again."

"Well, if she is determined, she'll get there," Kieran said.

He hadn't known my mom very well, other than the stories I used to tell when we worked together at the FBI. But then again, he was a profiler. "I think you're right."

"You take care, Val. Let us know if I can help you out with anything, and watch your back. I don't like that these notes are showing up in your hometown."

I don't like it either. "Will do. Thanks, Kieran."

"Don't be a stranger, huh."

"I won't. Thanks."

After hanging up, I let out a breath, trying to let the conversation sink in. Was Kieran being overly protective, or were there clues I hadn't pieced together yet? I knew the notes were from the same person. It wasn't completely unreasonable to assume that whoever had left the notes and broken into the Nelsons would be capable of setting a fire.

We still hadn't received the fire marshal's report on the origin and manner of the fire. It could have been something as simple as someone driving by and tossing a cigarette out the window, but that seemed unlikely, considering the location in the backyard. It was at least half a mile from the road. Or maybe a neighbor or someone hiking on the trails behind the house got a little too curious. Even as I thought through the scenarios, nothing seemed to fit.

I was about to climb out of bed to hit the shower and grab some breakfast when the vibration on my nightstand caught my attention once more. It was Brady. Feeling quite popular this morning, I answered with a chipper "Good morning."

"They found him."

"Jordan? Jordan Nelson?" I asked, my pulse quickening.

"Yes."

"Where is he?"

"Give me a sec." After a few moments, he relayed the address, and I knew there was no time for a shower or breakfast. "All right, I'll meet you there."

My heart racing, I slipped on a pair of jeans, a T-shirt, and a blazer to conceal my firearm, along with my running shoes. I needed to be ready for a fight.

FIFTY-TWO

VAL

Parked in the lot of a convenience store up north, I made my way toward Brady, who stood near a man with a shiny badge. "Hey, Brady."

"Val, you made it. This is Sheriff Deets of Shasta County. He's the officer in charge."

The man with a thick silver mustache said, "Nice to meet you. Your reputation precedes you."

Good. "What do we have?"

All I knew was that they had tracked Jordan to a convenience store in the city of Anderson in Shasta County. He had been inside, buying provisions, when the store clerk recognized him and called it in.

Sheriff Deets said, "When we arrived, Jordan had pulled the clerk out into the parking lot. He was holding a six-inch blade to the hostage's neck, telling us to stand back. It's been nearly an hour. He's not negotiating or wavering."

"What are his demands?"

"Just for us to get lost, so he can ride off into the sunset."

Not a chance. "He has to know that isn't going to happen."

"We have a negotiator on the scene. He's the one with the bullhorn."

Turning toward the scene, it was one that would be terrifying to anyone casually strolling by. Six members of the sheriff's department had guns set on Jordan and his victim, the poor clerk had terror and tears in his eyes.

Jordan had changed his hair from silver to dark brown but hadn't been able to entirely disguise his identity. The shift from hiking pants and a flannel shirt to skinny jeans and a turtleneck sweater was notable, but it was the beard that he had refused to rid himself of, now dyed brown, that still made him unmistakably Jordan Nelson. It was clear Jordan intended to go on the run.

The determination on Jordan's face told me he would kill the hostage to get away. But there was no way I would let him claim another victim.

"I want to talk to him."

"I'll introduce you to the negotiator."

We headed toward the man, who stood at well over six feet tall, with a bullhorn in hand, as he yelled, "Mr. Nelson, we need you to put down the knife and let the man go. We can talk about this."

He could try all he wanted, but I knew that approach wasn't going to work, not with someone like Jordan Nelson.

Sheriff Deets caught the negotiator's attention and made the introduction. After formalities, I said, "Can I talk to him?"

"You can have a shot at it," he replied, handing me the bullhorn.

Taking a deep breath, I raised the bullhorn to my mouth and yelled, "Jordan, it's time to tell your story. Let the world know what you've done. Leave your legacy. Let the man go and we can talk."

He turned his head toward me, a flicker of understanding in his eyes. Jordan Nelson was most likely a narcissist, and narcissists love the sound of their own voice. They take pride in their deeds, even though the words they utter make those around them cringe. "Jordan, you need to live. Your children need you. I can't control what happens if they find you to be a threat to this person. They'll kill you, Jordan. I don't want that to happen. Your kids need you. Don't make Jake and Sarah orphans. Be smart about this."

He shook his head defiantly, clearly not ready to surrender. He yelled out, "Get back, or I'll do it! Get back! You all need to leave or this man dies."

Jordan Nelson needed to be stopped, once and for all.

Despite the monster he was, his children didn't deserve to lose both parents. And I wasn't going to let him abandon his children any more than he already had by the choices he had made. That wasn't the only reason. I was nearly certain forensics would come up with evidence of more victims he'd held captive in his bunker, and I wanted to know what had happened to them. I lowered the bullhorn and turned to the negotiator. "Talk to him about his kids. See if you can distract him."

The negotiator glanced down at me. "What are you going to do?" he asked.

Resolute, I said, "I'm going to stop him. I want him behind bars, not dead. I need to find his other victims. He's not going out like this."

He nodded, and I handed him the bullhorn. I positioned myself strategically next to the officers at the front line. The sheriff and Brady followed. All guns were trained on Jordan.

The negotiator began, "Jordan, Sarah and Jake need you. Don't make them attend their mother's funeral without you. Let's end this now."

Jordan wavered a little and lowered his knife ever so slightly.

Brady, who was at my side, asked, "What do you think?"

"We need to take him down, but don't kill him. Do we have any sharpshooters?"

"How sharp?" the sheriff asked.

"I can do it if you don't have anyone else."

"Let me tell my men. And then he's all yours," he said.

As the negotiator announced, "We have Sarah and Jake on the phone. They want to talk to you."

Whether or not he believed him, it caught his attention and was enough to distract him.

The sheriff returned with a thumbs-up.

I rushed toward him and took aim. The shot fired out and Jordan went down, the knife skittering across the concrete. Officers rushed in, securing the victim and rushing him to safety. I tackled Jordan, handcuffed him, and began reading him his rights as he cried out in pain.

"You'll live," I said coldly.

FIFTY-THREE

VAL

After the chaos had subsided and the paramedics had bandaged Jordan Nelson's arm, he sat cuffed on the bay of the ambulance. The bullet had merely grazed his arm, but it had been enough to make him drop the knife and let go of his hostage.

"Hi, Jordan," I said, as I approached him.

"You don't know anything," he retorted defiantly.

"Oh, I know a lot, but I would like to know more."

"Well, I'm not talking to you, so you can just forget it. I want a lawyer," Jordan said, shutting down the conversation.

"You know, if I were in your position, Jordan, I'd want a lawyer too. But here's the thing. The only thing your lawyer's going to do for you at this point is negotiate the best deal. Is it going to be the death penalty, life in prison with no possibility of parole, or will it be life in prison in a segregated population? I hear people don't like that. It's pretty unpleasant. Or, if we can prove that you crossed state lines, my pals at the feds would like a shot at you. We're still waiting on all the details, but if we find out you took any of those women from outside of California, well, let me tell you, federal prison is no joke. I'm afraid, for someone like you, it's a fate worse than death. I wouldn't want to be in your position," I said, laying out the grim reality of his situation, hoping he would withdraw his request for a lawyer.

"You don't know what you're talking about. I'm done with you," Jordan snapped.

"That's fine, Jordan. I've got two witnesses—victims who survived your evil. We have DNA, we have trace evidence, we have your entire collection of photographs and videos. And you know what the worst part is? Nobody saw it coming. But you know who did see through your facade? Me. Because you messed up, you see. We now have an FBI profiler in Red Rose County, and I could see it in your eyes and in your mannerisms. You're not the person you said you were."

Jordan rolled his eyes like a petulant teenager.

"Here's what I want. I want names, I want dates, I want the number of women you tortured in your bunker. I want to know where they are. It's not a matter of if you're going to prison, Jordan, it's how bearable it will be once you're there. Keep that in mind."

"It isn't going to stick," Jordan retorted defiantly.

"We have physical evidence and witnesses. You're not smarter than we are—surprise, I know you think you are, but you're not. We can do this the easy way or the hard way. Do you want to do it the hard way and not talk, hide behind a lawyer like a scared little boy? That's your choice."

He smirked, but his true demeanor was on full display.

"Who was it? Who were you torturing over and over again? So far, the victims we know about have dirty-blonde hair, brown eyes, freckles. Did you pick them at random, or had you stalked them, watched them from afar? Did you take trophies, aside from the photographs? How long has it been going on? When did you start?"

"Are you going to talk at me all day or are you going to book me?"

"Oh, I'll definitely be booking you."

I called out to Brady. "Jordan says he's ready to go to county lockup. Do you want to take him in your car? Or do we have a black-and-white that can transport him?"

"We've got a black-and-white with his name on it. Special order," he said with a smile.

It was good to see Brady smiling with a job well done.

I said, "All right, well, let me help you down from there. I wouldn't want you to hurt yourself."

As Brady and I escorted Jordan from the back of the ambulance over to the patrol car with the door open, I said, "Your chariot awaits."

He looked me up and down like I was prey. I simply wiggled my fingers and waved. "Have a safe trip."

Brady shut the door and turned back to me. "I gotta say, I could get used to working with you, Val."

The feeling was mutual. "I appreciate that, but we're not done yet. We need to build a case against him. We have a lot, but not everything. I want to know what happened to his other victims. We have to get him to talk."

FIFTY-FOUR

VAL

Brady shook his head and said, "I just don't understand how Jordan could be this perfect family man and community member, go to church, have children, and at the same time abduct and torture young women."

It happened more than we'd like to believe. Most people tended to think that serial killers or other violent criminals had green skin and wild hair, like monsters in a movie. It simply wasn't true. Predators looked like everyone else. Like Ted Bundy, who was able to murder so many women because he was charming and attractive, and nobody suspected him until he had killed dozens. They were psychopaths who could pass for normal. "I suspect for most of them, it's like compartmentalization. They separate their normal life from their predator lifestyles, switching between the two but not letting them cross."

"Do you suspect that Jordan tortured animals, set fires, or was abused as a child?" Brady asked, referring to the serial killer trifecta.

Most people didn't realize that less than half of interviewed serial killers actually met all three criteria. "If he talks to us, we'll know, but until then, all we can do is guess." I paused, and said, "Think of John Wayne Gacy and Dennis Rader. They both lived seemingly normal lives. Nobody suspected them until their crimes were discovered. Each made one mistake that got them caught, blowing up their whole world—their spouses, their children."

"I can't believe there was a serial killer living two towns away from us, Val."

It was true. Our friends and classmates fitting Jordan's type could easily have been one of his victims. "It's true, although we're still not sure if he's actually killed anyone."

Lucy said, "True, but one of the contributors from the mattress got a match, and it's a missing female that's never been found. What's the likelihood she's alive?"

It was most likely she wasn't. The forensics had come back, and the blood on the wall belonged to Tally Blackwood. Everything else was relatively clean, aside from a mattress that looked about twenty years old and hadn't been cleaned very well. The lab came back with fifteen female contributors and one male. Not surprisingly, that one male contributor was Jordan Nelson.

How many victims were there? Was it only the fifteen we had found DNA for? The forensics team had uploaded all of the DNA profiles to CODIS and NamUs, hoping for some matches, other than the one we'd found so far. If the others weren't dead, where were they?

"Have we contacted the family of Naomi Carter?" I asked. Naomi Carter's DNA was found on that old mattress and was a match in NamUs.

Lucy nodded. "I sent a message through NamUs, letting the coordinator know we had a DNA match, but not a body."

Not yet.

If Jordan Nelson was a psychopath and narcissist, and had been abducting and holding women captive for years, then, like the others before him—the John Wayne Gacys, the Ted

Bundys, the Dennis Raders—he'd want to tell his story. But likely not until he understood that he would never get out of prison with the evidence we'd collected, and the testimony from his survivors that would be presented at trial. Not to mention, the hostage situation at the convenience store in Shasta Lake would get him several years in prison for that offense alone.

When I promised Tally that Jordan Nelson would never get out of prison, I meant it.

"How are we going to get him to talk? Tell us where they are, what happened?" Brady asked.

"We need to present all the evidence we have against him, make him see there's no way out, and it's time for him to tell his story. He's likely proud of everything he's done, as sick as that is. He'll want fame, notoriety, the whole nine yards, trust me."

Just then, there was a knock on our conference room door. All of our attention turned to the fire marshal who stood there.

"Inspector Chisholm. How are you?"

"I was told I'd find you here. We've got the report on the fire at the Nelson residence. I'm guessing it'll be important, considering the news."

"Yes. What did you find?" Brady asked.

Chisholm entered the room and said, "Long story short, the origin of the fire is in the backyard, near the opening to that bunker. It was as if somebody was trying to draw you there or trying to destroy it, but that doesn't make sense. If they'd really wanted to destroy it, they'd have set fire to the inside, not the outside, or both. In my professional opinion, I think somebody wanted you to find the bunker."

My thoughts went back to my conversation with Kieran and how he said I may have an admirer or stalker here in town. Perhaps it wasn't the Bear after all, or it was and he'd set up shop right here in Red Rose County. That would be something new for me to discuss with my therapist. Speculation wouldn't get me anywhere. I had to shake the idea out of my mind.

Lucy said, "Maybe somebody else knew about Jordan's extracurriculars, and was trying to expose him."

"It's possible, but who?" Brady asked.

Lucy shrugged. "I have no idea, but if somebody else knew, why wouldn't they have told the police? Why would they have set a fire? Or maybe, they didn't know what was inside but thought you should check there. Maybe it's the same person who broke into the house and left the note."

That, I thought, was a real possibility. Someone broke in, left a note, and set his backyard on fire to expose the truth. The note said they knew what he had done. It was likely we had a vigilante on our hands.

"Any questions for me?" Chisholm asked.

"Accelerant? Anything unusual?" I asked.

"Sorry, wish I had better news. Run-of-the-mill lighter fluid, the kind you'd pick up at any hardware or grocery store."

"Like the kind to get a barbecue going?" Brady asked.

"Exactly. Who knows, they could've even used something that the Nelsons already had in their garage."

Who was our little helper? Vigilante justice wasn't something that we could tolerate. Setting a fire like at the Nelsons was a serious offense, an escalation, and an indicator of more violence to come.

"Anything else I can help with?" Chisholm asked.

I shook my head. "Nope, you've told us somebody set the fire in the backyard and it was with run-of-the-mill lighter fluid. That will never trace to a specific individual."

"That's right. Y'all have a good day, and good job. That creep deserves to spend the rest of his life in jail. Still can't believe it though."

That was the sentiment from the community. Nobody could believe it. We had even invited a camera crew down to the bunker to dispel any rumors the story had been fabricated. We didn't want the community to go against the sheriff's department, claiming that one of their own was innocent when we had a mountain of evidence saying he wasn't. We needed to get him to confess, and armed with the forensic evidence, I would do just that. It was time to bring Jordan's reign of terror to an end once and for all.

FIFTY-FIVE

VAL

Through the two-way mirror we watched Jordan as he sat alone in the interrogation room, the new street clothes he had worn as a disguise now replaced with an orange jumpsuit. The plan was to interview him with his lawyer present, but he hadn't arrived yet. Thinking I could use that to my advantage, I told the team I was going in.

Inside the small interrogation room, I took a seat directly across from Jordan. "We meet again."

Jordan remained silent as he stared me down.

"Where's your lawyer?" I asked, looking around the cramped room.

Jordan said, "He'll be here shortly."

"Let's wait for him," I said, maintaining eye contact. "Or I can go ahead and give you the punchline. You don't have to say a word." Shrugging, I said, "It's a good one."

Jordan smirked, which I interpreted as consent.

"I'll take that as a yes." Tapping my fingertips on the file folder on the table, I said, "First, I'll tell you a little story." And then I explained the forensic evidence that had been collected from his bunker, home, and garage. "Not only that," I continued, "but we have also found two witnesses—victims of yours, who are still alive. They recounted every single thing you ever did to them, from their kidnapping to their captivity to the vile things you subjected them to. Want to know what else we found?"

Jordan shrugged, his gaze drifting away, feigning disinterest.

"They found fifteen female DNA contributors, and just one male on that dirty old mattress you had on the floor where you kept your victims, chained to the wall."

I finally got Jordan to speak.

He said, "Sounds like the team has been busy."

"They have," I said, just as the door opened.

In bustled a man, not a day under eighty, with silver hair and a dark suit. "Don't say another word to my client. He has invoked his right to an attorney. You should know better, Ms. Costa," the man scolded.

"I haven't asked him any questions. I was just letting him know what we have, that's all."

"Don't worry, Will, I haven't said anything," Jordan reassured his lawyer.

I shrugged and addressed the lawyer, "It's true. But the thing is, we don't really need him to say anything at this point. We've got tons of forensic evidence. We've got witness statements. We've got the whole hostage situation at Shasta Lake. Your client's never getting out of prison."

The lawyer glanced down at his client before taking a seat.

"You asked for this interview. What do you want, Ms. Costa?" the lawyer asked pointedly.

"I was just explaining to your client, our forensics team has completed testing of the evidence collected. Of the fifteen female contributors' DNA we found, one was linked to a missing person, Naomi Carter, aged sixteen. We have witness statements from two other contributors who claim your client kidnapped, held captive, and repeatedly assaulted them before they escaped. What I want to know is, of those fifteen women, we know the identity of three. We know the location of two. I want to know about the others. I want to know their names, where they were from, and where they are now."

His lawyer, old enough to be my grandfather, said, "That's quite the speculation, Ms. Costa."

"It's not speculation. We have evidence. And honestly, I've worked with a lot of people like your client here in my time at the FBI Behavioral Analysis Unit. I've got an inkling that Mr. Nelson would like to tell his story and get his name in the history books along with some of the greats like John Wayne Gacy, Ted Bundy, and Dennis Rader," I said, tipping my head toward him.

"My client is not a serial killer," the lawyer said. I wondered if he really believed that.

Jordan Nelson gave me the creepiest of smiles, his eyes glinting with a strange light. "You think I'd be among some of the greats?" he mused, his voice laced with a disturbing sense of pride.

If he meant the greatest abominations of humankind, then *absolutely*.

"You'd have your own Wikipedia page and everything. People are going to write books about you, probably make a movie, at least one, maybe even a miniseries."

"You think you know me, don't you?"

Will, the lawyer, said, "Jordan, don't say another word. I'll get you out of this."

Jordan cocked his head at Will, his expression shifting. "I'm not getting out of this, Will. Thank you for trying. You can go now."

"This is crazy, Jordan," Will protested.

"No, it's not crazy. It's just facts. You heard them. They have evidence, they have my mistake of holding that clerk hostage. I should've known better and just turned myself in. I don't want this to be any more painful for my children than it already is. It's okay, Will. I've got this. You can go," Jordan insisted, dismissing him with his hand.

With Will gone, it was just Jordan and me. "I'd love to hear your story," I said, locking eyes with him. "But first I need to remind you of your rights."

He nodded slowly, squinting at me. "I waive my right to an attorney." He knew, and I knew, he was going to relish every moment of this.

"How about you start from the beginning, Jordan? When did you first have thoughts about this type of thing? Did your mother abuse you? Did someone wrong you and you've been righting that wrong over and over? Did you set fires when you were little?" I asked, knowing Jordan likely had been fascinated by other serial killers and likely researched them.

He chuckled, a sound that sent chills down my spine. "I think you know none of that is true. No, I had good parents. They were strict. It was a different time, but I think the earliest I can recall having these fantasies..." He paused, glancing toward the recording devices. "Is this being recorded?" he asked.

"Yes, it is. All cameras are on you."

He waved at the glass, likely aware of the audience on the other side, waiting anxiously to hear his sick story. "Well, I wasn't always nice to stray animals, I'll tell you that..."

As Jordan recounted his early childhood memories, I felt my stomach turn. He spoke of frying ants with magnifying glasses and progressively moving on to dismembering frogs and wounded animals he found. He knew exactly the location of the missing pets in the neighborhood. His stories progressed to his fantasies, his need for bondage, the need to control others, and how he got off on the fear in their eyes.

His account was disturbing, and I knew he was nearing the part I needed to hear: about the first time he took someone, what he did, who they were, and where they were now. He stopped, and I said, "Can I get you a drink of water, tea, coffee, soda?"

"I am parched. I could use some water," he said.

Raising my hand, the pretense that there wasn't an audience for all of this now long gone, I signaled for the refreshments.

A few moments later, Brady walked in, providing Jordan with a water bottle. "Anything else you need?" Brady asked.

"I think this is all for now, but I can imagine being hungry after I finish," Jordan said.

"Okay, well, when you're ready let me know."

Jordan took a sip of water, and said, "Thank you, Deputy Tanner."

Glancing up at Brady, I gave him a nod to let him know I understood the pain of having to cater to this monster. He gave a tight-lipped smile and exited.

Alone with Jordan again, I said, "So, tell me about your first."

Jordan looked up at the ceiling with a smile on his face before returning his focus to me. "You never forget your first. She was young. I don't know exactly how old. I think she said she was sixteen, maybe seventeen. She was living on the streets, and I saw her, all by herself. You know, she looked kind of sad, like nobody would miss her. That was, gosh, thirty years ago."

He had got married and started killing all in the same year? "What was her name?"

"Tanya. She was my first. I made a lot of mistakes with her that I've since corrected. After I took her down into my special room, she cried at first. Eventually, she calmed down and did what I wanted. For a while. The camera loved her," he said, smiling with a far-off look as if fondly remembering the moment.

"Was she someone you'd seen around, or had you been watching her for a while?"

"No, I just happened to see her there. She captivated me because of her vulnerability. It was a crime of opportunity. I suppose that's what you'd call it."

"Where did you meet her?"

"Temecula. I was away on one of my trips."

"When you say one of your trips—were these the supplier trips?"

He smiled. "You are clever. Yes, during my supplier trips."

"What happened to her?"

"You mean, what kind of fun did we have?" he asked.

I nodded and braced myself.

As he gleefully recalled his capture and torture of Tanya I listened, trying to remain calm and collected, knowing this would ensure he never got out of prison. "How long was she with you?"

He let out a breath. "Almost a year. I would have kept her longer, but she was getting unruly. So, I had to get rid of her. It was so disappointing."

The poor woman had been tortured for a year. "How did you get rid of her?"

"I strangled her to death. Boy, does it take a long time. Not in reality, but in the moment, you know? You'd think it would take about thirty seconds. But it was closer to five minutes for her to finally die, even in her weakened state."

I had figured he'd killed his victims, but until his confession we didn't know for sure. "Tell me about your second victim."

"The second girl, I met a few hours away on one of my trips. But after Tanya, I had a second purpose. One, meet with a supplier and two, hunt for my next prize. I had been so enamored by Tanya, I wanted to find someone who looked like her. I really did care for her. I did. And I wanted her over and over. That's what the textbooks will say, I'm sure."

"What was her name?"

"Loretta, Lori. She cried all the time, so irritating. She was a mistake. That's when I got the ball gag, to shut her up, you know. But then I found I liked it. Anyway, she refused to eat or drink anything. It really was a shame, so I had to get rid of her too."

As I continued to question Jordan about the details of his victims and crimes, he revealed that not only had he killed his victims, but he'd also buried them on his property when his wife was at work teaching high school students.

If he was telling us the truth, we could search the property and hopefully find those women and bring closure to their families. "All thirteen are behind your house and in the forest?"

"Yes. I wanted them close, and well, it was convenient."

"Did Claire know about the girls?"

He shook his head. "Oh, no. I don't think so."

"She never mentioned seeing Tally, finding her, or finding the bunker?"

Jordan shook his head again. "No, she must've been as surprised as I was when Tally came into the house. But for the life of me, I can't figure out how she did it. I always locked up afterward."

I leaned forward, and selfishly knew I'd enjoy this part. "I might be able to help you out with that. You see, we talked to Tally. She told us what happened."

Jordan raised his eyebrows. "Oh?"

"Yes. You see, Claire did know about Tally. She knew for weeks. She would go down and visit her but would never help her escape. One day, Claire didn't relock the bunker. That's when Tally made her escape. She'd been planning it for a while and had been practicing freeing herself from her restraint."

Jordan's face morphed into that of a grieving husband. And he shook his head in disbelief. "Claire knew, and she never said anything. Oh, my... what that must have done to her. I bet that nearly destroyed her."

"It did destroy her. Tally begged Claire for help, but she

refused. Instead, she tried to kill Tally to keep her from leaving and exposing your secret, but Tally was able to get the knife away from Claire. And that is how she died." I'd seen this change in demeanor before, but for those behind the glass, they were probably shocked. "Your children are also grieving. They know what you did."

He nodded. "I hope they don't hate me. I really do love them. Claire... She was a great wife and mother."

"Then why the girls?" I pressed.

"I just had to have them. I wanted to do things that I knew Claire wouldn't want to do. Things I wouldn't want to do to Claire. Claire was so pure, a beautiful mother. I couldn't do that to a mother."

A mother was off limits, but teenage girls were okay? I could never understand the logic of these types of people, and nor did I want to. "So, what happened when you did find Claire? There was a forty-minute gap between when you supposedly got home and when you called 911."

He lifted his hands in an almost silly gesture and said, "You got me. When I arrived home and saw what had happened, I was devastated. I tried to think of who could possibly have done that to Claire. Then I realized I needed to check if Tally was still in the bunker. But to my shock, she was gone. So, I knew it must've been her. I searched the house to make sure there was no trace of Tally, aside from the crime scene in the kitchen. I went out and relocked the bunker, waited in the house, cried over my poor sweet Claire, and then I called the police."

"I have to ask, your home was broken into, a note was left, and there was a fire in your backyard. Did you have anything to do with those?"

He shook his head. "No. At first I really thought it was you."

It would have been nice to attribute the note and fire to Jordan. No such luck. "Did anybody else know about the girls who might have been trying to expose you? Anyone who could have known?"

"No, it's strange. It wasn't you?"

"It wasn't, but we think there's somebody who knew what you were up to."

"Maybe it was somebody who suspected me. I knew you suspected me the first day I met you. You gave me a look."

Interesting. "You had said teenagers are temperamental. You were referring to Tally."

"You are a clever one, Valerie. May I call you Valerie?"

Why not? "You may."

"Boy, I'm starved, Valerie. You know, I could go for a burger."

With a fake smile plastered on my face, I excused myself to get the worst serial killer and human being who had ever lived in Red Rose County a Happy Meal. His confessions, if true, were critical for the investigation. We needed to get the search team out to his property as soon as possible to find those girls and bring them back to their families.

FIFTY-SIX

VAL

With a glass of wine in hand, I joined Lucy and Sally in a solemn toast. "To the missing who are now found," we said in unison, each of us taking a sip from our drink.

The three of us had decided to go out after an arduous few weeks. We were the only ones from the department who had worked on the case and opted out of attending Claire Nelson's funeral earlier that day. Honestly, I wasn't sure she deserved our respects. She had allowed her husband to hold a girl captive and torture her and then tried to kill her. In my book, that was unforgivable. Instead, we stayed in contact with the rest of the team while on-site with the dig team in the backyard of the Nelsons. We were searching for the thirteen missing women Jordan claimed he had buried there, one of whom we believed was Naomi Carter.

The team had found thirteen graves, with the bodies in various stages of decomposition. Some were just bones. Dental records and DNA would help identify each of them, along with the names Jordan had provided. But our work wasn't done yet. We needed to find the families of those missing women and let them know their fate, to allow them to move on with their lives and stop wondering if they would ever find their missing loved one. Sometimes knowing was worse, but not knowing was a torture that lasted a lifetime.

The district attorney assured us that Jordan would never get out of prison, and I doubted he would want to. But he wouldn't be happy. He had a craving, a need for something much darker, something he could only get when he took it forcefully and locked it away in a bunker. The plea deal Jordan agreed to included taking the death penalty off the table. It was a win, considering that meant Laney and Tally wouldn't have to go through the ordeal of a trial.

I planned to call Kieran the next day to update him on all the details we had found, unsure if any of the missing persons were part of any of their cases. We hadn't needed their assistance after all, but it was good to know he was willing to lend a hand despite my resignation.

"When you first met Jordan, is this what you expected?" Lucy asked, breaking the silence.

"I knew there was something off about him. Something he was hiding, that was clear to me the first time I met him."

"What was it, his eyes?" Sally asked.

"Yes, exactly. Studies have proven that adrenaline can make the pupil larger, physically making the eyes appear black or dark. The phenomenon is common with killers. The other thing was how quickly he changed his demeanor from grieving father to cold and detached," I explained.

Sally nodded. "Well, it's a good thing we had you on the case. Nobody else suspected him."

"Forensics would have caught up with him eventually. Speaking of forensic testing, how's Jonathan?" I said, eyeing Lucy, and shifting the topic to something a bit lighter.

"I like him a lot," Lucy said, her face lighting up at the mention of his name.

"So, what's the story? How long has he been here? What's

going on? Does he have a past?" I asked, trying to sound casual; I still wanted to look out for my friends. Lucy and Sally were my new friends, and their well-being mattered to me.

"Well, he grew up in Southern California, went to school down there, then moved up here about five years ago. He'd been on a camping trip and fell in love with the area, so he decided to change jobs and work for Red Rose County."

"Any developments in the relationship?" Sally prodded.

"There's definitely been kissing, and hopefully more pretty soon," she said, wiggling her eyebrows.

Sally said, "Good for you, Lucy. He seems like a good guy. I've worked with him for a few years now, and I've never heard a bad word about him."

"Good," Lucy responded, taking another sip of her drink. "And your new boyfriend, Sally?"

"I think that's DOA," Sally said with a frown.

"Did you do a postmortem?" I asked, half joking.

She chuckled. "Only in my mind. I think he just wasn't what I thought he was. Seemed nice, clean-cut, maybe genuine, and someone I could see myself with in the future. But I think I was more serious about him than he was about me."

"So it's over?"

"It's over. If they're not in it for a relationship, I'm not in it," Sally declared.

"Good for you," Lucy said. Turning to me, she asked, "And you and Brady?"

I shook my head. "Honestly, the last few weeks have been so crazy, I just... I don't know. I've got a lot going on, so for now, we're just friends."

"But you see how he looks at you, like you're a mythical being, like the greatest thing that's ever lived, right?"

I swatted at Lucy. "Oh, he does not."

"I don't know, Val. We're going to keep an eye on that one for you," Sally added.

We laughed, but then my phone vibrated on the table. I excused myself.

"Hey, Mom."

"I know you're out with the girls, but could you come home?" she asked, her voice tinged with concern.

"Sure, what is it? Is something wrong?"

"I'm not sure. I think you should come home," she replied, her tone serious.

"Okay, I'll be right there, Mom."

"Sorry, gals, I gotta go. My mom sounds weird. She says I need to get home."

"Do you want us to come with you?" Lucy offered.

"No, I'm okay, thanks," I replied, trying to hide my concern.

"Then you go. We'll take care of the check."

As I left, my mind raced with thoughts of what could have upset my mother. I hoped she hadn't had another stroke or a mini-stroke, like the doctor had warned us about. As I hurried out of the restaurant, I thought, *Please let my mother be okay*.

FIFTY-SEVEN

VAL

Rushing through the front door, I quickly armed the security system and dashed into the kitchen where I found Julie, Diane, and Mom. Their expressions were solemn, something terrible had happened, yet Mom appeared fine.

"Hi. I got here as quick as I could. What is it? Are you okay? Did something happen?"

"It's not your mother, honey," Julie said, her tone serious.

"Then what is it? Is it Harrison? Have you heard from Harrison?" My heart raced, nearly beating out of my chest as I reached for my phone, ready to call him.

"No, no, it's not Harrison," Julie replied. She gestured toward an envelope lying on the dining table.

A sense of dread washed over me, my heart nearly stopping as I struggled to catch my breath. Another note. "Did you look to see what it said? Where did it come from? Was it in the mailbox?" I questioned urgently.

Julie said softly, "I found it tucked under the doormat."

"So, it was hand-delivered? Did you check the cameras? Was there anybody on the camera?" I asked.

The three women exchanged glances, their faces reflecting

a growing sense of unease. "Somebody had obscured the cameras, sprayed them with black paint. We couldn't see who," Mom said.

The person leaving these notes knew about our security system and how to avoid being captured on camera. My heart raced. "What does it say?" I asked, but they shook their heads.

Mom said, "We didn't open it."

Had this been the first note, I would have rushed to put on rubber gloves and placed it in an evidence bag. But at this point, we knew better. I swallowed hard, stepped forward, and picked up the crisp white envelope. In block letters, it was addressed to Valerie Costa. I opened it, revealing a white note card with black lettering typed on it.

It read:

I'm glad you found it. Happy to help. Good work. S.

Like the last one.

I showed the note to my mother and her friends.

"What does it mean, Val?" Julie asked.

"It means it's likely from the person who sent me the original note, the note at the Nelsons, and I also suspect, the help they're referring to was the fire. The fire led us to the discovery of the bunker on the Nelson residence."

"Do you still think it's the Bear?" Mom asked.

I lowered my head, pondering the implications. If it was the Bear, he had changed his tactics, but if it wasn't, then I had a vigilante admirer who might be just as dangerous.

But what was more disturbing was that whoever had sent this had to be local or live nearby. If they had set the fire, they had been in Hectorville, two towns from my home, and then came to our property to black out the cameras. "I need to call Kieran," I said decisively.

They nodded in agreement.

As I waited for Kieran to answer, I realized it was nearing eight o'clock in the evening. He was likely to be concerned at the late hour, but I supposed it didn't matter. The urgency of the situation outweighed any concerns about it being too late.

"Hi, Val, what's going on?" Kieran said.

"I got another note." And I quickly briefed him on the situation: the disabled cameras, the contents of the note, and the bodies discovered on the Nelson property. "Have there been any developments on the Bear? Do you think he could've done this?" I asked. The behavioral analysis team were experts at profiling criminals, but I wondered if I was too close to see things clearly.

Kieran said, "There hasn't been a peep from him. We've completely lost his scent."

Was the Bear in Red Rose County keeping an eye on me? Involving himself in my investigations? "Do you think it's him leaving the messages?"

Kieran sighed. "I'm not gonna lie, it's a possibility."

I felt short of breath and overwhelmed by trying to figure out how to protect my family. My son was starting college next week, and I needed to fly out to Washington, DC, to help him move into his dorm. These were events I couldn't miss, and I had arranged for Julie and Diane to stay with my mother. I needed to talk to Brady, to ensure he would check on them and make sure no strangers came near the house.

"How do you want to handle this?" I asked Kieran. "I've got the note. I've got my fingerprints on it. I figured at this point we know he didn't leave a trace, but we should keep them in evidence. Do you want me to store it in Red Rose County? Or, if the FBI really think this could be the Bear, we should be storing it in the FBI files."

"Send it to us. We'll keep it at Quantico, do some more testing, but also take photos for Red Rose County, in the event it's not the Bear and it's a local nut."

Moments before, I had been celebrating finding the graves of thirteen young women. It was a sad victory, but it meant a solved and closed case.

Mom was happy and healthy, getting stronger every day.

My baby boy was starting college in just over a week, and I was going to be there for him. Like any mother, I would witness my little boy, now a young man, move into his first independent living space. In all the commotion, I had tried my best to push the Bear, and my own captivity, to the back of my mind, but it kept rearing its ugly head at every turn. When would it stop, if ever?

"I'll be in DC next week. I'll bring it by."

"Good. Let's have lunch and catch up," Kieran suggested.

"Thanks, Kieran," I said and ended the call. I sat at the table with Mom, Julie, and Diane, feeling a mix of emotions.

Kieran's advice weighed heavily on my mind as I sat with Mom and her friends. "He thinks it's something to be concerned about. While I'm gone, I'm going to ask Brady to come by the house every day to make sure everyone's safe and that no unauthorized people get near the house."

Mom seemed hesitant. "I'm not sure that's necessary, Val."

"If nothing else, it'll make me feel better. I'll be gone for a few days, but I want to make sure everybody's safe."

"And, Val," Mom added with a slight smile, "keeping people safe is one of your greatest strengths."

"I hear it's hereditary," I quipped, trying to lighten the mood.

"Why don't I make some tea, and you can fill us in on everything that happened today at work?" Julie suggested.

I welcomed the distraction. It might help keep my mind off the thought of being chained up in that barn, those eyes, and that voice telling me all the horrible things he was going to do to me.

I spent the rest of the evening with my mother and her

friends. We celebrated the lives of the young women who had lost theirs to Jordan Nelson, honoring their memory in our small way.

Before I went to bed, I called my son just to hear his voice and to let him know I loved him. The Nelson case was a stark reminder that our lives could change in an instant, and everything we thought we knew could vanish. We needed to cherish every moment. We only get one shot at this life, and I wasn't going to waste it.

A LETTER FROM H.K. CHRISTIE

Dear reader,

Thank you for reading *Don't Make a Sound*. I hope you enjoyed reading it as much as I loved writing it. If you did enjoy it, and want to keep up to date with all my latest releases, you can sign up to my author mailing list, where you'll be the first to hear about upcoming novels and other author news. Your email address will never be shared and you can unsubscribe at any time.

www.bookouture.com/h-k-christie

If you're interested in exploring more of my books, or you'd simply like to say hello, visit my website and drop me a message. I love to hear from readers! You can also sign up for my H.K. Christie Reader Club, where you'll be the first to hear about upcoming novels, new releases, giveaways, promotions, and a free eBook of *Crashing Down*, the prequel to the Martina Monroe crime thriller series. You can also follow me and reach out on social media.

Thank you,

H.K. Christie

KEEP IN TOUCH WITH H.K. CHRISTIE

www.authorhkchristie.com

 facebook.com/AuthorHKChristie
instagram.com/authorhkchristie

ACKNOWLEDGMENTS

The most terrifying thing about this story is that Jordan's character was inspired by an actual person. As part of my research I read *Confessions of a Serial Killer: The Untold Story of Dennis Rader, the BTK Killer*, by Katherine Ramsland, PhD. This book was difficult to get through, because it changed POV from Dennis Rader to that of the author. Rader's proclivities and thoughts were difficult to stomach and I often had to take a break from reading. The book was well done, but I won't be rereading it anytime soon as it gave me nightmares! Like the fictional character Jordan Nelson, nobody would have ever thought Dennis Rader, a family man and active member of the church, was capable of the atrocities he'd committed until he was finally linked to a crime scene. It goes to show, you never really know anyone. My gratitude to the author, Katherine Ramsland, for writing such an outstanding account and explanation for one of the most prolific serial killers in the US.

Many thanks to my editor Billi-Dee Jones and the team at Bookouture for helping bring this story to life.

And of course, a big thank you to my emotional support team. My fellow author Sara Ennis Henderson, for her support and guidance (like when she tells me, "I'm older and wiser, and I demand you take a break!"). For Charlie, my little Yorkie Poo, for always being by my side. Always. And to my friends, family, and husband for the endless support over the years.

Last but not least, I'd like to thank all of my readers. It's because of you I'm able to continue writing stories.

PUBLISHING TEAM

Turning a manuscript into a book requires the efforts of many people. The publishing team at Bookouture would like to acknowledge everyone who contributed to this publication.

Audio
Alba Proko
Sinead O'Connor
Melissa Tran

Commercial
Lauren Morrissette
Hannah Richmond
Imogen Allport

Cover design
The Brewster Project

Data and analysis
Mark Alder
Mohamed Bussuri

Editorial
Billi-Dee Jones
Ria Clare

Made in the USA
Las Vegas, NV
18 September 2024